Secrets in the Cottage

A Rosemary Mountain Mystery

Book One

Nicole Gardner

For Brandon
You gave me the courage to chase my wildest dreams.

CHAPTER ONE

WHY ISN'T IT RAINING?

It was supposed to rain at funerals. In every TV show or movie I'd ever watched, funerals were held on overcast, dreary days, the gray skies reflecting the fact that someone had lost their light, their love, their everything.

Yet, as I stood beside Dad's grave, only half listening to the minister drone on in a sermon that was somehow supposed to be comforting, the sun shone brightly on my face. So brightly, in fact, that I found myself wishing I had brought my sunglasses.

It felt wrong.

How dare the sun have the audacity to shine?

"My deepest condolences, Ms. Sullivan." The words snapped me out of my thoughts.

"It's Daphne," I said automatically, as the minister reached out to shake my hand.

"Yes, Daphne." His smile was mixed with recognizable pity. "I remember you coming to services with your father. Please don't hesitate to reach out if there is anything I can do for you."

"Thank you. I appreciate it."

I stood awkwardly as the minister continued pumping my hand, gazing at me with that same look of pity. It made me feel like a lost little child. I didn't want to be here accepting condolences and smiling politely. I wanted to rip my hair out of its painful bun, shed my high heels, and run barefoot through the grass. I wanted to get away as fast as I possibly could. Hide behind a tree somewhere, until everyone disappeared, and I could finally let the tears come.

But grown women weren't allowed to do that. So, I continued to stand there, wishing I knew how to escape.

Thankfully, Mom stepped in, grasping his hand and telling him what a lovely service it had been. He turned his attention to her, and I slipped away, my heels sinking into the dirt with each step as I made a beeline for my car.

"Daphne!" Mom's voice was scolding as she hurried to catch up to me. "You can't leave yet. You need to wait until everyone else has left. Others want to offer their condolences to you."

Tears welled up and threatened to spill.

"I can't," I said. "I just can't stand there anymore. I can't shake hands and hear anyone else tell me how sorry they are. If anyone really cares about how I feel today, they'll let me get away from all of this and try to-try to..." The words came out in a rush, as I fought so hard to keep my voice from breaking.

"You can, and you will," she said firmly. "I know this is awful for you. But you're not a child anymore. It's time to grow up. You're an adult. Now, act like it."

She took my arm and led me back to the people gathered around the gravesite. I swallowed the lump in my throat, along with the resentment threatening to surface.

The truth was that I hadn't wanted her to come to the funeral at all. She and Dad hadn't spoken in years. My own relationship with her had always been difficult, and it had only gotten worse when they divorced. Dad wanted full custody, and she had immediately agreed, happy to move on and live her life without me weighing her down. Things had been more than a little rocky between us since. But she had insisted on being at his funeral to support me. At least that was how she phrased it. Knowing her, she was likely there to make sure I didn't embarrass her too much by crying publicly or failing to observe the proper social customs.

It felt like hours before the last mourners drifted away, leaving me alone with my grief. I made a beeline for my car and finally let the tears come.

I DROVE STRAIGHT TO DAD'S HOUSE AND SAT IN THE driveway, staring mindlessly at the front door. All day, I had felt desperate to be alone.

But now, facing his empty house, I felt lonelier than I would ever have imagined possible.

All I wanted was to see him walk out and wave, waiting for me to walk up the steps, the way he always did when I came to visit. I still couldn't believe that I would never see him again, never catch up over takeout, or play another game of chess.

The house felt so cold and empty without him. After ditching my heels and purse, I poured a large glass of Merlot and headed to his study. It was where he had spent most of his time, poring over maps and books, always with a snifter of brandy nearby. Being in there made me feel less alone, somehow. I sank down into my favorite spot, a corner chair that had often been my refuge from the world. How many times had I plopped myself down in that chair to discuss something I was thinking with him? It seemed that all my important life decisions had been made right here in this chair, with him listening patiently from his desk.

Wiping the tears from my cheek, I offered up the glass as a toast. "Here's to you, Dad." My voice broke, so I left it at that, even though there were a thousand other things I wanted to say—things I should have said long before we got to this day.

I sighed, looking around the study. I dreaded the decisions I needed to make. The house was mine now, but keeping it wasn't really an option. It was too much for me to maintain. Dad had always liked having a large house. He was a bit of a packrat and enjoyed having the space for his many collections. Mom had apparently loved large houses too, having purchased a giant, sterile house in the suburbs after their divorce. But I couldn't imagine living in this empty house by myself, nor could I imagine being responsible for its maintenance.

The house would need to be sold, and therefore, so would most of his things. I could never squeeze everything into an apartment, even if I rented an additional storage unit. But there were things I couldn't bear to part with, like this chair, and Dad's collection of leather-bound classic novels. Even the brandy snifter and antique chessboard would need to come with me wherever I landed.

I walked over to Dad's desk, running a finger along the edge before sitting down in his high-back desk chair. Rather than delay the inevitable, I decided to make a list of what needed to be done. I pulled open a drawer in search of a pen and paper. As I shuffled through the mess—organization had not been a quality he possessed—my fingers landed on something cold and oddly shaped. I pulled it out from underneath the mess of loose papers.

It was a key, but not to anything I recognized. It was a beautiful antique with intricately carved details on the handle. That in and of itself wasn't odd, as Dad was always collecting unique historical pieces. But it was strange that I had never seen it before. He usually couldn't wait to show me his finds.

I pushed away from the desk and began scanning the room for anything the key might fit. It was possible, of course, that it didn't belong to anything at all. It wouldn't be unlike him to pick up a solitary key from a flea market just because it was beautiful. But my gut said that if it was just a random purchase, he would have shown it to me and displayed it inside one of his many display cases. That it was tucked away inside a desk, out of sight, meant that it opened something.

Something he hadn't shared with me.

Chapter Two

I drained my glass of Merlot, then began searching his office for whatever the key might fit. There were so many nooks, corners, and hidey-holes that it took a while. Ultimately, the search was fruitless. Whatever the key went to, it wasn't here. I plopped back down into my chair and mulled it over.

The next most logical place to search was his bedroom. The idea made me feel guilty, though, as if I would be invading his privacy. It was a silly notion, since I would soon have to sort through everything in the house anyway. *The dead have no privacy.* The startling realization made me want to go home and burn several of my journals on the chance that I died before Mom did.

Since I couldn't bring myself to invade his bedroom yet, I did a quick search of the rest of the house. It was also fruitless. I was about ready to give up for the night when it hit me that if he had wanted to keep something private, he might have hidden it in the attic. The thought made a chill run up my spine. As a kid, he had teased me that the attic was full of ghosts and had warned me to stay out of it. I was old enough to know that ghosts weren't real, but I still felt like I was breaking a commandment by going up there.

Dad's "attic" wasn't really an attic at all, at least not compared to the modern attics I had seen with hatch openings and pull-down ladders. His was really a partial third story, more like a large, unfinished bonus room. I had gone up there once as a little girl, before he had scared me off it. I had found it so charming that I wanted to turn it into my "princess" bedroom. That is, until he had filled my head with stories of ghosts and goblins haunting the corners.

With a thrill of rebellion, I climbed the stairs and flicked on the light to the dusty room. The place was a mess of boxes, stacks of books, and old furniture he had stored away. I imagined that this was how his office would look as well, if not for the weekly housekeeper who forced him to maintain at least a basic level of tidiness.

First, I checked the furniture for any cabinets that might have a lock. Nothing. I started opening boxes and moving things around. I told myself all of this was pointless, that I was wasting time and energy looking for something that probably didn't even exist. But my gut said to keep going. It was practically screaming at me that the key was important and that I needed to find whatever it unlocked.

Finally, just as I was about to give up, I found what I was looking for. Hidden in a trunk in the corner was a wooden box, carved with stunning Celtic knotwork. My heart began beating faster as I pulled it out of the trunk and ran my fingers over the top. I was both excited and terrified to open it. My suspicion that it must hold something Dad had deliberately hidden from me felt confirmed. Celtic antiques were his favorite, and he would never have been able to contain his excitement over a piece like this.

My body vibrated with anticipation as I knelt on the floor and inserted the key. I opened the top to find a stack of letters, yellowed with age, tied together with a piece of old twine. I read the addresses and realized they were a series of letters between Dad and a woman I had never heard of named Eileen. *Love letters.* It was startling, but also sweet. Dad had never been the sentimental type, at least when it came to Mom. Their marriage had always appeared to be one of strict practicality, a mutually beneficial partnership until they dissolved it. Yet, here in my hands was evidence that he once had a real romance.

I put the letters aside and pulled out the next packet in the box. It was also tied with twine and wrapped in old lace. I gently untied it and let the lace fall to the side.

At first glance, I thought it was a photograph of me and Dad. Only it wasn't me at all. It was him—a much younger version of him—with a woman who could almost be my twin. She was shorter than I was, with the kind of curves I would kill for, but we shared the same pale skin and long, wispy, strawberry-blonde hair. Our faces were nearly mirror images. I traced my finger over the photograph. She felt so familiar.

As the ramifications of this washed over me, so did feelings of shock and betrayal.

I shook myself, insisting that there must be another explanation. My Dad would not—could not—have lied to me my entire life about my mother. Maybe this was a photograph of a cousin on his side I had never met, or some other relative I simply looked a lot alike.

With a shaking hand, I went to the next picture. It was her again. She was alone this time. She wore a long, flowing dress and was twirling in a field of flowers. When the shutter had snapped, she had been staring right at the camera, caught in the middle of a laugh. She looked like a hippie from the 70s, the kind of girl you would find singing around a bonfire with friends.

What I'd always loved about photography was how a well-taken photograph could capture someone's essence. The woman in this photo was so very vibrant. Unrestrained. Joyful. I found myself absolutely fascinated by her.

I flipped slowly through more photos. They put to rest any notion of this being one of Dad's relatives. It was clear from the pictures of them together that this must be the Eileen from the letters. If he was looking at the camera, his arm was around her waist, and on his face was a clear expression of pride. But in most of them, he was looking directly at her, as if he couldn't take his eyes off her for even a moment. In those, his face shone with absolute adoration.

My father had once loved deeply—and the woman he had loved looked exactly like me.

. . .

WITH THE THRILL OF THE SEARCH OVER, I WAS LEFT WITH nothing but waves of grief and exhaustion. I wanted out of the dusty attic and away from its ghosts. But I couldn't bring myself to leave the box up there. I carefully placed everything back inside and carried it to my bedroom, where I could read the letters in better light.

I slipped out of my black dress, now covered in dust, and changed into leggings and a sweatshirt. Then I grabbed the box and took it to my bed, slipped the letters out of the twine, and began reading.

The letters began shortly after Lonnie, my dad, had met Eileen. The first few were timid, sweet, as they got to know each other. They mentioned going for walks together and fishing at her neighbor's pond. Over time, the letters grew deeper as they wrote of their dreams. They both expressed great love for Rosemary Mountain, the town where they apparently both lived. Strange that Dad had never mentioned the place.

In the later letters, they were obviously engaged and wrote of their plans. They were going to move into Eileen's house, which her parents had given them. Eileen wrote about planting a garden and raising children in the same house in which she had grown up. Dad wrote of taking his future sons fishing at the neighbor's pond, and how excited he was to be starting their lives together.

One of the last letters made me catch my breath.

Dear Eileen,

I'm so overjoyed by the news. I know we planned to wait a few years to start our family, but this happy surprise makes the idea of waiting seem silly. All we've ever wanted is to raise a big family here on the mountain. Let's move up the wedding. I don't want to wait any longer.

A baby! Can you believe it? I will be the proudest man on earth watching you walk down the aisle toward me, knowing that inside you grows the child we made together. It's all I've ever wanted. You are my every dream come true.

Yours forever,
Lonnie

. . .

THE DATE ON THE LETTER WAS APRIL 14, 1998. SIX MONTHS before I was born.

Only two things remained in the box: a velvet pouch and a solitary envelope. I opened the envelope first, assuming it was another one of their love letters. But this one was different. It was written by Eileen—my mother, I corrected myself, with a wave of disbelief—but it wasn't a love letter. In a shaky, erratic hand, she had written words that shocked me to my core.

LONNIE,

I'm sorry. Please keep Daphne safe. Protect her. Move somewhere lovely, start over, and be happy. And please forgive me.
Eileen

I STARED AT THE WORDS, WILLING THEM TO MAKE SENSE. Had she left us and run away? Committed suicide? Confessed to some crime and gone to prison? Or was she simply ending things and sending him away? Was it possible that my mother—my *real* mother, the love of Dad's life—was alive out there somewhere, maybe still living in the same cottage where I had been born?

With trembling hands, I replaced the letter in its envelope and turned to the final object in the box: the velvet pouch. I pulled open the strings and shook the contents into my hand. When it touched my skin, a wave of terror and darkness washed over me, along with flashes of images and sound.

Soft crying. "Please," in a woman's voice, a voice that sounded so familiar and yet so strange. "Please don't. I'll do anything."

I dropped the object like it was a hot coal and forced my eyes open. It was a delicate gold band. My heart thudded in my chest as I fought to slow my breathing.

I felt certain it was Eileen's wedding ring. And I was even more certain that something terrible had happened to her.

CHAPTER THREE

I woke the next morning in a haze, feeling as if I had barely slept at all. Yesterday's events had left me more shaken than I would like to admit.

Clairvoyance, visions, intuition—whatever you wanted to call it—had come so naturally to me as a kid that I assumed everyone experienced the world the same way. I learned my mistake the day I announced to my parents that the neighbor next door was in the hospital, hooked up to a machine, and that he was scared and couldn't breathe.

"How do you know that, Daphne?" Dad had asked sternly.

"I saw it," I said with a shrug, thinking it was a stupid question.

"How did you see it?" he demanded.

"You know," I said, shrugging again. "Like a dream, only you're awake." I couldn't understand why Dad was being so weird.

I still remember the fear in his eyes when he heard my answer. He knelt on the ground, eye to eye, and told me that visions were dangerous. He told me to do whatever was necessary to stop having them—to block them and kill them. He was so serious, so earnest. It was completely unlike him. He had always encouraged me to explore the world and told me not to be afraid. His reaction was totally out of character. It terrified me. So, I listened.

Two days later, when we found out that the neighbor had died in the ICU from pneumonia, we pretended it was a shock. We all acted as if I had never said a thing. And somehow, over time, I learned to block out the visions altogether, until they finally stopped coming.

Truthfully, I had thought that part of me was dead. It had been years since I had experienced anything like this. It felt as if the grief that had broken my heart had also cracked the walls I'd so carefully built around that part of myself.

Losing Dad was bad enough. But finding that box, and the experience after, raised a thousand questions for me. I wasn't sure if I really wanted the answers.

Why had Dad never told me about my real mother? For that matter, why had Mom never told me the truth?

I didn't like the ideas that were forming in my head.

I felt angry and impulsive.

Betrayed.

I wanted answers.

I paced around my room, mulling over the situation. The easiest way to get answers would be to call my mother—correction, my *step*mother—and confront her with what I had found. But there were two problems with that. First, it would require speaking to her, and frankly, I wasn't sure I had it in me. Second, I knew I wouldn't trust anything she said. She and Dad had apparently lied to me my entire life. Why would she suddenly tell me the truth now?

It dawned on me that she might not even know the real story. Obviously, she knew I wasn't her biological daughter. But what if Dad had never told her the truth about Eileen? If he had lied to me, he could have lied to her.

If I wanted the truth, I was going to have to find it myself.

A nagging voice inside me raised an uncomfortable question. Did I actually want the truth? If he had kept a secret that big for that long, he must have had a good reason. It might be better to just take the box back up to the attic and pretend I had never discovered it. If I kept telling myself it was all a mistake, that I had imagined the whole thing because of the trauma of Dad's death, I knew that eventually I would believe it. Eventually, I could forget about the woman who looked just like me, who stared straight at the camera, laughing...the woman who wrote a goodbye note that gave me chills.

I sank down onto my bed, holding my head in my hands. I didn't realize I was sighing until the audible sound of it hit my ears. It was a deep sigh, one of resignation. I knew that sigh.

I wasn't going to bury the box and carry on Dad's deception for him.

I wanted the truth.

AFTER MAKING A STRONG POT OF COFFEE TO COMBAT THE fatigue of a night spent tossing and turning, I sat down with a steaming cup and opened my laptop. My first search was simply for her name: Eileen Sullivan. I said the name aloud, feeling it on my tongue and listening for it in my ears. I hoped it would stir some sort of recognition, maybe even trigger a memory. It didn't. The name didn't seem to mean anything to me.

The internet search was fruitless. The name Eileen Sullivan apparently also belonged to a journalist, which meant that she dominated the results. But it was clear from her picture that she wasn't my mother.

I tried again, adding the words Rosemary Mountain to the search. This time, I found an obituary. It gave little information, only saying she "died suddenly" in September 2001. That especially hurt. For three years, she had been my mother, yet I couldn't remember her at all.

It wasn't a surprise, but it stung more than I expected. A tiny part of me had been hoping she was still alive out there, that we had a chance of reuniting. Maybe in the same way that we looked alike, we would also be alike. Maybe we would share similar interests. Maybe we would both prefer staying home with a good book instead of making the rounds at a party. Maybe we would both prefer being in the background instead of front and center.

Maybe she would actually be proud of me, instead of looking at me with barely disguised disappointment, the way Mom always had.

I blinked away the tears that came unbidden.

"This is ridiculous," I spoke aloud, giving myself the emotional equivalent of a slap in the face. "You can't lose something you never had."

Still, my voice broke when I said the words.

Next, I searched for the return address from Eileen's letters. That search produced surprising results. I was expecting to just look at some satellite images or something, but instead, I found a current real estate listing. My parents' old house was on the market.

I'd never been one to believe in fate, but what bigger sign could the universe possibly give me? I had decided to get answers about my mother, and her cottage—the cottage where I had spent my first three years of life—just happened to be on the market and available for showings. If I wanted to trigger any early childhood memories that were still lingering somewhere deep down, what better way than to revisit where they had been formed? And while two decades was a long time, it was likely that someone living in the area had been there back then. Even if I couldn't get all the answers I was looking for, maybe I could at least find out more about her.

I scrolled through the pictures, again searching for any feeling of recognition. Nothing. But being there in person might be a whole different story.

I wrapped both hands around my warm coffee mug and took a deep sip, letting my gaze drift off out the window. Dad's elderly neighbor was outside pruning her rose bushes. She had lived in that house since her husband had brought her there as a young bride, and she always maintained an old-fashioned cottage garden, even as the neighborhood built up around her. A memory came to me of how I used to slip over there when she was working in her garden. She was always patient and had even tried to teach me a few things, although I had no desire to actually learn or help. I just wanted to be there with the flowers and herbs. The scent of them had always conjured up warm feelings inside of me, like being wrapped in a cozy blanket on a snowy day.

Was that somehow connected to my mother? Was it possible that those scents were triggering sensory memories of time with her?

I clicked open a new tab and searched for driving routes to Rosemary Mountain. It was nearly a ten-hour drive. I had never traveled that far by myself, and the thought of doing so was unnerving.

Before I could talk myself out of it, I went back to the real estate website and clicked "request a showing."

Chapter Four

Three days later, I was on the road headed toward Rosemary Mountain. I rolled down the windows and turned up the radio, enjoying the thrill of the curvy roads. The late afternoon sun lit up the trees, making the landscape glow with warmth. I tried to absorb as much of the scene as I could, keeping one eye on the narrow mountain roads. The pictures I had seen online hadn't done this land justice. It was simply beautiful.

Rosemary Mountain. The name had haunted my dreams the last three nights.

I drove straight through town, wishing I had left early enough to stop. It had an old-fashioned town square with an actual soda shop and barber. I wondered if they were original or if they were a tourist draw. Either way, it was like driving through a movie set. For such a small town, there were a surprising number of people on the square, popping in and out of adorable storefronts. I spotted a bookstore and a local art gallery. This was definitely somewhere I would enjoy exploring when I had time.

The road got steeper on the other side of town, as I exited the main highway and began the climb toward my destination. The realtor had given me detailed instructions, telling me the house was easy to find, as it was at the very end of a dead-end lane. Still, I would have missed the turnoff had my GPS not alerted me to its location. Lonely Oak Road. The name suited it perfectly.

The lane turned to gravel, and I winced at the cloud of dust blowing up behind me. My small car rattled so hard I worried it would fall apart on the drive up.

A fresh wave of butterflies hit my stomach. What on earth was I doing? This whole thing was crazy. But just as I started talking some sense into myself, the wooded lane made its final turn, and I saw the cottage—my mother's cottage.

Home.

I stepped out of my car, immediately recognizing the soft scents of lavender and rosemary carried on a warm breeze. I breathed them in, basking in the warm sunshine, and let that old feeling of comfort embrace me. Something in me shifted, relaxed.

Birds chirped and squirrels chased each other on tree branches. This was nothing like the manicured, sterile lawn at my old apartment. This place, this little piece of land, was alive. I could almost feel the pulse of the earth beneath my feet.

A quick glance at my phone told me I had just a few minutes to explore the grounds before the realtor arrived. I changed into boots, tossed my ballet flats into the back of the car, and headed straight for the area that had caught my attention. It seemed to be the overgrown remains of the garden that had appeared in my mother's pictures.

I stepped past the broken gate onto what had almost certainly once been a pathway. It overflowed with overgrown rose bushes, lavender, and masses of rosemary. It was all a mess now, full of weeds and grass and broken-down beds, but it had obviously once been someone's pride and joy.

My fingers reached out to stroke a sprig of rosemary, releasing even more fragrance. It was as if I was starting to remember everything I had once forgotten.

The sound of tires on gravel broke my thoughts. I walked back to the driveway just in time to meet the realtor. I shoved down the guilt I felt about wasting her time by pretending to be a potential buyer and pasted a smile onto my face.

"Hi, Daphne!" She waved with a mess of papers in her hand. I got the impression that she was someone who was always in a hurry.

"Hey, Sandra," I replied. "It's nice to meet you in person."

"Have you been waiting long? I tried to beat you out here so I could have it open for you!" She pushed her sunglasses to the top of her head and started digging around in her massive handbag.

"I've only been here a few minutes," I answered. "I took a look at the garden." I gestured back at it.

Sandra's confused gaze followed to where I was pointing. "What garden?"

"It's there. It's just a bit overgrown."

"Hm. I'd say. Looks like a big mess to me." She returned to digging in her purse and finally emerged with a fob in hand. "Here we go! Let me open the lockbox to get the key."

"Sure," I answered, turning back to glance around the rest of the front. The surrounding woods were so gorgeous. I had always thought of woods as dark and foreboding, but these seemed positively happy. Inviting.

"I am so sorry," Sandra apologized, hurrying back toward me. "I guess they must have put the wrong key in the lockbox. The lock won't turn at all. Unfortunately, the owners are not actually located in the area, so we're out of luck. I'll have to get in touch with them and have them mail me the right key. I could arrange to see some other things today, if you want?"

I wasn't ready to give up. Something inside me whispered that the lock would open if I tried it, that the cottage was just waiting for me. I wasn't willing to walk away.

"May I try?" I asked, somewhat timidly. "It's an old lock. It may just need a little finagling. Sometimes I have a way with these things." I smiled, hoping it didn't sound too odd.

"Be my guest!" Sandra shrugged and handed me the keys. "Maybe you'll have better luck than I did."

I slowly climbed the faded steps up onto the porch. I had dreamed of this moment so many times over the last few days—had dreamed of touching something tangible that was connected to my mother. Here I stood on the threshold, staring at an old wooden door that my mother had walked through. I had goosebumps just thinking about it.

I put the key into the lock. It turned easily.

"It's open!" I called back to Sandra, who was standing at the car, absorbed in typing on her phone.

"Oh!" She looked up at me with obvious surprise on her face. "Well, I guess you do have the magic touch!" She slipped her phone into her purse and made her way back up the stone walkway to the front of the house. "Shall we?"

I pushed the door open and almost gasped. The house was filthy, and in much worse shape than the listing pictures showed. I had never seen such a thick layer of grime. Cobwebs haunted every corner. Paint was peeling from the walls, and by the smell, I could only assume that some small animals had made their home there.

"Well, it's a little rougher than I expected," Sandra said.

"How long has it been empty?"

She consulted her paperwork. "Not as long as it would appear. It came on the market almost two months ago. I'm guessing the previous owner didn't live here full time though. Probably used it as a hunting cabin. A lot of these smaller places out in the county get used by hunters. Some of them get taken care of, but this one obviously didn't."

"That's sad," I commented. "You can see this place used to be gorgeous." I walked around the front room, tracing my fingers over the antique windows. "Shall we see the rest of it?"

I glanced back at Sandra, whose face betrayed her surprise that I wasn't running out the door. She quickly erased the look and slipped back into professional mode. "Sure! Let's take a look!"

We walked through the house, with Sandra offering a monologue about its features. I mostly tuned her out, lost in my own thoughts. An idea was forming in my head. I didn't have any serious ties in Fayetteville. Honestly, I hadn't even missed it since moving back home to take care of Dad. My work could be done almost entirely at home. I had Dad's life insurance money coming, and there would be more after I sold the house.

Maybe it was grief. Maybe it was fate. Either way, I was seriously contemplating the most impulsive, ridiculous decision of my life.

The inside of the cottage was a major disappointment, but it had good bones and some nice features. If nothing was seriously wrong with it, I could probably handle the rehab. The living room had a fireplace built from massive stones, which I assumed were probably local to the area. Everything was outdated, yes. But I could make it work without spending a ton of money. The kitchen cabinets were high-quality wood and would look great painted white to brighten up the place. The hunter green carpet was awful, but I could envision the hardwood floors that almost certainly existed underneath. It would be a lot of elbow grease. But I didn't mind the work. There was something compelling about taking something so neglected and making it beautiful again.

I gasped for different reasons when we walked upstairs. Here, there was no hideous carpet. The original wood floors were intact, and the plaster walls had been left untouched. It completely changed the character of the house. When we walked into the main bedroom, I couldn't believe it. There was another fireplace, something I had never seen in an upstairs bedroom. The windows were larger than the ones downstairs, flooding the room in the most beautiful light. Best of all, a door led to a private wood deck overlooking the forest. *My* forest. It was incredible, and something I hadn't expected at all.

"I'd like to make an offer." The words spilled out of me, startling Sandra, who was still talking.

"Are you sure?" Sandra hesitated. "I mean, I'm glad you like it, and of course we'll make the offer if you're certain. But for your budget I could find you something much nicer in town. This is the first place you've even looked at, and honestly, it's priced a little high for what it is. Don't you want to see a few more houses before you decide?"

"No, this is the one," I answered. I shrugged again. "It feels like home."

Sandra's micro expression revealed that she thought I was crazy. Frankly, I was starting to wonder about that myself.

Chapter Five

After Sandra and I worked out the details of my offer, I drove to Rosemary Mountain's only motel to check in for the night. It was an older place and looked more than a bit rundown on the outside. Definite "Bates Motel" vibes. I cringed and wished I had done some more research. Surely there was a nice inn or even a cute bed-and-breakfast somewhere in town.

I pulled out my cell phone to do a quick internet search and realized I had missed three calls from Mom.

I leaned my head back on the headrest and let out a deep sigh. I dreaded talking to her. I was still so angry about being lied to that I didn't know how to be normal with her. But I wasn't ready to confront her with what I knew.

As the phone rang, I mentally crossed my fingers, hoping she wouldn't answer. It would be so perfect if I could just leave a voicemail letting her know I was returning her call. She never left voicemails. She would simply keep calling until I answered.

"Hello?" Mom answered as if she didn't already know who was on the other line. I stifled my sigh and made my voice as normal as possible.

"Hey, Mom, just calling you back! Everything okay?"

"Where are you?" she demanded.

"What do you mean?"

"I went by the house twice today, and you weren't there. I called you three times, but you never picked up. I was worried sick."

"I decided to go on a little road trip. Just an overnight getaway. I'll be back tomorrow."

"By *yourself?*" Her tone was incredulous.

"Yes, by myself. It's no big deal. I just needed to clear my head and make some decisions."

"Well, I wish you would have told me. I could have come with you."

I rolled my eyes. *That would sort of defy the point of getting away alone.*

"I didn't want to bother you. Besides, you know me, sometimes I just need a little space to process things."

"Well, when are you going to be back? I know you have a lot of big decisions to make, and, frankly, a lot of *stuff* to deal with. And I mean that quite literally. I remember how difficult it was to get your father to get rid of anything. I cannot imagine how full that house is now."

This time, I could hear her own eye roll as she said the words, and I couldn't help but grin. "It's nice of you to offer. I really appreciate it. But I don't expect you to help me with all of that."

"Don't be silly. Lonnie and I may not have been on speaking terms, but I'm still your mother. Of course I'm going to help you deal with his things."

I winced and bit my tongue. Just hearing the word "mother" reignited my anger. Part of me wanted to confront her right then and there. But I knew that was a terrible idea. This wasn't the kind of conversation we could have over the phone. So, I swallowed my feelings, and managed to keep my voice light.

"Well, thanks, I appreciate it. I'll be back in town late tomorrow, maybe around eight."

"Okay, I'll bring dinner over, then we can get to work."

"Thanks, Mom." The word felt bitter on my tongue.

The phone call drained what little energy I had left, and I decided that compared to driving around trying to find somewhere better, the rundown motel on the outskirts of town didn't look quite so bad after all. And it wasn't. It may have been old, but the room was well kept and felt surprisingly fresh and clean. I placed my overnight bag in the corner chair and immediately went to the window. The view nearly took my breath away. While I had been busy checking in, the sun had started to set behind the mountains. The sky had changed to vivid warm hues. The mountains cut against the bright colors in a blue silhouette, and the sun was a glorious ball of orange, disappearing slowly behind the highest peak. It was the most astonishing sunset I had ever seen in my life. I quickly grabbed my camera and ran outside to capture it before it was over.

I found the perfect spot to sit behind the back of the motel and snapped an entire series of photographs that would be worthy of a coffee-table book. I had long harbored a secret dream of creating and publishing a book of my photos, and it was exhilarating to see what amazing material I would have in Rosemary Mountain. I couldn't help but scroll through the images on my camera as I walked back to my room. I was so distracted that I nearly ran into another motel guest.

"Oh, I'm sorry," I said with a quick laugh, holding up the camera for him to see. "I was still caught up in the sunset and wasn't paying attention to where I was walking."

The man didn't reply. He simply stared at me with his mouth gaping open. The color drained from his face as if he had seen a ghost.

A nervous tingle ran up my spine.

"Are you alright?" I asked, taking a small step backward.

He continued to stare. A wave of fear washed over me as I realized just how isolated we were out here in the middle of nowhere. I edged away from him and headed for my car instead of my room. There were only two cars in the parking lot, mine and his, so there wasn't any hiding which car was mine. But I didn't want him seeing what room I went to if I could help it.

"Well, goodnight," I said awkwardly, trying to act as normal as possible. "I just pulled over to see the sunset. I'm heading out now. Have a great night."

I slipped into my car, with him still staring at me, unmoving. I shivered under his gaze and locked the car door, not caring if he noticed.

Then I put my car into reverse and headed back toward Rosemary Mountain.

I watched my rearview mirror more than I watched the road as I drove into town. I couldn't quite say why the man had unnerved me so much. There was an obvious explanation for why he would look as if he had seen a ghost. If he were a longtime resident, it's possible that he knew my mother. And based on the photos I had seen, we shared a remarkable resemblance.

On the other hand, why would a Rosemary Mountain resident be staying at the local motel? And if it was as simple as him noting a resemblance to someone he had known years ago, why not say anything about it? I went round and round in circles, arguing with myself about the whole encounter.

By the time I made it into town, I decided I had simply overreacted about the whole thing. There was no need to get so worked up over something so minor. This was exactly why Mom and Dad were always telling me to stop letting my imagination get the best of me. I had probably just startled a man who wasn't expecting a woman to whip around the corner of a dark building.

Still, I shivered every time I thought of him.

ROSEMARY MOUNTAIN HAD QUITE A FEW RESTAURANT options for a small town. I pulled into one of the busiest—a sprawling fish house boasting the best fried catfish in the state. My appetite had been almost non-existent the entire time I had been taking care of Dad, watching him deteriorate each day. But here, in the fresh mountain air, I felt ravenously hungry for the first time in months, and by the time I finished my meal, I was ready to name them the best fried catfish in the whole country.

It was seriously dark when I was ready to leave, and I discovered that small towns didn't have anywhere near the amount of light pollution that the city did. I wanted to appreciate the stars, but the darkness was too unnerving. I shivered again, with the face of the man from the motel flashing before my eyes.

The restaurant had been packed when I arrived, so I had parked at the back of the lot, on the opposite side of the solitary streetlight. I paused at the entrance, unwilling to step outside of the light and take those steps into the darkness toward my car. Bad guys aside, we were also in the mountains. What if there was a bear lurking in the shadows of the tree line, just waiting for his next meal? *You're being ridiculous, again.* Ridiculous or not, I still wasn't moving.

I'm not sure how long I stood there, but it was long enough to be noticeable, because I soon felt a light touch on my elbow.

I jumped out of my skin.

"Is everything okay? Are you waiting for a ride?"

I looked up at the man who had nearly given me a heart attack. When our eyes met, the noisy restaurant faded away. He was tall, with dark, wavy hair and a scruffy beard. His eyes, deep brown with flecks of gold, seemed as kind as his voice. He was, quite simply, the most attractive man I had ever met in my life.

He cocked his head and asked again, "Are you alright?"

I suddenly became embarrassed, realizing how silly I must look.

"Yes. No. It's just, well, it's really dark, and I parked all the way over there." I felt my cheeks flush. "City girl," I said, with an embarrassed laugh.

He grinned in a way that made me feel instantly more comfortable.

"Let me walk you to your car," he offered.

I hesitated. He seemed like a gentleman. But wasn't that how women were killed? By trusting men who were perfectly charming?

He seemed to sense my hesitation. "Hey, Greg," he called to someone I couldn't see. "Come here a sec."

Another man joined us. This one was a bit older and shorter, with a few lines starting to show and a bit of gray in his temples.

"Greg," the first man said, "Ms.—" he paused, waiting for me to fill in the blank.

"Daphne," I said.

"Daphne parked over on the other side of the lot, and she doesn't feel comfortable walking out there alone. Think you can help her out for me?"

He turned to me before Greg had a chance to answer. "Greg's the County Sheriff," he explained. "Keeping everyone safe is literally his job, and, well, he could use some work to do around here." He grinned again as Greg rolled his eyes.

I noted the holster on Greg's hip.

Greg whipped out his wallet and showed me his identification. "That's right, Ma'am. Happy to help." He gestured with his hand for me to lead the way.

I felt both embarrassed and grateful.

"Thank you," I said, making eye contact with the first man, expecting him to go back inside the restaurant. But he fell in step with me as Greg followed us.

"No problem. Here for the festival?"

"What? Um, no. What festival?"

"The Folk Music Festival. It's an annual thing. One of the biggest events in town. It draws a lot of tourists from the city who want to come get a taste of the simple life."

"Oh, I didn't know about it." I paused for a second, wondering how much I should share with a total stranger. "I was here looking at some property. I'm moving to the area. Hopefully, anyway."

"That's great!" He sounded surprised. "It's a nice place to live. You'll love it here. I'm Emerson, by the way."

"I'm Daphne," I said automatically.

"I remember," he said with a chuckle.

We reached my car, and the men stood there waiting for me to get inside. "Well, thank you both. Really." I laughed again and shook my head. "I'm sorry you had to walk a city girl across the parking lot. Ridiculous, I know. I'll remember to park underneath the light next time."

"Nothing ridiculous about it," Emerson said, his eyes conveying understanding.

"Have a good night now." Greg gave me a two-fingered salute.

"And welcome to Rosemary Mountain," Emerson added with a grin.

"Thanks." I returned his smile, feeling a rush of anticipation as our eyes locked again.

Rosemary Mountain was going to be a very interesting place to live.

Chapter Six

When I pulled back into the motel's parking lot, I was relieved to see that the black BMW from before was no longer there. I breathed a sigh of relief and switched my mental focus to getting some quality rest. The strain of the last few days—months, really—was beginning to show, both in my body and in my mind.

I ran a hot shower and let the water wash away all my thoughts. Then I curled up in the motel's bed, my wet towel still wrapped around my hair, and fell into the deepest sleep I had experienced since before Dad got sick.

I was normally an early riser, so I was shocked to find that the sky was already bright when I woke. I decided to forgo any town exploration and just hit the road.

The drive gave me time to think. I needed to gather my own thoughts and make a tentative plan for Dad's belongings that I felt comfortable with. I knew all too well that once Mom arrived, she would push her own plan. It would probably be a good one. But I needed to make sure I was okay with whatever we were going to do.

My mind drifted back to the cottage. If my offer was accepted, I would have room for Dad's book collection. I could turn the second bedroom into a study, or even just put the bookshelves in the living room. There were also practical things I could keep. The cottage was significantly larger than my old apartment, but I could easily furnish it with pieces from the house. It would mean a lot to me to be able to keep more of Dad's beloved things.

It surprised me to realize just how much I wanted the cottage. It had been such an impulsive decision to go see it, and an even bigger one to make an offer. But I didn't regret it.

I HAD BARELY DROPPED MY LUGGAGE WHEN THE DOORBELL rang. Mom bustled in, with a bag of takeout in one hand and a bottle of wine in the other.

"Oh, goodness." Her eyes widened. "It's been a few years since I've been in here. He really went crazy without me here to curb his collecting. It's like an episode of *Hoarders*."

I couldn't help but laugh. It was true that Dad had a lot of things, but it was nothing like *Hoarders*. It was more like an antique store, with eclectic furniture and display shelves of prized finds. Mom preferred more austere spaces. In her home, the kitchen counters were always bare and shiny. Even her fruit bowl stayed tucked into a cabinet. It was one of the many points of conflict between her and Dad before their divorce.

We carried the takeout to the kitchen. Mom began dishing pasta and breadsticks onto plates while I poured the wine. We both dove in, and once again, I was surprised to remember how delicious food actually tasted when you had an appetite.

Mom watched with approval. "Good. Eat up. You are way too skinny."

"It's been a long few months," I said.

"I know. I can't imagine, really." She sighed, looking around. "I'm assuming you're selling the house?"

"That's right. I feel a little guilty about it, though."

She waved her hand. "Don't. Your father wouldn't want you to work yourself to death and go broke trying to keep up with this place. It was his great love, not yours. I think the best thing to do would be to hire one of those companies to put on an estate sale. Lonnie has exactly the type of things that people look for at those. It will be quicker and easier than trying to sell things piece by piece."

"That's a good idea," I admitted. I had imagined listing things online one by one. An estate sale sounded much better.

"Also," she went on, "one of my good friends is a realtor. I called her to come evaluate the house and help you put it on the market."

"Thanks."

"I also told her you'll need a new apartment. Or you might consider buying something, either a townhouse or a small home in a nice neighborhood. I asked her to send over a list of options for you to see. I'm hoping you'll stay here, of course, but she works in Fayetteville as well if you're thinking of moving back. I'm not sure why you would, though, now that you're done with college. Little Rock has so many more opportunities, and of course I'm here, and—"

"Well, actually," I interrupted, avoiding her eyes and picking at my pasta nervously. "I made an offer on a house yesterday."

"Really?" She frowned. "I wish you had come to me first. I hope you didn't offer too much. And it's a bit fast, isn't it? You won't have the proceeds from the sale of this one for quite some time. What neighborhood is it in?"

"It's not in a neighborhood."

"Well, where is it then?"

I kept my eyes fixed resolutely on my fork while answering. "Rosemary Mountain, Tennessee." I looked up and met her gaze, my eyebrows raised.

Her face paled as her fork dropped to her plate. "How long have you known?"

"Four days now."

"Then he wasn't the one to tell you," she said, her tone flat.

"No, I had to find out all on my own," I answered, unable to keep the bitterness out of my voice. I picked up my wineglass and took a long swallow.

"I told him to tell you. For years, I told him you had the right to know."

I stayed silent. I wasn't in the mood for excuses.

"How did you find out?" she asked.

"I found a box in the attic. It had pictures of her and the love letters they wrote back and forth."

"Ahhh, yes," she said, an edge in her voice. "I've seen those too."

That felt like a stab to the heart. How was it that I was the last person to get to know my own mother's face?

I took another long sip of wine, then put down my glass, steeling myself. "Why did he not tell me about her? Why all the secrecy? I don't understand."

It cost me something to ask her these questions. I wanted the answers desperately, but I didn't want them from her. Beggars can't be choosers though, and I had to start somewhere.

Watching her, it was clear that she was highly uncomfortable. The always calm and collected Janet was unnerved. Knowing that gave me just the tiniest edge, made me feel a bit more in control of the conversation than I had before.

"Tell me the truth," I said. It may have been the first time in my life that I had ever given her an order.

"Eileen—your mother—" Janet stopped, seemingly unable to get the words out.

"Yes?"

"Well, Eileen had some mental health issues."

"What kind of mental health issues?"

She reached out and put her hand on my forearm. "Are you sure you want to hear all this?" I felt her almost pleading with me to just let it go.

"Yes, I want to know. I should have been told the truth from the very beginning."

"Your father was only trying to protect you."

"From *what?*"

"From your mother. From what happened to her."

"Please," I said, losing patience. "Just start at the beginning and tell me everything."

"If you're sure," she said, still uncertain.

"I'm sure." My voice was firm. I could feel myself losing that edge of power. She was gathering herself. If I didn't get her to tell me what she knew while she was still a bit off balance, she might decide that I didn't need to know after all.

"Okay," she said, raising her palms, with an unspoken *but don't blame me when you decide you should have stayed out of it* hanging in the air.

"Your mother was the love of Lonnie's life," she said flatly. "I never compared. I could never hold a candle to her in his eyes."

Please, stay on track. This is not about you! I bit my lip and forced myself to be patient.

"Lonnie adored her," she continued. "But she had, as I said, some mental health issues. She became increasingly paranoid, obsessive, and anxious. Thought she had some special intuition. Visions or some such nonsense." She snorted, as if it was the most ridiculous thing in the world. "Of course, in reality, it was hallucinations and delusions of grandeur."

My heart pounded in my chest.

"Anyway, they were happy at first. But eventually Lonnie realized that something was wrong. He tried to get her help, really. After all, he still loved her. But she continued getting worse, and well, she committed suicide."

No. She couldn't have. The conviction rose up in me. That wasn't what I felt when the ring touched me. Something terrible had happened, but it wasn't suicide. I refused to believe it.

Refused to believe that two mothers willingly chose to leave me.

Mom went on, without realizing that my heart was being ripped to shreds. "It broke your father terribly. He couldn't live there anymore, couldn't continue in that nightmare. Everything there reminded him of her. So he moved here. Wanted a fresh start. A few months later, he met me. We had a whirlwind romance, and before I knew it, I was playing the role of wife and mother for a man who would never really think of me as more than a housekeeper and babysitter."

It wasn't just an edge of bitterness anymore. The hurt was so clear. It didn't erase my own issues with her. But I felt a pang of sympathy for her even so.

"I still don't understand the secrecy."

She sighed. "To be frank, I never fully understood it either. But he was adamant that it would be better for you this way. He was worried that you would become some sort of, I don't know, self-fulfilling prophecy or something. As if you would follow in her footsteps if you knew about her."

She waved her hand, dismissing his ideas, and took a long sip of wine.

"I didn't understand, but you were *his* daughter. He made that very clear from the start. I was to just go along with how he wanted to raise you, and he was certain you would be healthier and happier not knowing any of the drama that happened in your early years. He wanted you to believe the three of us had been together from the start. He wanted you to forget. And you did. Maybe he was right." She shrugged. "You grew up healthy and happy enough. I don't know why you need to go digging up the past now."

The dismay I felt must have shown on my face, because Mom shrugged again and said, "I warned you that some things are best left unsaid. Especially after all this time."

The sympathy I felt toward her vanished and anger rose again in its place. Not that I really blamed her. If she was telling the truth, the secrecy had been entirely Dad's fault. I couldn't blame her for that.

I couldn't even blame her for not understanding what I needed in a mother.

"Let's just talk about something else," I said, returning to my pasta.

"Well, wait a minute. With what I just told you, do you really think it's a good idea for you to buy property in Rosemary Mountain? What an impulsive, ridiculous thing to do. I really don't know what you were thinking."

"I was thinking I wanted answers about my mother, and that I didn't have anyone here I could trust to give them to me."

"That's not fair— " she started.

"Please don't," I interrupted. "I don't want to fight with you. The offer is made. If they accept, then I'm moving there. At least for a while. Maybe not forever. Just long enough to come to terms with all of this and get the answers I'm looking for. If they turn down my offer, then I'll take it as a sign that I'm not supposed to go. I'll let go and try to figure out some other way to come to terms with all of this."

She let out a deep breath. "Well, I really don't think it's a good idea for you to go there. I may not understand all the details, but I know

Lonnie wouldn't want you to. And he had faults enough, but one thing was true. He loved you, and he always wanted what was best for you."

"Wanting what's best for someone and knowing what that is aren't always the same thing."

She half-nodded in assent. We both fell quiet as we finished our pasta, silently agreeing to let everything else go unspoken.

MOM CAME BACK EARLY THE NEXT DAY TO HELP ME START sorting Dad's things. Our unspoken truce held. We ignored the elephant in the room and ended up working well together. By the time we were ready for a break, we had worked our way through three rooms.

We were debating takeout options when my phone rang. *Sandra.* I bit my lip, wondering how I could excuse myself to answer it without starting anything with Mom.

"Just answer it." She rolled her eyes. "I can tell by the look on your face that it's your realtor."

I raised my eyebrows and answered the phone, walking to Dad's study for privacy.

"Hello?" I settled down behind the desk, grabbing a pen and notepad, hoping I would need them. I knew my offer was solid. I wanted to avoid negotiating back and forth.

"Daphne! It's Sandra. Great news! Your offer was accepted! You're going to be a homeowner!"

I let out an exhale. "That's great, Sandra. Thank you. So, what's the next step?"

I was so busy taking notes as Sandra explained the process that I didn't notice Mom slipping into the room to listen.

When I hung up the phone, I finally saw her. She broke the silence first.

"I suppose *congratulations* are in order."

"Mom."

"All I'm saying is that this is a terrible idea. Why on earth you have to go running off to live in the wilderness to figure things out is beyond me." Her voice softened. "And, well, I'll miss you."

I cocked my head at the last comment. *Miss me? We barely see each other as it is, and we always fight when we do.*

But I wasn't going there with her.

"It's not the wilderness. It's an adorable little mountain town with cute restaurants and local shopping. You'll love visiting. And like I said last night, I don't expect this to be forever. It's just something I have to do. I hope you can understand that."

She shook her head and left the room.

Alone, I finally allowed myself the grin I had been holding back. Everything that was happening felt like fate.

But I couldn't possibly explain that to Mom. What was the phrase she had used last night about Eileen? *Delusions of grandeur.* That's exactly how she would describe what I was feeling right now.

I ignored the little voice inside that whispered she might be right.

CHAPTER SEVEN

THE NEXT FEW WEEKS FLEW BY. EVERY DAY FELT LIKE A marathon as I pushed to settle everything of Dad's while also handling the cottage purchase long-distance. I could not have done either without Mom and Sandra. Sandra more than earned her commission by handling all the details for me, even video conferencing with me during the inspection so that I wouldn't need to be physically present. Meanwhile, Mom showed up every single day to help me take care of things at home. It was the most I had seen her since before the divorce.

The to-do list seemed endless, but I was grateful for it. It kept me so busy that I didn't have time to grieve. I had done so much of that in the months leading up to Dad's death that I was thankful for the reprieve. At some point, I knew I would have to deal with the grief, as well as the sense of betrayal still simmering under the surface. But whether it was emotionally healthy or not, I wasn't ready to face either of those things. A to-do list felt much more satisfying.

When moving day finally arrived, Mom showed up with drinks from our favorite coffeeshop. We stood together in the garage, watching the team load up everything I had chosen for the cottage. I took a sip of my drink and realized that, at some point over the past few weeks, Mom had memorized my order. A pang of regret made my heart ache. *Why did she have to start acting like a mom* now, *when I'm leaving? Why couldn't she have been like this before?*

"So, I can't change your mind?" she asked, as if sensing my thoughts.

"I'm afraid not," I answered.

"I'd like to visit sometime, if that's okay."

I still hadn't told her that the house I was buying was actually Dad and Eileen's old home. I couldn't imagine what she would say to that.

"Give me a little time to settle in, then let's plan it."

"So you're leaving in the morning?"

"That's right. I'll have to head out before dawn to get to the closing on time. They scheduled it as late as they could for me, but it's a long drive."

"Are you going to stay at a hotel or something until your things arrive?"

I laughed. "No, I'm actually going to stay at the cottage. I'm packing a sleeping bag and everything I need for the weekend. The movers should be there by Tuesday."

Mom looked at me like I was crazy. But to her credit, she didn't say a word.

There was a benefit to leaving before dawn. In the haziness that came from not feeling entirely awake, I was on autopilot, focused entirely on what I needed to do.

Even so, I felt a wave of emotion wash over me as I backed out of the driveway one last time. I would be back, yes. But if all went according to plan, the next time I returned would be to do a final walk-through before new owners took the keys. It would never again be my home.

I paused at the end of the driveway and gave the house one last look, saying goodbye in my heart before hitting the road.

With every mile I drove toward Rosemary Mountain, my sadness diminished and my excitement grew. By the time I exited the interstate, I felt pure joy. I loved this last stretch of drive, through rolling hills dotted with picturesque farms and the mountains in the background. It felt as if they were beckoning me home.

The last few months had been the hardest of my life, harder even than the turmoil-filled days of my parents' divorce. Whatever Rosemary Mountain held in store for me, it was a fresh start. And man, did I need a fresh start.

I drove straight to the loan office to sign, having entrusted Sandra with the final walk-through the day before. She had also negotiated professional cleaning services into the contract so that the home would be move-in ready upon closing. Before I knew it, I was pulling into my driveway with the keys to my new home in hand.

My breath caught at the sight of the cottage. It made a perfect painting, with autumn blue skies and the trees exploding in a symphony of gold and scarlet. It was mine. My very own home.

I had never been prouder in my life.

The evening was a cool one, but I was still dripping sweat by the time I finished hauling my plastic tubs and suitcases inside. I was also starving. The reality of country life hit me when I realized I had forgotten to buy groceries, and ordering delivery wasn't an option. I plopped down onto the floor with a groan, taking a swig from my water bottle. The last thing I wanted was to drive back into town. But it was that or make do with the granola bar in my purse.

I was still mentally weighing the options when I heard a tentative knock on the door. My heart nearly stopped. With every murder mystery I'd ever read broadcasting in my mind, I tiptoed over to the window to get a glance out front.

I felt silly when I saw a tiny woman standing on my porch. She had snowy white hair worn in a waist-length side-braid. She was dressed unlike anyone of her age that I had ever seen before, wearing a black sweater and denim overalls that were tucked into green rain boots. I jumped when she knocked again, realizing I should let her in instead of staring at her.

I opened the door, curious about this strange woman on my steps. When I did, she dropped the plate she was holding and stared at me as if she had seen a ghost.

"My word," she said in a whisper, raising a hand to her mouth. "Eileen?" The question was tentative. "No... Are you Daphne? Can it be?"

"That's right," I said, as she continued to stare. "I'm Daphne."

Her eyes filled with tears. She shook her head. "I can't believe it. I just can't believe it. For a minute there, I thought it was your mama." She wiped her eyes and seemed to remember herself. "Oh goodness, I'm sorry about this mess."

I looked down and saw that the pie plate had broken, leaving a mess of glass and ruined apple pie all over the porch.

"It's fine," I said, as she stooped to pick it up. "I'll take care of it, no worries."

She stood back up and stared at me again, her face unreadable.

I knew the polite thing would be to invite her inside, but I wasn't exactly set up for company. I didn't want her to leave, though. Here was someone who had known my mother—and, apparently, me. I desperately wanted to find out more.

"I would love for you to come in, but I don't actually have any furniture yet." I opened the door wider and gestured at the tubs in my living room. "I'm making do with an air mattress and a camping chair temporarily."

She peered inside, then looked back at me with a quizzical look on her face. "So, dear, does that mean you're my new neighbor?"

"Well, yes, I guess I am. I just bought the place."

Her eyes held a mixture of joy and amusement. "Well, I'll be. My new neighbor is Daphne Sullivan. I just can't believe it. But I'm so very glad. It's time this house had a woman like you looking after it again. And as for furniture, that's quite alright. We can sit on the fireplace!"

With that, she walked right past me and was in my home. She peeked around, taking in everything with her sharp eyes, then perched herself on the stone hearth.

I was speechless. I closed the door and followed behind, taking a seat cross-legged on the floor.

"I tell you, I'm just so happy you're the one who bought the place!" She slapped her hands down on her thighs. "I have a million questions for you. But that can wait. I know you were too young to remember it, but this used to be the prettiest house on the mountain—except my own, of course. But it's been nothing but hunters for ages now."

The last thing I wanted to do was make small talk. But I let her take the lead. "How long have you lived here?" I asked.

"Oh, decades! Too many to tell without giving away my age," she said, laughing. "I'm one of the long timers. There's some houses here that seem to change hands every few years, and some of us who have been here since the beginning. Tell me, do you plan on living here full time, or is this a vacation cabin for you?"

"The first one," I answered. "I'm moving here full time. At least for now."

She clapped her hands together in excitement. "Oh, I'm so glad! Usually, the young ones run away from places like this to the city. Well, goodness, Daphne, you were just a wee thing the last time I saw you! I can't believe you're all grown up now. Tell me all about yourself. We have so much catching up to do!"

It felt strange talking to a complete stranger who seemed to know me and a part of my life that was a total mystery to me. It was a little like being a child at a family reunion full of elderly aunts, all of whom know you and want to pet you, even though you don't have the slightest clue who they are. But there was something about her that seemed oddly familiar. I couldn't put my finger on it. But it was as if part of me, deep down, remembered her somehow and felt completely safe and at ease.

"Well, I'm a photo editor," I said. "I contract with several busy wedding photographers. They shoot the weddings, then turn the photos over to me. I do all the post-processing work and set up their client galleries."

"Oh, now that sounds like an interesting job! Do you take photos, too?"

"Well, not for work, no. But I do love photography. I just haven't figured out how to make a decent living shooting landscapes and flowers." I blushed, surprised I was about to admit a personal dream to someone I had just met. "I was actually hoping that I might be able to do some photography here, maybe sell prints to tourists. Maybe even put together a coffee-table book someday."

"Is that what finally brought you home to our little mountain? I have to say, it surprised me that Lonnie never brought you back to visit. I know you were too young to remember, but you were like my own grandchild. Toddled around in the garden with me and your mama." Her smile faded. "When Lonnie left, he swore he'd be back to visit. But he never came, and you were just gone. Just like your mama. It was one of the saddest years of my life. Oh, I don't expect you to remember old Fiona. But I'm just glad you're here. It's so good just to look at you! Goodness! You really look just like her." She gazed at me, shaking her head in amazement.

"What was she like?" I asked tentatively.

"Your mama?" she asked, surprise in her voice.

"Yes."

"Why, didn't Lonnie tell you all about her?"

My face flushed. "No. In fact, I didn't even know about her until a few weeks ago."

She gasped. "How could he let you grow up not knowing a thing about your own mother? Why, when I see him, I'm going to give him a good talking to!"

"He died. Just before I found out."

"Oh." Her voice grew quiet. "Well, I'm sorry to hear that. It's not right for someone your age to have lost both their parents. But you asked about Eileen. Where do I even start?" She smiled again.

"Well, like I said, you look just like her. She and her parents moved into this very house when she was a young thing, maybe eight or nine years old. She was lonely a lot, being one of the only children here on our road. Every day, she would come to my place to visit. I suppose I was like a second mama to her. Anyway, she was real sweet. Loved being outside. Loved everything, really. Had one of those spirits that was just happy to be alive. And when you came along, you were the apple of her eye. She was one of the proudest, happiest mamas I've ever seen."

"I wish I could remember her." It was an odd ache, a hole in my heart that it didn't seem anything else could fill.

"That's a hard thing," she agreed.

"What about her parents?" I asked. "My grandparents. Are they still alive?"

"I'm afraid not. We kept in touch over the years, and they came back to visit often. But they passed away, oh, maybe three years back."

Another loss of family I would never know. There were a million more things I wanted to ask her, but she changed the subject before I had a chance.

"You sure didn't bring much with you." She surveyed the cottage.

"Yeah, I didn't have room for much in my car. The movers picked up my things yesterday, but they won't be here until after the weekend."

She wagged a finger at me. "It seems, dear, that you don't quite have a kitchen set up yet. Let me treat you to dinner! It will be a welcome to the neighborhood gift."

"Oh, no," I started to protest.

"Now don't argue," she interrupted. "It's plain to see you don't have a lick of food inside this house. There's a little Italian place in town. Doesn't look like much, but we have us a real Italian chef running it. Marco and his wife came here from Sicily back in the 90s, and their tiramisu is so good it will make you cry. They call it a pizzeria, for the tourists, but Marco makes all sorts of wonderful things."

"Well, okay then." I threw up my hands in surrender. "Let me just wash up real quick."

"You do that. I'll just pop over to my place for my truck, and I'll be back to pick you up in twenty minutes."

"You walked here?" I asked, surprised. Come to think of it, I hadn't seen a car out front. But I wasn't used to seeing someone her age be quite so active. My guess was that she was at least seventy.

"Well, of course I walked here! I've got to get my exercise, don't I? Besides, your property is right next to mine, and it's only a minute if you cut through the woods."

"You cut through the woods?" I thought my jaw would hit the floor.

"It's the fastest way." She waved it off as if it were nothing. "You wash up and I'll be back in a jiffy! Oh, I can't wait. There's so many people for you to meet!"

And with that, she was off. I watched her out the window, and sure enough, she quickly disappeared into the trees beside the house, as if she were a wood nymph. In all my life, I had never met such a fascinating person.

I began, even then, to have a sense of foreboding that my life on Rosemary Mountain was going to be more of an adventure than I had bargained for. Still, nothing could have prepared me for all that was to come.

Chapter Eight

Fiona drove slowly, taking the time to point out the houses on the lane as her antique truck bounced over the gravel.

"You can't see my house from the road, but it's just down that drive to the left," she said, showing me. "And that house on the right belongs to the Reverend Don Kistler."

It was a gorgeous home, one that reminded me a little of Dad's. It was interesting how the houses here on the lane were all so different from one another. I was used to cookie-cutter neighborhoods, where all the houses were of similar size and were built in the same era at least.

"He's one of the long timers," Fiona continued. "Moved here back in the 90s. His wife is Patricia, and they have two sons, a bit older than you. Their oldest, Matthew, lives in town with his wife, but their youngest, Luke, still lives with them. Thirty-five years old, and still living with his parents! Can you imagine?"

I replied that no, I couldn't.

"Just between me and you, I don't think he's quite right, if you know what I mean."

I nodded and murmured assent, even though I really wasn't at all sure what she was getting at.

She pointed to a showstopper on a hill. "That house belongs to the

Rogers family. Dave's been a family doctor here since the days when the town was so small we only had one! His wife passed on a few years ago, and I thought he would remain a dignified widower. But no, he had to go get himself married again." She lowered her voice as if she didn't want anyone to overhear, even though we were clearly alone in the truck. "His new wife, Katie, is young enough to be his *granddaughter.* Can you imagine? She's a pretty one all right, and happy enough to score herself a doctor, I'd imagine."

"Maybe she loves him," I suggested.

"Oh, that she does, that she does," Fiona agreed. "She acts downright devoted to him. But all the same, you can tell she loves putting on airs. Refers to herself as 'Mrs. Doctor' all over town, when Dave's always gone by his first name, ha!"

It was clear that Fiona enjoyed gossip. I had a feeling she would soon tell all of her acquaintances about Daphne Sullivan returning to Rosemary Mountain. I wasn't quite sure how I felt about that.

"Now those houses over there sit empty most of the time. Just like your house was, they're hunting cabins now. I hope someone nice will buy them sometime. I don't like these hunters that pass through and never really put the time in to be part of things." She sighed. "This used to be such a nice place to live. We all had enough land to feel like we lived in the country, but we were as close as any neighborhood, just the same. Had to rely on each other. Now we're all getting old, and I just can't stand thinking about all the houses getting sold to people who don't care to even live here."

"I imagine it's sad to watch things change."

"Yes." Her face brightened. "But you're here now, and you'll make yours a home. And that one right there was bought just a year or two ago by a single man. Emerson." She pointed to a log cabin sitting back in the trees. "He's a male nurse. Isn't it funny how the world changes? Anyway, he moved here when we got the medical helicopter program. He's what they call a flight nurse. They fly people out to the bigger hospitals when something is too much for our little one."

The name Emerson triggered the recollection of my rescuer at the fish house. "I may have already met him," I said.

"Now, how can that be?"

"It's a long story. And it may not be the same guy. But the name Emerson isn't too common, is it?"

"There's only one Emerson in these parts, so I reckon it's one and the same." She shot me a sly smile. "Well, that's nice that you two have already met. I suppose you'll be spending some time with him."

I blushed as I realized her meaning. "Oh, no," I said. "I'm not really looking for a relationship right now."

"You might change your mind when you see him again. If I were forty years younger!" She cackled in laughter. I just shook my head.

Next, she pointed out an adorable A-frame house on the right. "Now, that house belongs to Sheriff Joe. Except he's not the sheriff anymore. He retired at least ten years back or so, but I still think of him as the sheriff all the same." She gestured to another showstopper on the left. "That house belongs to Bill Brinksley." She had a tone of disgust in her voice. "We don't like him."

"Why not?"

"Oh, he thinks he owns the whole mountain, just because he's rich. Made a small fortune back in the 80s, buying and selling land all over the state. I don't know why he's stayed here all these years. He could move just about anywhere. But no, he stays here, and constantly tries to 'improve' us. Wants us to have rules, like we live in some uppity neighborhood or something. Well, we don't. Most of us chose to live in the county for a reason, and that reason is so that we can do what we want on our own land without anyone giving us what for. But Bill just keeps pushing."

"What is he trying to change?"

"Oh, he wants our land annexed into the city so that we have to abide by city laws. I'd only be allowed to have five chickens! And no one could shoot on their own property. Can you imagine?"

I could easily imagine, as I had grown up without chickens *or* a gun, but I could tell this was important to her. I agreed he was obviously being unreasonable.

I had to ask, though. "Do people shoot their guns out here often?"

Fiona looked at me like I was crazy. "Well, of course they do. Dave even has a cannon! Likes to shoot it off on holidays. It'll shake the walls of your house!"

Yes, I had certainly found myself an interesting place to live.

Fiona wasn't exaggerating when she said Marco's Pizzeria didn't look like much. It was on the corner of an old storefront strip and looked as if it hadn't been updated in decades. The green leather booths and faux Tiffany-style light fixtures screamed 1990s.

But the aromas of roasted garlic and freshly baked bread had my mouth watering before we even opened the door.

"Marco!" Fiona called out.

An older man in the open kitchen looked up from stirring a large pot. "Fiona! Hello there!"

"We're heading to the booth in the back," she said. "I brought someone for you to meet! Come see us when you get a minute."

She led the way to a cozy corner booth at the back of the restaurant. No sooner than we had sat down, a heavily pregnant waitress brought us bread and peppered olive oil for dipping.

"Hey, Fiona!" She leaned over and gave her a hug.

"Christie, this is my new neighbor, Daphne! She just bought the old house next door."

Christie turned to me and smiled. "Welcome to the area. You'll love it here."

"Thank you." I returned her smile. She had a gentle, kind way about her. She was quite pretty, with gorgeous blue eyes, rosy cheeks, and soft blonde curls swept up messily into a clasp. She also seemed entirely too young to be pregnant.

"Let me get you some drinks. Your usual, Fiona?"

"Yes, that will be fine. But first, how are you feeling?"

"I'm hanging in there!" she laughed and patted her bump affectionately.

"Are you drinking your tea every day?"

"Yes, Ma'am, every day, just like you said."

"Oh, good, good. Won't be much longer now." Fiona smiled and squeezed her hand.

"I hope not!" Christie laughed. "I'll be happy for him to come any day now."

"A few weeks left, I think. But you know to call me if anything changes."

"Of course, I will."

Christie took my drink order and left us, then Fiona explained.

"I'm a midwife. This is Christie's first, but she's doing just great. I'm hoping she'll have an easy time of it."

Fiona became more fascinating every moment I spent with her. I tried to imagine any of the other elderly women I knew doing something like delivering a baby, and I couldn't. I'd always assumed that when you reached a certain age, you just sort of stopped living, but Fiona's life was more interesting than my own.

"Wow, that's amazing," I said. "How long have you been a midwife?"

"Oh, ages!" She laughed. "I delivered you, don't you know? I've been helping birth babies practically my whole life. There was a spell when midwives went out of fashion and most women wanted to have their babies in a hospital, thank you very much. But times are changing again, and young people especially want to do things more like the old way. Seems I've been busier the last few years than ever!"

"Wow." I was truly impressed.

She leaned forward, whispering conspiratorially. "But with Christie, it's less about wanting to do things the old way and more about not having much of a choice, money-wise. I'm helping her out, trying to make things as easy on her as I can. She doesn't have anyone taking care of her, see. Won't tell us who the baby's father is. I get the feeling he's married." She raised her eyebrows.

Before I could ask more, Christie came back with our drinks, followed immediately by Marco. He welcomed me to the restaurant like a king welcoming a visitor to a palace. He was a short, stocky man with a deep tan, white hair, and muscles that belied his age.

"Welcome!" he said, arms open, before planting kisses on each side of Fiona's face.

Fiona made the introductions, and Marco immediately planted kisses on my cheeks as well.

"Welcome to Marco's!" he repeated. "I made *sfincione*! I will bring it to you; you will like it very much!"

I had never heard of *sfincione* and had absolutely no idea what it was, but I smiled appropriately and thanked him. When he left, Fiona explained that it was a Sicilian-style pizza. It wasn't on the regular menu. Marco only made it when he felt like celebrating.

He brought it out quickly. The square dish was covered in melted cheese and anchovies and was topped with crispy bread crumbs. It was unlike any pizza I had ever tried and was one of the most delicious things I had ever tasted. So far, Rosemary Mountain was blowing me away with their food. Who knew that such a small town would have food that rivaled the most expensive restaurants I had ever been to?

Our dinner conversation was limited, mostly because we were interrupted every few minutes. Fiona seemed to know every single person in town, as well as every single thing about them. Virtually everyone who came in to eat had to come say hello, which meant that I spent most of the evening trying desperately to memorize faces and names. I couldn't remember the last time I had met so many people in one night.

Only one person ignored our little table. Fiona pointed him out with a whisper. "That's Luke, the boy—man, I guess—who still lives with his parents on our lane. The one I told you about."

I studied him from across the room. I could see what she meant. He seemed sullen and angry, a different picture altogether from everyone else in the restaurant.

"What does he do?" I asked.

"Beats me." Fiona shrugged. "Something with computers. Works from home. But I'm guessing it's not much of anything, since he can't seem to afford a place of his own."

I made up my mind to avoid him, if possible. The vibe he was giving off gave me the creeps.

After dinner, Fiona drove me back home. I thanked her for dinner, but I really wanted to thank her for so much more than that. She had given me a link to the mother I couldn't remember. I didn't have the words for that, though, so I just said thank you for the pizza. She squeezed my hand, and I felt that somehow she understood what I couldn't say.

I stood in my doorway, watching her back out of my driveway. I shivered as the light from her truck disappeared around the bend. It was so *dark* in the woods. Anything could be lurking out there in the inky blackness. I felt exposed under the brightness of my porch light, surrounded by a world I couldn't see.

I stepped into the protection of my house, closed the door, and double-checked all the locks. But the cottage didn't feel cozy anymore. It felt more like Dad's attic, full of ghosts.

A shiver moved down my spine.

Stop it. You're just scaring yourself. You're perfectly safe. Stop being ridiculous.

Still, I left the light on when I snuggled down into my sleeping bag for the night.

Chapter Nine

The morning brought gorgeous sunlight shining through the windows of my room. I stretched in my sleeping bag, happy to have made it through my first night unscathed. All my fears from the night before felt silly now that I was bathed in that glorious morning light.

I let myself out onto the deck and gazed at the stunning view. How could I have feared these woods? *My woods.* They were beautiful.

I was just going to have to get comfortable with them, that was all.

Feeling better, I jogged down the stairs to the kitchen. I may have forgotten to bring food, but I had packed my French press and a bag of coffee. Priorities.

While my coffee steeped, I changed into leggings and a sweatshirt. I poured that first cup—*glorious*—and decided to have it out on the deck upstairs. The deck was quickly becoming my favorite place. I made a mental note to shop for some outdoor furniture. A bistro set, perhaps, or a nice lounging chair. It would be the perfect place to have coffee and plan my day each morning, and to relax with a glass of wine at night.

In the city, my routine was to hit the stationary bike after my morning coffee. But here, I decided I would go for a walk down the road. The thought unnerved me just a bit. I made a mental note to ask

Fiona if this area had any bears. But I knew the only way to get comfortable with the woods was to actually experience them. Walking on the road wasn't exactly the same thing as a hike, but it was a first step.

I stretched quickly on the front porch, then headed out. I had watched a documentary on bear attacks once that mentioned calling out "hey bear" in a loud voice every so often to avoid surprising them. To be honest, I wasn't sure if that was a good idea or not. Wasn't that basically just announcing myself to them? *Hey bear. I'm here. Come get your breakfast.*

I settled for something in between. "Hey, bear," I called in a low voice, as I jogged down the lane. "I'm not your breakfast. Hey, bear. Just ignore me."

"Hey, bear," I called a little louder as I approached a blind corner. "Not your breakfast."

As I came around the bend, I ran into another morning jogger. Of course, I was so hyper-focused on bears that I let out a scream when I saw her. She just giggled.

"Hey, there," she said, laughing. "Don't worry, I know you're not my breakfast."

I clutched my chest. "I almost had a heart attack."

She giggled again. "I'm Katie," she said, with a little wave. "Are you visiting someone out here or something?"

I mentally ran through the list of names Fiona had given me last night. *Katie. The doctor's wife.* That made sense. Fiona wasn't kidding about the age difference. Katie couldn't be much older than I was. I pegged her as early thirties, maybe. She definitely looked the part of the woman who would marry a much older man. Her blonde hair was perfect, even in a ponytail, and she was jogging in full makeup and false eyelashes. Even her outfit was stylish. She looked like a model. I suddenly felt plain and shabby in contrast.

"I'm Daphne," I said. "And I actually just bought the house at the end of the road."

"Oh, that adorable little cottage? I'm so glad! We'll be neighbors! I've just been dying for someone our age to move out here. It's all old people. No one to talk to. Except Emerson, of course, but he barely counts because he doesn't like to talk at all." She laughed again and reached out to grab my hand. "Tell me we'll be friends. I've been so *lonely* out here."

I couldn't help but like her. If I were judging based on looks, I would have immediately written her off. But her openness and warmth won me over.

"I'd love a friend," I said. "And as my friend, you can just keep the whole bear thing between us."

She threw her head back and laughed again. "Deal. And as *my* friend, you can agree to skip our workouts and head back to my place for coffee and cheesecake."

"Cheesecake? At 7:30 a.m.?"

She shrugged. "We're celebrating a new friendship."

"Deal." I grinned.

"Ohhhh, speak of the devil," she said in a stage whisper. "Here comes the man himself. If I wasn't married…"

My eyes followed her gaze, directed at a familiar man jogging our direction down the lane.

"Ahh, the famous Emerson," I stated.

"That's right."

He was quickly approaching us, but by the look of it, he didn't intend to stop. He nodded our direction but maintained his pace.

"Emerson! Yoo-hoo!" Katie stepped toward him and flagged him down. He wore a polite expression when he stopped, but I could almost feel his annoyance as he greeted her.

"Emerson, this is our new neighbor, Daphne!"

He turned to face me and his eyes lit up in recognition. "Daphne? From the fish house?"

"One and the same." I smiled. "Thanks again for coming to my rescue that night."

"Anytime," he said, his eyes never leaving my face. I blushed, feeling a wave of butterflies. I had forgotten just how gorgeous he was.

"Wait, you two already know each other?" Katie interrupted, her disappointment obvious.

"We met when I was here looking at properties," I explained.

Emerson spoke up. "Listen, I hate to be rude, but I only have a few minutes before I have to be back at the house for a conference call. Daphne, I'd love to take you to dinner tomorrow night if you're free."

"I'd like that." The words tumbled out of my mouth before I had the chance to even think about it.

"Great!" He smiled. "I'm assuming you're in the house that just sold at the end of the road?"

"That's me," I said, returning his smile.

"Pick you up at seven?"

"That sounds great. See you then."

He gave us a little wave, then returned to his run. I turned to Katie, whose jaw was practically on the floor.

"What?" I asked.

"Every single girl in Rosemary Mountain is going to hate you. Hell, I hate you at this point."

I just laughed. "Oh, come on."

"No, I'm serious. Every girl in town has tried to get that man to bite. He's been here for over a year and hasn't gone on a single date. We were starting to wonder if something was wrong with him."

"How do you know he hasn't gone on a date?"

"You must not be from a small town, huh? Honey, everyone knows everything about everybody here. And after tomorrow, everyone in town will be talking about how Emerson Jones took you out to dinner on your first week here."

"Hmmm." I wasn't sure how to feel about that. On one hand, I was loving all this small-town hospitality. I had never made friends so quickly in my life. But I was used to privacy— anonymity even—and I didn't know how long I would last in a town where, as Katie said, everyone knew everything.

But maybe that meant that the long-timers, as Fiona called them, would know everything about my mother. Getting those answers would make a lack of privacy worth it—for the short term, at least.

Katie and I walked up the driveway to her gorgeous home. It was a large Tudor-Revival style house. The architect had done a marvelous job at making it stand out from the many cookie-cutter Tudors I had seen before. It was a true classic.

"I love your home," I said.

"Thank you!" She was obviously pleased. "I love it too."

She punched in her garage code. "Come on in," she said, waving me to the door.

I stepped into her kitchen and immediately gasped. It looked like something from a magazine. The granite countertops and dark walnut cabinetry were obviously modern, yet had been chosen to complement the Tudor-style architecture perfectly. I had to swallow down a bit of envy when I compared it to my cottage.

"This kitchen is fabulous," I said. "You have amazing style."

"Thanks." She giggled. "But I can't take credit. It was like this before my time. Dave's the one with all the style." She pulled a bag of coffee from the pantry. "Is decaf okay? I'm trying to cut out caffeine."

"Yes, fine," I answered, my eyes still taking in all the details of the house.

"Oh, good," she said. "I still haven't managed to get rid of my morning cup of regular, but I'm sticking to decaf after that. I hate it, but Dave says I need to kick the habit if we're going to start a family." She blushed, perhaps not intending to have said so much.

"Dave is a doctor, right?"

"That's right," she said proudly. "People here just love him. He's practically a fixture in the community." She pulled a cheesecake out of her refrigerator and dished up slices on two gorgeous dessert plates.

"I'm going to have to be careful," I said. "I think I've eaten more rich food here in twenty-four hours than I normally eat in a week."

"I know what you mean! I've gained five pounds since I moved here. We have the best restaurants. Things are slowing down right now, but just wait until the summer season. Town will be packed with people. They say they come for the mountains, but we all know they really come to eat!"

"I don't blame them." I tasted a bite of the cheesecake. It practically melted on my tongue, with tangy notes of sweet and sour. The raspberry and white chocolate topping was perfect. "Oh my goodness. This is heavenly. The best I've ever had, and I've been to New York."

"Isn't it amazing? I'm addicted. It's from the bakery downtown, *CoCo's*. They did our wedding cake, too."

"How long have you two been married?"

"Almost a year. Our anniversary is next month. He's taking me to Paris to celebrate." Her whole face pinked up in happiness.

"Wow, that's amazing!" I took another bite of my cheesecake and almost moaned in pleasure. "How did you guys meet?"

She giggled again. "At a hotel in Vegas."

I raised my eyebrows and cocked my head.

"I love telling people that. It sounds so scandalous. But it really wasn't like that at all. He was speaking at a medical conference," she explained. "I was there for a friend's wedding. We ended up sitting next to each other at one of the blackjack tables." She blushed. "He was just so charming and intelligent. And sweet. We talked all night. The rest, as they say, is history!"

Small town dynamics were new to me, but even so, I could see why the locals might share Fiona's attitude about Katie. Older doctor, a staple in the community, comes home from Vegas with a much younger woman who looks like a lingerie model. Yes, I could see why there would be instant judgment and an assumption about her motives. But from where I was sitting, it wasn't fair. Katie seemed genuinely sweet.

"Well, that's wonderful," I said. "I can't wait to meet him."

"Yes!" She brightened. "I've always wanted to have a cocktail party or something for the neighbors. Maybe even a progressive dinner where we do different courses at different houses. But I wasn't sure anyone would want to come. With you here now, though, and you and Emerson already becoming friends..." She gave me a wink.

I laughed. "It's one date. I wouldn't get too excited yet. I've gone on plenty of first dates that ended there. Actually, come to think about it, the vast majority of first dates I've been on have ended there. Unlike you, I've never found that charming, intelligent, sweet kind of guy you want to talk to all night."

She wrinkled up her nose. "Well, if that's what you're looking for, I don't know that Emerson is the guy. He's real quiet. I can't imagine him talking to anyone all night. No one here really knows much about him, except that he loves his job and is good at it. But enough about Emerson," she said, dismissing him. "You'll catch me up to speed on him after your date. Tell me about you! What made you move out here all by yourself? I know you're not one of those people who moves out here for the hiking." She giggled again and winked at me.

I debated internally about how much to tell her. Part of me wanted to keep everything about Eileen to myself. The little pieces I had of her felt so precious, so rare, that I didn't want to share them with anyone. But if I wanted to find out more about Eileen and what had happened to her, I was going to have to have conversations about her. And next to Fiona, Katie was probably the best place to start. She obviously hadn't lived here at that time, so she wouldn't know much. But she was married to the town doctor, which meant she had access to what was probably the best source of information possible.

"Well," I started. "This is a little hard to talk about."

"Go on." She took a long sip of coffee, her eyes never leaving my face.

"My mother used to live here. In the same house, actually. It was hers—ours, I guess. I don't remember it. I didn't even know she existed until recently. But when I found out—"

"You wanted to find her."

"Well, sort of. I mean, she died when I was little. But I wanted to get to know her somehow. I guess I thought that living where she lived, seeing the mountains she loved so much, and getting to know people who knew her back then would somehow give me a piece of her back. I don't know if that makes any sense."

Katie reached across the island and squeezed my hand, giving me a look of understanding.

"Actually, it does. I lost my mom when I was young, too."

"Really?" I was astonished that we shared that in common.

"Yeah. I was twelve when she died." She fell silent for a moment, her eyes drifting away from me as if she was remembering. "It was awful. And my father hadn't been in the picture much. We were never a real family, and he had left altogether a few years before that. So, when Mom died, I was completely on my own. Twelve years old, living alone in a dump of a town in backwoods Pennsylvania." She shook her head, seemingly snapping herself back to the present.

"Anyway," she continued. "All I'm saying is I get wanting to have that connection."

My heart went out to her. "Thanks for understanding. I was afraid people would think I was crazy, uprooting my life and moving somewhere just to find out more about her. In fact, I'm pretty sure Mom—my stepmother—really does think I've lost it."

"Anyone who thinks you're crazy just hasn't been through it themselves. When a kid loses a parent, it's like—" She paused, searching for the right words. "It's like there's a hole inside. A part of you that's missing or broken. And if moving here is going to help you fix that, then moving here is what you need to do."

I felt so grateful to find someone who understood.

"You know, I'm really glad I ran into you," I said. "Even if you never let me live the bear thing down."

She erupted into giggles, breaking the melancholy mood that had descended upon us.

Chapter Ten

I said goodbye to Katie and jogged back home for my car. *Home.* The word still felt surreal. But with the welcome I had already received, it was feeling more like home than my apartment ever had. I had lived there for weeks before the first neighbor had bothered to say hi. It was different here. Fiona was right. The lane was like a little community. And for once, I actually felt like I fit into it.

I grabbed my keys and a notepad and headed into town for supplies. Thanks to Fiona and Katie, I hadn't needed to make use of my lone granola bar yet, but I was ready to stock the pantry with more than coffee. Fiona had warned me that flash floods, snow, and broken tree limbs frequently made the lane impassable. She advised me to always keep at least two weeks' worth of food and supplies at the cottage, just in case. That would take some getting used to. I rarely had more than coffee, yogurt, and a box of cereal stashed in my apartment. I had a feeling I was going to regret my lack of interest in cooking over the years.

Rosemary Mountain was a small town, but thanks to its status as a vacation destination, it had a surprisingly good shopping selection. I started at a home goods store, where I purchased fluffy new bath towels, a shower curtain, and some cute kitchen utensils. A fresh start was worthy of some new things.

Out of curiosity, I popped into a local artists' gallery. When I saw a set of wine glasses featuring hand-painted black bears, I had to splurge. Katie would love the joke.

Next on my list was the hardware store. I had brought Dad's toolbox and paintbrushes, planning to get a start on renovations before the movers arrived. I chose samples in blue, white, and grey, hoping to give the cottage a brighter feel. At the last minute, I added a sample of pale sage green as well. Green had never been my favorite color, but I suspected it might look nice in the cottage.

I treated myself to a burger for lunch, then finished my shopping with a trip to the grocery store. I filled my cart with everything I thought I could possibly need for a week. It was the largest grocery trip I had ever made for myself, but at least I wouldn't go hungry if I was trapped at the cottage for a few days.

By the time I got back home, I was exhausted and had spent a ridiculous, head-spinning amount of money.

But I also felt happier than I had in weeks.

WHAT I WANTED MORE THAN ANYTHING WAS TO SPEND WHAT was left of the afternoon playing with paint samples, but I still needed to earn a living.

Photographers hired me because of my eye, speed, and consistency. I loved editing photos nearly as much as I loved taking them, and I enjoyed the freedom of working from home. My current project was a bit tricky, though. The ceremony and reception were both indoors, and the photographer was inexperienced and had struggled to nail her lighting. Her ISO had been set too high, making the pictures grainy and dark. But in my hands, the photographs transformed into what I hoped would be treasured heirlooms for the bride and groom. I liked to imagine all my couples still looking over their wedding albums together on their 50th anniversaries, even though the cynical side of me knew that at least half of these marriages would end in divorce. I could usually predict which ones, too, just by looking through the pictures.

My gut said this couple wouldn't last more than two years.

But I always did my job to the best of my ability, no matter my feelings about the couple. Several hours later, I had a beautiful gallery ready for the photographer. I stretched, feeling the satisfaction of a job well done, then realized I was starving. The day had flown by.

I started heating the carton of clam chowder I had bought at the grocery store that afternoon and poured a tall glass of Cabernet into one of my new wine glasses. Nothing could make a more perfect first dinner in my new home.

Already in a great mood, I brightened even more when I heard a knock at the door. Fiona had probably cut through the woods again to say hi. I opened the door with a smile on my face and my wine glass still in hand.

"Oh," I said, surprised. "Hi. Can I help you?"

It wasn't Fiona after all. A couple was standing on my porch, holding what appeared to be some brochures. My gaze went from the woman to the man, and I nearly jumped out of my skin. It was the man I had seen in the motel parking lot a few weeks prior, and he was staring at me with the same expression as before. All the color had drained from his face.

The woman, however, didn't seem fazed, and she took the lead in the conversation.

"Hello," she said. "This is Reverend Kistler, and I'm his wife, Patricia. We heard that a new neighbor had moved in next door, so we just wanted to come introduce ourselves and extend an invitation for you to join us in church tomorrow."

She passed me the pamphlet, which turned out to be an advertisement for their church. It was flashy and colorful, splashed with photographs of the Reverend preaching and praying for people. It was fascinating, in an odd sort of way.

"Thank you," I said, tearing my eyes away from the pamphlet and meeting her gaze. "I appreciate the invitation."

She smiled, but it didn't quite reach her eyes. I studied her while she began explaining my attendance options (*there were two morning services, young people usually liked the later one, potluck after in the fellowship hall, lots of young people like myself for me to meet, she was sure I would love it, they were a real Bible preaching church, not like the other churches in town, yada yada*). She seemed nice enough, but there was something off. She spoke with a deliberate meekness and obvious deference for her husband. When she looked up at him, her gaze was almost worshipful. The whole dynamic between them made me feel more than a little uncomfortable.

The Reverend finally recovered himself while his wife was talking. He cut off her spiel, for which she seemed grateful instead of annoyed. When he spoke, she seemed to shrink, almost pulling back as if to let him shine.

"Well, we won't take up any more of your time," he said in a confident voice. He reached out and grasped my hand in a firm handshake, his eyes piercing mine. I automatically shivered and felt myself shrink, too. He carried himself the way I imagined a U.S. President would. There was something so, well, powerful about him.

"We'll see you in church tomorrow," he continued, as if it were a foregone conclusion.

"Oh," I said, my mind racing to formulate a decent excuse. "I'm afraid I can't make it tomorrow, but thank you anyway. The movers haven't arrived with my things yet. I'm roughing it out here for a few days with nothing nice to wear."

"God doesn't need you to be dressed in frills and finery," he said. *Says the man wearing a well-cut suit and leather dress shoes. In the woods.*

"God simply needs you to come with an open heart, willing to hear and receive His message. Don't you agree, Ms.?"

"Sullivan. Daphne Sullivan."

His face paled again, but he recovered more quickly this time.

"Oh," said Patricia, "Sullivan. There were some Sullivans who lived out here years ago, weren't there, Don?"

"That's right," he said, slowly.

Patricia started in on another pitch, but Don cut her off again, and she instantly hushed.

"We hope you'll change your mind," he said, reaching out to shake my hand again. I grimaced at the feel of my hand in his. "Patricia, I think we have dinner guests waiting?"

"Oh, yes!" she said in a flutter. "Well, goodnight."

"Goodnight," I said. I went back inside, but held the door open a crack, watching them walk down my driveway toward their own house.

They were a picture in contrasts. He was tall, at least six two. She was short. His haircut looked fresh and expensive, while her own badly-permed hair looked like it hadn't seen the inside of a decent salon in years. He was dressed impeccably, while she appeared almost shabby in a long denim skirt and a faded sweater. His posture was perfect; her shoulders stooped. *I guess it's true that opposites attract.*

When they disappeared around the corner, I locked the door. I shivered again, although I couldn't say why.

Chapter Eleven

Sunday morning brought dreary skies and the threat of thunder in the distance. I had my morning coffee on the deck anyway, enthralled by the visual play of fog over the treetops. The whole feel of the woods was different, like a woman who had traded her sundress and bare face for a slinky cocktail dress and smoky eye. It was fascinating. I made a mental note to find a scenic outlook, somewhere I could compose a nice photograph and capture the mountain in its various moods. Seasonal shots could be gorgeous as well. The transition from spring to winter and back again, death and rebirth playing out in front of our very eyes. Oh yes. There was plenty of inspiration for a book here. A thrill ran through me just thinking of what it would be like to flip open a book of *my* images.

An hour had passed, coffee long gone, before I said goodbye to the woods and returned to what felt like an endless task list. I had another wedding that needed my attention, and I was determined to get some paint samples on the wall. I also had a date that night with Emerson, I remembered, my heart quickening. It had been a long time since I had been on a date. There had been little time for that kind of thing when I was starting my business and working long hours to prove myself to the photographers who gave me a shot. Then Dad got sick, and there wasn't time for anything at all.

I changed into my work sweats and grabbed my paint samples, adding swatches in different rooms to see how they looked. When I walked into the second bedroom, the empty room in front of me faded and I was blindsided with images—visions or memories, I wasn't sure. They were broken, disjointed, but clear. Eileen was walking around the room with me in her arms, bouncing and singing to me, her face a picture of joy. The scene changed to her rocking in a corner chair, her mind a million miles away as I played alone with toys on the floor. Next, she was writing furiously in a journal, glancing around as if she didn't want to be seen, then hiding it underneath a floorboard.

The empty room returned and I slid bonelessly to the floor, my heart pounding. I wanted to weep and scream at the same time. I wanted to crawl back into the first moments, the ones where Eileen had been happy holding me. Those moments were infused with a love I had ached for my whole life. I craved more of it.

But the others. I hated the others. Eileen had been deeply afraid. The fear had been so strong I could almost taste it as bitterness on my tongue. And I had been helpless, watching, unable to protect her from whatever had happened so many years ago.

But I wasn't helpless now.

I was more determined than ever to find out exactly what had happened to my mother.

If nobody else knew about the journal, there was a strong possibility it was still hidden in the house. Finding it might give me every answer I was looking for.

The only problem was that I had no idea where to start. I didn't get any sense of place during that flash. All I saw was Eileen lifting a floorboard. Everything around her was dark.

The easiest place to start was here, upstairs, where the floors had never been carpeted over. I crawled around on my hands and knees, testing for loose spots.

Nothing.

I went to my bedroom next and repeated the process. There was a loose board in the corner. I ran downstairs to the toolbox and grabbed a hammer, thinking I could use the claw end to pry up the board. It took a few tries, but it worked.

Nothing.

I sat down, defeated. If the journal had been underneath this one, it was gone. If it was downstairs, I would need to rip out the carpet to get to it.

Adding insult to injury, someone chose just that moment to knock on the door. I looked down at my clothes. I had managed to get myself filthy while crawling around on the floor. The last thing I wanted was to meet any more neighbors. Actually, that wasn't true. I would take meeting more neighbors over another encounter with Don any day.

The knock returned, more persistent this time. I sighed, dusted myself off as best I could, and headed down to the door.

"Oh, my!" Fiona clucked her tongue, looking me up and down. "What on earth have you been doing?"

"Oh, just a little head start on painting," I said weakly. "Come on in. Coffee?"

"Daphne," she said hesitantly. "You know you can tell me anything, right?"

"What do you mean?"

"Well, it's just that most people don't cry over testing out some paint samples."

"How did you know I was crying?" I asked, startled.

"Honey, those tear tracks are as plain as can be with as dusty as your face is. Plus, your eyes are all red and you haven't smiled once."

I stepped into the downstairs bathroom to look in the mirror. She was right. I was more of a mess than I had realized. I ran some cold water and washed my face quickly. Even with the dust and tear tracks gone, I still looked terrible.

I returned to where Fiona was. "Sorry about that," I said. "You just caught me at a bad time."

"Or the right time." She cocked her head. "How about some hot tea instead of that coffee? Something a bit more soothing, perhaps. Sit down, honey, and let me handle things in the kitchen."

I nearly collapsed into my camping chair and nodded. "I grabbed a couple of hot teas at the grocery store. The boxes are in the pantry."

She came back a few minutes later, holding two steaming mugs.

"Here you go," she said, her voice soothing. "Drink up. It will do you good."

She perched back on the fireplace hearth and watched me, nodding in approval as I sipped the hot liquid. The tea was smooth and fragrant. Nourishing. I took a deep breath and felt steady.

"Which one is this?" I asked. "It's delicious."

"Oh, it's one of my own," she said. "I always carry a few herbs in my bag. Trick of the trade." She patted the fringed crossbody bag that hung around her slim frame.

"Well, thank you. It's just what I needed."

"I thought it might be," she said, winking. "Now, I think we need to talk. What's going on, honey?"

I hesitated. As if she could read my mind she said, "Oh, I know what you're thinking. But town gossip is one thing." She waved a hand through the air, dismissing it. "Anything real though? You can trust old Fiona with your secrets. Your mama did, you know." She cocked her head again and gazed at me intently.

Some sort of communication passed between us and I found myself wondering.

"What secrets did she trust you with?" I felt sure I already knew.

"Well, for example, I know she had the second sight. And for another, I know you do, too," she said, pointing a finger at me.

"How do you know that?" I stammered.

"Well for one thing, it's written all over you. For another, it's often passed down from woman to woman, and your mama's was so strong it would be shocking for you to not have at least a little. But mainly, because you told me so."

"What? No, I didn't."

"You did," she insisted, cocking her head again. "Back when you were a wee thing, coming with your mama to visit me in the garden. Oh, but you were a solemn little babe! You'd look up at the sky, then look at me and tell me 'snow.' And by golly, that night it would snow. Then there was the time you brought me my midwifing bag and told me to go, and five minutes later the phone rang to tell me Mrs. Clemens was in labor and needed me right away." She chuckled at the memory.

I was astonished, and frankly relieved.

"Do you also have the second sight?"

She shook her head. "Oh, no, not me. My gifts are different."

"But, my mother, too? For sure?"

"Oh, yes, honey. It was strong in your mama."

I gathered myself. "After I found out about her, I talked to Mom— my stepmom, that is. Janet. She said that Dad told her my mother was mentally ill. That she thought she had intuition, but it was really paranoia and hallucinations. That..." It was so hard for me to speak the words. "That she killed herself because of it."

"Hogwash." She was emphatic. "Lonnie knew about the second sight. He had seen evidence of it aplenty, let me tell you."

"Then why would he say that?"

She shrugged. "Why does anyone do anything? Lonnie loved your mother, maybe more than a man should ever love a woman, if that's possible. When she died the grief nearly killed him. Turned him into someone I barely recognized. Maybe he needed something to blame and that's all he could come up with."

I was struggling, torn between believing the Dad I had always trusted or what my own heart was telling me.

"But if she wasn't mentally ill, then why would she kill herself?" *Please, tell me you doubt it too.*

Fiona frowned. "I've always struggled with that one myself. To tell you the truth, I can't give you a single reason for that. When they investigated, they said it was a clear suicide. There was a note—" she paused, glancing at me. "Are you sure you're okay to talk about this, honey?"

"Yes. Please. I need to know. And I've seen the note."

She nodded and continued. "Well, I saw it too and it was definitely in Eileen's hand. It was just you and her here at the house. Lonnie was gone on a weekend fishing trip. There wasn't any sign of a struggle."

"How did she..." I didn't want to hear it, didn't want to have that image in my head. But I needed to know.

"Sleeping pills." Fiona frowned again. "That was another thing that always bothered me. Why did she even have them?"

"I think it's fairly common for them to be prescribed. My college roommate had them."

Fiona shook her head. "Common for some people, maybe. But your mama wasn't one for western medicine. Like me, her medicine came from the garden. If she was having trouble sleeping, she would have brewed up some chamomile tea or taken some valerian tincture. If that didn't work, I would have given her a stronger concoction. In all the time I knew her, I never knew her to take sleeping pills."

"Fiona," I paused. "Do you think there's any chance she was murdered?"

Fiona sighed. "I wondered, that's for sure. But everyone told me it was a straightforward case. And who on earth would want to kill her? There was no motive. Everyone loved Eileen. She was such a sweet girl."

With a painful stab of guilt for the betrayal in even thinking it, I asked the question that had haunted me ever since I found the box.

"Fiona, is there any chance at all that my dad..."

She shook her head emphatically. "Absolutely not. I would never believe it. Your daddy loved your mama like she was the sun, moon, and stars all wrapped together in one. They were happy. You can rest on that."

I nodded, relieved. I let out a breath I didn't realize I had been holding.

"Your mama did change in those weeks leading up to her passing. She was worried about something." Fiona frowned again, remembering. "It's the one time she didn't open up to me. Something was bothering her and she wouldn't tell me what. But if it had been about Lonnie, I would have known."

"I had a couple of visions of her." The words came out, surprising me even as they did. After years of denying them, blocking them, being ashamed of them even, it was so strange to discuss them openly.

"Did you now? Tell me about them." Fiona's eyes were curious.

"It was her, in this house. With me. And yeah, I saw that she had become worried about something. She was writing in a journal. She hid it."

Fiona gasped and leaned forward, her eyes locked on mine. "Did you see where?"

"It was under a floorboard. I checked the ones upstairs, but it wasn't there."

"Maybe it's down here." She looked at the carpet in disgust.

"Unless her killer took it."

Our eyes met with silent understanding.

Chapter Twelve

Two hours later, we both plopped down on the fireplace hearth, exhausted. We had turned the house upside down searching for the journal. We had even ripped up the carpet in the living room. Now, I was left with a colossal mess to take care of before the movers arrived on Tuesday. It would have been worth it if we had actually found the thing, but we had come up empty.

I grabbed us each a bottle of water and greedily gulped mine down.

"Would you like something to eat? I have sandwich fixings and chips. There's also some leftover clam chowder to go with it."

Fiona waved me off. "Thank you, dear, but some of the ladies are having a potluck lunch today." She checked the delicate gold watch she wore on her wrist. "In about an hour, in fact. You'd be welcome to come if you want."

Her mention of potluck reminded me of my visit from the Kistlers. "Fiona, I'm so sorry, I wasn't even thinking. Did I make you miss church?"

An amused look crossed her face. "I'm right where I'm supposed to be today. Don't you worry about that."

"Okay. It's just that the Reverend and his wife came by last night to invite me to theirs. They mentioned a potluck lunch after, so I wondered if it was the same one."

Her amused look quickly turned to something different. "Did they really? No, not the same one. This is a group of ladies that get together once a month for lunch, which really means to catch up on town gossip." She winked. "Don't worry, I meant what I said—your secrets are safe with me."

"So you don't go to the Reverend's church?"

She threw her head back and laughed. "Hardly. Don doesn't want me around any more than I want to be there."

"What do you mean?"

"I'm not the kind of woman he wants as a parishioner."

"Why not?"

"Because I have a brain," she cackled. "It's hard to explain if you don't know him and how his particular brand of religion works. I visited once, back in the day. They were new, and I was trying to be neighborly. I felt uncomfortable pretty much the moment I walked in. And then he started preaching."

I leaned forward, interested.

"You know what he said?" she asked.

I shrugged. I couldn't even imagine.

She leaned forward, too. "He said that it was crucial to be in church every time the doors were open, because that's where God *lives*. He said that people who think they can skip church and go out into the woods to meet with God are fooling themselves, cause God ain't out there." She leaned back again and pointed her finger at me. "And that's when I realized we didn't actually worship the same God."

A grin spread across my face. I found myself liking Fiona more and more.

"I'm pretty sure he spells God *D-O-N*. Or maybe *M-O-N-E-Y,*" she said, spelling out each letter with emphasis.

"You know, that's interesting. I got a really weird vibe from him, but I don't know how to explain it."

This time, she was the one leaning forward in interest. "Go on."

"Well," I lowered my voice slightly, feeling the tiniest bit guilty for indulging in this type of gossip. "My first encounter with him was actually a few weeks ago. I had come to town to check out the house, and I was staying at the motel out on the highway. Anyway, he was there. I ran into him in the parking lot. He acted like he had seen a ghost."

"Well, now, isn't that interesting?" Fiona's eyes narrowed. "You know, there's been rumors now and then of him indulging in some *extramarital recreation,* shall we say? It never gained any traction, though; he's always claimed that people are just trying to persecute and slander God's anointed one." She rolled her eyes.

I laughed. "Well, I didn't see anyone else there. There wasn't any other car in the parking lot, and he didn't have a woman with him. So I don't know for sure that he was there for that purpose. But it was weird. Gave me the creeps, for sure. He just stared at me in the weirdest way. Then, when they came over last night, he did the same thing. Patricia did the talking at first, while he stood practically frozen with his mouth gaping open."

Fiona frowned. "Now that is extremely interesting. I've never known him to let Patricia take the lead on anything. You do look just like your mama, though. I thought I had seen a ghost when you answered the door for me! Did he mention that?"

"No, not really. When I gave them my name, Patricia mentioned some Sullivans used to live here, but neither of them mentioned my mom or asked if there was any relation."

"I don't like it," Fiona said. "Something about all that just don't seem right."

"It felt odd," I agreed.

We left it there and said our goodbyes, both of us in desperate need of a shower. After I cleaned up, I surveyed my house in dismay. Pulling up the carpet was an improvement, for sure. The hardwoods eventually needed to be refinished, but there was no way for that to happen before the movers came. Thankfully, they were in decent shape, considering. But I had no idea what to do with all the carpet and carpet padding that was now in a pile in my living room. I doubted that leaving it by my trash can was an option, and I had no idea where to dispose of it—or how to get it there inside my small car. But I needed to figure out something, even if it was a temporary solution, before the movers arrived on Tuesday.

. . .

THE AFTERNOON SLIPPED AWAY MUCH TOO QUICKLY, BUT I didn't really mind, considering it made waiting for my date with Emerson go by that much faster. It felt strange to be doing something as normal as getting dressed for a date. The last few months of my life had been anything but normal. In fact, they had been the most dramatic, strange, emotional months of my life. And yet, even in all the chaos, life somehow went on.

My wardrobe was temporarily quite small, but Mom had taught me one truly useful skill: the capsule wardrobe. Despite what I had told Don and Patricia, my wardrobe in a suitcase would accommodate most occasions.

The problem was that I hadn't thought to ask Emerson where we were going or what we were doing.

I played it relatively safe, with black skinny jeans and a camel-toned cashmere tunic that I knew brought out the warmer tones in my hair. Black leather ballet flats and smoky quartz jewelry completed the outfit. I looked in the mirror, satisfied. It was dressy enough that I would feel comfortable at a nice restaurant, but casual enough not to feel too out of place at the fish house.

I took extra care with my makeup and even ran a curling iron through my hair for some extra waves. I relished the thrill of butterflies. It had been too long since I had something to look forward to.

I WAS READY WHEN THE DOORBELL RANG. WHEN I OPENED IT, the butterflies went crazy. Emerson was standing on the porch with a bouquet of wildflowers in hand. He looked fantastic, in dark jeans and a hunter green sweater. The green suited him perfectly, just like the landscape behind him.

"Come in," I said, welcoming him inside.

He passed me the flowers. "These are for you."

"They're gorgeous. Thank you." I breathed in their scent.

"Goldenrod and Purple Aster," he said. "They bloom this time of year. I came across a big patch this morning on a hike and thought you might like some.”

“I do like them. They’re beautiful.” My mind flashed back to one of the pictures of Eileen. She had been standing in a field of purple and yellow flowers just like this. The wildflowers felt like one more strand connecting us. I turned and walked toward the kitchen, so Emerson wouldn’t see the emotion I was sure was all over my face.

“I’m just going to put these in water,” I called. “I’m so sorry about the mess. Make yourself as comfortable as you can. There’s a camping chair in there.”

When I walked back to the living room, he was perched on the fireplace hearth, just like Fiona always did. I couldn’t help but grin.

“Doing some renovations?” he asked.

“Sort of,” I said, laughing. “I think I made an error in judgment, though. I pulled up this carpet without thinking it through, and I don’t have the slightest clue what to do with it now that I have.”

“I can take care of it for you,” he offered.

“Oh, no.” I blushed. “I wasn’t trying to hint around for help.”

“I know you weren’t. But it’s not a big deal. When we get back from dinner, we can throw it in the bed of my truck. I drive by the county landfill on the way to work. I’ll drop it off for you.”

“Thanks. That’s really nice of you.”

“No big deal. We all take care of each other out here.”

That was the second or third time I had heard that same sentiment in my short time on the lane. I was starting to believe it.

“Well,” he said, standing. “Are you ready for dinner?”

“Sounds great.” I grabbed my purse from the corner and pulled out my keys to lock up.

His hand lightly brushed the small of my back as I walked out the door, sending a thrill up my spine.

“It seems like everyone up here has a truck, except me,” I commented, as he helped me into his.

He glanced at my own sporty compact sitting in the driveway. “Well, four-wheel drive is a good thing to have up here when the weather starts changing. You don’t need a truck necessarily, but they are convenient for hauling firewood or supplies. Or carpets." He winked before walking around to his side.

"Exactly how bad does the weather get up here?"

"I'm not the one to ask. I've only had one winter here so far, and the locals said it was a mild one. We got snowed in a couple of times, and we had one ice storm. It was pretty nasty, knocked out the power for a few days. Then spring comes, and you have to worry about flash floods."

"I'm not sure what I'm getting myself into."

He glanced over at me, a reassuring smile on his face. "It's all part of living on the mountain. It's worth it."

"I hope so." I returned his smile. His eyes lingered on mine for just a second before he turned them back to the road. My heart flip-flopped in my chest.

"So what brought you to the mountain?" he asked. It was a question I had grown to expect. I gave him the same true, but limited, version that I had given Katie.

It was getting easier. I no longer feared I would lose part of Eileen by sharing her. By telling the story, it was actually becoming more real. More solid. She had only felt like a phantom before, a wispy ghost of an idea. Stepping into my identity as Eileen Sullivan's daughter was bringing her to life somehow, if only in my heart.

The drive into town felt all too short. Before I knew it, we were pulling into a restaurant I hadn't seen before, tucked out of the way of the main streets through town. A small sign identified it as O'Malley's Irish Pub.

"This is my favorite place in town," Emerson explained. "It's almost all locals. He owns a second, bigger one back there on the main strip. It's done up big time for the tourists, with a gift shop and everything. It's always packed during the summer. This one, he kept quieter. Wanted it to be a place the locals felt was their own."

"Wow, I love that."

"Me too. And since you're a local now, it's only fitting that you should know about it too." He shot me a quick grin.

I felt flattered. I didn't really think of myself as a local yet, but it felt fun to be included in one of their secrets.

Emerson came around and opened the truck door for me, his hand resting lightly on the small of my back as he guided me to the door. I felt acutely aware of his fingertips, like my senses were heightened just being around him. The faint scent of his cologne made me want to bury my face in the crook of his neck.

Oh, I was in trouble.

He opened the door to the pub and guided me in, greeting the man behind the bar as he did. He gestured toward a booth in the back corner. I slid in and watched him take his place across from me.

A waitress appeared out of nowhere with menus.

"Well, hey there, Emerson," she said, giving him a flirtatious smile. Katie wasn't kidding. The waitress was at least ten years older than he was, but her body language made it clear that she was interested.

"Hey." Emerson's smile was polite but not warm.

"What can I get you?" She leaned over, resting her forearms on the table, giving Emerson a clear view down the front of her shirt. I could see her black lace bra peeking out. My jaw nearly hit the table.

Emerson, bless him, kept his eyes on her face. "I'll take a pint of Guinness. What about you, Daphne?" As he said my name, his smile warmed.

The waitress stood up and looked me over. No smiles for me, just a thinly disguised look of contempt.

"A glass of your house red, please," I said. She spun on her heels and walked away without a word.

"Sorry about that," Emerson said, his expression pained. "They must have changed her schedule. She normally has Sundays off."

I giggled. "That was interesting."

He shook his head. "It's mostly retirees who move here. I'm pretty sure I'm the only single man under forty who has moved to the area in the last couple of years. It has its downsides."

"Or its perks?" I shrugged.

"Some might see it that way. But I moved to the mountain for solitude, not to be the center of attention."

Solitude. So, probably not looking for a relationship. Not that I was either. *Liar.*

"So, where did you move from?" I asked.

"Well, technically, I moved here from Ohio. I was stationed there, at Wright-Patt. But I'm originally from Madison, Wisconsin."

"Stationed? Were you in the army?"

"Air Force."

"Oh, that's cool." I felt completely out of my element. I knew next to nothing about the military or how it worked. Compared to him, I suddenly felt young, stupid, and inexperienced.

"What about you?" he asked. "Where did you call home before deciding to make the move out here?"

"Little Rock, Arkansas," I said.

"Wow. So this will be more of a winter than you're used to, huh?"

"I guess you could say that. It certainly will be a different kind of one, for sure."

"There's nothing like it. Everyone comes out here during the fall to see the leaves turn. And yeah, it's beautiful. But when the mountain is covered in snow and the road hasn't been plowed yet? Man. It's a different world. Everything slows down, and the forest comes alive in a whole new way. We don't get near as much snow as I'm used to, growing up in Wisconsin, but I love it just the same. Have you ever snowshoed?"

I shook my head no with a laugh.

"I'll teach you."

He smiled at me and held my gaze. My heartbeat picked up as he leaned forward slightly. The spell was broken by our waitress practically slamming my wine glass onto the table. Emerson's pint was placed much more gently, with another pose obviously meant to put her best assets on display. A giggle escaped before I could stop it. She glared at me.

"Sorry," he apologized—again—when she left with our orders.

"It's fine." I waved him off. "Honestly, it's kind of funny."

"I'm glad you think so." His grin returned.

I loved his grin. It went up slightly higher on one side, showing off his dimples. They were in stark contrast with the rest of him. He carried himself in a stoic, rugged manner. His face was often serious. But when he grinned, it was like seeing a different part of him altogether. It was a part of him I desperately wanted to know better.

DINNER WAS, OF COURSE, EXCELLENT. I HAD COME TO EXPECT nothing less from the restaurants here in Rosemary Mountain. I tried the shepherd's pie. It was made with real lamb and fresh herbs, and beat every single shepherd's pie I had ever eaten.

"The food in this town makes me want to learn to cook," I said in between mouthfuls.

"But why learn when you can just eat your way through the town?"

"Excellent point. Thanks for making me feel better about my lack of skill in the kitchen. I'll just do my part and support the local economy."

"There you go." He grinned. "That's certainly how I like to look at it."

"I do need to learn a few kitchen skills before we get snowed in, though. Canned soup can only get you so far."

"That's where learning to snowshoe will come in handy." He took a long drink from his beer mug. "You can just snowshoe down to my place and eat a home-cooked meal with me." He winked.

"I thought you didn't know how to cook either!"

He leaned forward conspiratorially. "I never said I didn't know how. I just don't do it every night. But if there's a beautiful girl on the mountain going hungry with nothing but canned soup and crackers, you better believe I can put together a killer beef stew."

The waitress had chosen that exact moment to slap our ticket down on the table. She flounced off without so much as a word. Emerson just groaned.

A RAINSTORM HAD MOVED IN WHILE WE SAT IN THE restaurant.

"This is a heavy one," Emerson said. "I'm afraid we'd better head back in case the road becomes impassable." He opened the truck door for me, and I slid in, nervously watching the rain. Growing up in Little Rock, I knew all too well the damage that flash floods could do. When the rains came and the river rose, it was always shocking how quickly the roads would disappear under the rushing water.

"This is a stupid question," I began.

"Haven't you heard? There are no stupid questions."

"Well, this one is. I guess I just don't understand. Why is flooding such an issue on the mountain? With the elevation, I would think the water would just run off. We had bad flooding in Little Rock, but it was a low-lying city on a river."

"Well, you're dealing with a couple of things on the mountain," he said, driving more quickly than he had before. "There are streams and creeks all over that thing. And because of the steep run-offs, heavy rain can turn those streams and creeks into raging rivers before you know it. The other issue up there is that storms can send boulders or tree limbs into the road."

"So our road becomes impassable often?"

"More often than you'd think."

We made it to the turnoff for the lane, and I saw for myself exactly what Emerson meant. I had barely even registered the small creek that normally ran under the road at the bottom of the hill. But you couldn't miss it now. It had risen and swelled to three times its normal width and was threatening to cover the road.

Emerson let out a relieved sigh. "Looks like we made it just in time."

Once the creek was behind us, he relaxed. "That was the only spot I was really worried about. They really need to do something about the road right there, with as often as that creek floods like that."

"Yeah, I see what you mean."

I wasn't quite ready to relax, though. The rain was still driving down in sheets, making visibility nearly impossible, yet I was more aware than ever of Lonely Oak Road's steep climb and treacherous curves.

"Hey," Emerson said, reaching over and covering my hand with his. "You ok?"

"Yeah," I said unconvincingly. "The road. It just makes me nervous. I'm not quite used to mountain driving, even in good weather."

He squeezed my hand, a nice, if momentary, distraction.

"Don't worry," he said. "I know this road like the back of my hand, and I've driven it in weather that's a hell of a lot worse than this."

His tone was reassuring and confident, but I noticed he slowed down anyway.

The road seemed to stretch out forever, but finally he turned into the clearing that held my cottage.

I let out a sigh of relief.

Emerson frowned. "Your house is all dark."

"I didn't think to leave a light on." I realized now what a silly mistake that had been. Without the light from his truck's headlights, the house would have been swallowed in darkness. I wasn't sure I would ever get used to just how dark it got up here on the mountain.

"Just a sec," he said, leaning over toward my seat. I thought, for a moment, that he was leaning in to kiss me. But he went for the glove box instead. He pulled out a large flashlight and handed it to me.

"I'll leave the truck going while we make a run for your door, but carry that just in case." Next, he leaned into the backseat to grab something else. "Here you go," he said, handing it to me.

"What is it?"

"Rain jacket. You're probably going to get wet anyway in this mess, but it will at least help."

This man thought of everything, it seemed.

"Got your keys ready?" he asked.

"Oh, good point." I fished them out of my purse and found the right one.

"Alright, let's go."

I grabbed his arm. "Emerson, you don't have to walk up there with me. This rain is ridiculous. Stay here in the truck where it's dry."

He flashed that grin at me, the one I was finding impossible to resist. Then he was out of the truck, completely ignoring what I had said. He ran around to my side and opened it for me.

The jacket was no match for the driving sheets of rain hitting my face. He grabbed my hand and we ran for the protection of the covered porch. He took the flashlight from me when we got there and shined it on the lock so that I could see. With freezing hands, I fumbled with the lock, but finally got it to turn.

"Do you want to come in?" I managed to get out through chattering teeth. The temperature had also dropped significantly during the storm. I half expected the rain to turn to snow.

"Under just about any other circumstances, I would say yes. But I'd better get back to the cabin while I know I can. I need to make sure my animals are safe and settled."

"Animals? Plural?"

"I've got a couple. I'll have to introduce you sometime." He grinned again.

He ran his hand down the side of my arm and leaned forward. This time, I knew he was going to kiss me. My heart raced.

But before he could, a flash of lightning hit somewhere close enough to shake the porch. I screamed and grabbed onto him, my heart now pounding for a different reason altogether.

"Wow, that was a close one," he said. "The animals..." His voice trailed off, and he looked at me helplessly.

"Go," I said. "Before the storm gets worse." I pulled off the rain jacket and handed it to him with his flashlight.

"Just a sec," he said, pulling his cell phone from his pocket. He quickly typed in his code and handed it to me. "Can you text yourself so that I have your number and vice versa?"

"Of course." I quickly sent a text to my phone and handed his back to him.

"Good. I don't know how long this storm is going to hang around. Hopefully, it's just a quick one and we'll be back to sunshine tomorrow. But you call me if you need anything, ok?"

"Okay. Hey, Emerson?"

"Yes?"

"Will you let me know you made it home safe?"

A wave of emotions I couldn't quite place passed quickly across his face before being replaced by his characteristic grin.

"Yeah. Sure thing."

He squeezed my elbow and gave me a quick kiss on the cheek. It wasn't quite the ending to our date that I had been hoping for, but it sent thrills up my spine just the same.

Chapter Thirteen

The next morning, the storm was just a memory. The sun rose bright and beautiful, and the mountain air felt crisp and clean. I was more than ready to start my day with another jog. I told myself that my eagerness to hit the pavement was due to my love for exercise. That was surely also the reason I swiped on a touch of mascara and lip gloss first.

I jogged just past Emerson's cabin before turning around and heading back. Out of pride, I wanted to go farther—I would die of embarrassment if he was watching out a window and saw my obvious attempt to run into him—but the grade was significantly steeper past that point, and the climb was already going to kill me on the way back. Thankfully, there was no sign of his truck, so my secret was safe—from him, at least.

When I circled back, I saw Katie at the top of the hill, folded over in laughter. I jogged toward her, my face flushed from humiliation as much as exertion.

"I know what you're doing," she said in a sing-song voice when I reached her.

I shook my head with an embarrassed shrug.

"I'm glad I ran into you. I'm dying to hear about your date last night. Come have coffee with me and tell me every little detail."

"There's not much to tell, really." I laughed at the disappointment on her face.

"Oh, come on. Seriously?"

"Well, the storm kind of rained on our parade, so to speak. We had to rush back home after dinner to beat the flooding."

"Sounds perfect to me," she said, a mischievous look on her face. "Come home, curl up in front of a fire to dry out, open up a bottle of wine..."

"More like rush home, get drenched running to my door, attempt to kiss but get interrupted by a freak bolt of lightning, then say goodnight so that he can go home to take care of his animals."

"What a bummer. No kiss at all?"

"He kissed me on the cheek before he left." I smiled at the memory.

"Well, that's sweet," she said, in a tone that suggested otherwise.

"It was. Really. As crazy as it sounds, it was sort of the perfect first date. He was really kind and considerate..." My voice trailed off as I remembered the way it felt when he would look at me, his eyes meeting mine in a way that made me feel like he really saw me.

"So you really like him?"

This time, I broke into a full-blown grin. "Yeah, I do."

"Hmmm."

I glanced over at her. She had a serious look on her face, almost as if she was worried.

"What?" I asked. "What is it?"

She hesitated for a moment. "Well, it's just, I don't know. I mean, he's totally gorgeous, I'll give you that. I thought it would be great for you to go out and have some fun. But I don't think he's really, well, *relationship* material."

"What do you mean?" I was truly confused. Other than his comment about seeking solitude, he seemed like perfect relationship material to me. It wasn't as if he was just looking for a one-night stand. It was obvious he could easily have those. He was respectful and considerate, and he seemed to genuinely like me. The chemistry between us seemed to go both ways. He had a job and owned a house. If that wasn't relationship material, what was?

"Forget I said anything," she said, opening her garage door for us. I followed her inside to the kitchen, where she started a fresh pot of coffee.

"No, I want to know what you mean. What is it?"

"I've just heard things. Things I wasn't supposed to hear. It's part of being a doctor's wife in a small town, I suppose."

"Well, what did you hear?" I was starting to feel alarmed.

"I can't say. I shouldn't have said anything at all. I need to stop opening my big mouth. All I'm saying is this. Go out with him. Have all the fun in the world. Just don't expect more than that."

She placed a cup of coffee in front of me with a sympathetic look on her face.

"Okay. Well, thanks for the heads up, I guess." I didn't bother keeping the sarcasm out of my voice. I didn't know what else to say. What on earth could she possibly know about him from being a doctor's wife? My mind went crazy with possibilities, most of which were probably far worse than the truth.

I was sick of it.

Once again, I found myself in the dark while someone else withheld information affecting my life. Once again, I was sitting across a table from someone who knew more than I did, but who had all the power to decide how much information to trickle down to me. Once again, I had been thrown into a situation where I would now question everything.

I knew it wasn't fair to be angry at her. There were rules surrounding medical confidentiality. My brewing anger wasn't really about Katie at all. But I didn't feel very rational at the moment.

I lowered my eyes and took a long sip of coffee, avoiding her gaze. I knew I was overreacting. *Stop being ridiculous, Daphne.* Mom's favorite phrase echoed in my mind.

Katie looked at me with frank curiosity.

"You're really upset," she said. "I'm sorry. I just don't want you to get hurt, that's all."

"It's fine," I said.

"Then why do you look like you want to throw daggers right now?"

I put my coffee down, put my head in my hands, and sighed. The anger dissipated, leaving a sad, empty feeling in its place. It was not an improvement.

"It's not about you, or even this," I said. "It's hard to explain."

"Try." She took a seat across from me and leaned forward.

"Okay. But it stays between us, right?"

"Of course." She made the scout's honor sign.

"Well, you know how I told you that I came here to find out more about my mom?"

"Right."

"And how I didn't even know she existed until just a few weeks ago?"

"Right..."

It was clear she had no idea where I was going with this.

"The way that whole thing went down still makes me angry. My dad and stepmom both decided I didn't need to know this whole part of my life and history, so they just kept it from me. Like they could erase it. Erase *her*. And she's part of me."

"So it feels like they tried to erase part of you," she said softly.

"Yes." I hadn't realized I felt that way until I was saying it, but when I spoke the words aloud, my heart ached with the truth of them. "There's more. More of me that they tried to erase."

"What do you mean?"

"Katie, you have to promise me that this stays between us. Seriously."

Her eyebrows knitted together in concern. "Daphne, whatever is going on, I'm here for you. You can tell me."

"Well, I've always been a little bit, well, what some people might call psychic. Fiona calls it the second sight."

Her eyes widened, but she stayed silent, allowing me the space to continue.

"And it turns out that my mother was too. At least, that's what Fiona told me. Anyway, my dad tried to erase that part of me. He told me to kill it. And he told my stepmom that it wasn't real, that my mom had hallucinations and delusions—" I stopped, registering the look on Katie's face.

It hit me how crazy this sounded.

No wonder Katie was drawing herself back.

"I know how this sounds," I said.

"No, it's just, well, a lot. It's a lot to take in. Although I'm still not sure how this relates to you getting angry about the Emerson thing."

"Right." I still owed her an explanation for that. "It's because you knew something that affected me, but instead of telling me, you just told me what to do instead. Made the decision for me, so to speak." I saw she was starting to interrupt, so I held up my hand. "No, it's okay. I get it. You really can't tell me, and that's fine. I wasn't really mad at *you*. I just haven't yet dealt with how angry I am at my parents. I'm really sorry."

"No, *I'm* sorry. I shouldn't have said anything at all."

"We'll just forget it ever happened."

"Deal." She smiled. "But help me understand. Your dad lied to you —by omission, at the very least—about your mom. You're psychic…" She trailed off there, obviously unbelieving.

"I don't think the word psychic is actually the right word. I'm not sure how to explain it. I just see things sometimes. Things that already happened, like a glimpse of the past, or things that are going to happen shortly. I can't control it or predict it or make it happen. It was more frequent when I was a kid, before I blocked it. It didn't happen at all for years, and it's only happened a couple of times since it started again."

"But your Dad said they were hallucinations?"

"He never said that to me, no. He just told me to stop them. But apparently he said that about my mother's visions."

"Daphne," she said hesitantly. "I have to ask. Do you think there's any chance he's right?"

"No," I said firmly. *But there was a chance, right?* The doubt surprised me, like a snake striking before you even knew it was there.

"Okay," she said simply, accepting. "So, can you tell me my future?"

I laughed. "No. It doesn't work that way. Like I said, I can't control it at all, other than blocking it out, I guess. I just sometimes see things. Sometimes hazy flashes, sometimes more."

"Like what?" She was obviously curious, not that I could blame her.

I hesitated. It was one thing to tell Fiona my suspicion that my mother was murdered. It was another thing altogether to tell someone who had never met her. If Katie didn't already think I was crazy, she probably would after that revelation. But she was my friend. She hadn't run away screaming yet.

"The real reason I came here is because I had a vision about my mother. A vision that makes me think she was murdered."

Shock rippled across Katie's face. "*Murdered?*"

"I know. And I know this all sounds seriously crazy."

"A little, yeah. But, I don't know, I guess I just believe you."

"Thanks. Really."

"So if she was murdered, do you have any idea who did it?"

"No, I don't." I let out a breath. "Fiona said my mother didn't have a single enemy in town. Everyone loved her. And honestly, everyone I've met seems really nice. I've only gotten weird vibes from one person."

Her eyes widened again. "Who?"

"The reverend who lives down on my end of the lane."

"Don Kistler?" Her voice changed as she said his name.

"Yeah."

"Huh. That's interesting." Her brows knit together again, with a look of someone whose mind was racing furiously.

"Why do you say that?"

"I mean, I don't know him very well, but he is definitely odd. To say the least. I guess he's always given me a weird vibe, too. Do you know what year your mother died?"

"2001. And yeah, from what I understand, they lived next door back then. When I met them, Patricia mentioned they had known the Sullivans. She didn't seem to put it together that I was related to them, though."

"They definitely would have been here in 2001. Don has pastored that church since it was founded in 1995. The house belongs to the church, but it was built specifically for them."

"Wow. That's a very nice parsonage."

She rolled her eyes. "Tell me about it. Well, that's very interesting. Do you think he was involved?"

"I don't know." I raised my shoulders in a shrug. "I really have no idea. All I know is that he looks like he's seen a ghost every time he sees me."

"Really?" She leaned forward again, her eyes widening.

"Yes. He's never mentioned my mother, but Fiona says I look just like her. And both times he's seen me, he's had a weird reaction."

"Both times?"

"Oh yeah. I forgot to tell you. The first time I ran into him, he was in the parking lot of the motel." I wiggled my eyebrows at her.

"The motel?" Her mouth dropped. "You're kidding."

"Maybe he was helping a church member with something."

She rolled her eyes again. "Please. Everyone in town knows that men go to that motel to rent rooms by the hour. And most people won't mention this, but everyone knows Don used to be one of those men. But I'm surprised he has the balls to keep doing it. He got into big trouble years ago for the same thing. He's supposed to have 'account-ability partners' keeping him on a leash these days."

"Really?" Now I was the one with wide eyes.

"Yeah. He could get in big trouble if anyone knew." She held up her hand when she saw my face. "Don't worry. I won't tell a soul."

I breathed a sigh of relief. I didn't want to get him in trouble. Unless it turned out that he really was the one who murdered my mother.

In that case, I would take him down so hard he never saw it coming.

Chapter Fourteen

I walked back to my house slowly, giving myself time to think. The picture I was getting of Don Kistler put him at the top of my potential suspect list. Of course, truth be told, he was my only suspect so far. I hadn't met anyone else who raised any red flags where my mother was concerned.

But I didn't have much to go on. If he had hurt my mother, I needed to prove it. The only problem was that I had absolutely no idea where to start.

Think it through.

I could talk to more people who lived here back then, see if anyone mentioned anything relevant. I could try to find out where the sleeping pills had come from, although I had no idea if a record of that even existed anywhere. Or how I would get it if it did.

I sighed in frustration. The journal must hold the key. There had to have been a reason I had seen that. *Maybe the whole thing was a figment of your imagination. If it were a real vision, you would have found the journal.* There was that snake-like doubt again, striking when I least expected. It had taken up residence in my mind.

I needed to find the journal.

If only to prove to myself that I wasn't crazy.

. . .

I turned down the long driveway to Fiona's house, hoping that talking to her might spur some new ideas.

She was out in her garden, hard at work clipping dried flower tops into a brown paper bag.

"Good morning, Daphne!" she called, her hands continuing to move quickly.

"Good morning!" I found the row she was on and joined her. "What are you working on?"

"Saving seed. I don't know why I go to the trouble every year; this yarrow is quite happy to spread itself without my help. But I always like to put away some extra seed, just in case."

I ran a hand across some of the white, lacy flower tops that were still fresh.

"I thought this was called Queen Anne's Lace."

"Different plants," she explained. "They look some alike if you don't know them. But this one has feathery leaves, see? The flowers are formed differently, too, if you know what you're looking for. Queen Anne is a wild carrot, but yarrow is in the sunflower family. Used to be called 'Soldier's Woundwort' because it could stop bleeding on the battlefield. But listen to me yammering on, you don't want to hear about all this."

"I don't mind," I said truthfully. I thought it was fascinating. Besides that, there was something that had always felt so right about being out in the garden. The scent of herbs, the feel of the warm sun on my face—they had always brought me comfort. Now that I knew about Eileen, I felt certain those feelings were connected to the time I had spent with her.

"What's bothering you, dear? You've got worry written all over your face."

"I just wish we could have found the journal yesterday. I need to find out what happened to Eileen. That's the only real clue I have to go on. I felt certain we would find it under one of the floorboards. I can't believe that after all that, it wasn't there."

"Well, that would have been nice, but sometimes life isn't quite so neat and tidy, now is it?"

"I guess not."

Fiona dropped her scissors into her apron and put her hand on my shoulder. "You'll find it. When you're meant to."

"How do you know?" The anguish was building up in my heart. "Fiona, if I really have the 'second sight,' if this is a real gift, then shouldn't it have been there? We ripped the house apart because of something I saw. What if it really was just a hallucination? What if…" I couldn't finish the sentence.

"What if you're crazy, and what if your mama was, too?"

I swallowed hard. "Right."

"I already told you, that's hogwash. And you know it. You're just frustrated, is all. Where is this coming from, anyway?"

"I don't know. Just thinking about how all of this must sound to someone. It *sounds* crazy."

"Lots of things that are true in this world sound crazy. Doesn't make them any less true."

"I guess you're right," I admitted.

"Daphne," she said, looking me straight in the eye. "I figure I knew Eileen better than any other soul on this planet did, except for maybe Lonnie. And I don't know why he would say the things he said, unless he was out of his mind with grief and just couldn't think straight. But I'm telling you, she wasn't crazy. And neither are you. So, you just put all this 'hallucination' nonsense out of your mind, okay?"

I breathed in deeply and nodded. "Okay. And thanks."

She squeezed my shoulder, then rolled up the top of her brown paper bag and tucked it into a basket sitting near her feet.

"I have some carrots to harvest," she said. "Feel like helping?"

"Sure." I shrugged.

"Good!" She smiled. "It will be good for you. Come on, then."

She led me over to a raised bed full of bright green carrot tops and handed me a pair of gardening gloves. "Use these if you want, or just get your hands dirty. I grow the carrots in this bed because the soil is nice and loose, which makes them easy to pull," she explained. "But if you get a stubborn one, you can loosen the soil a bit with this garden fork. Just be careful not to stab the carrot."

I reached for the first one. After a gentle wiggle, it slid easily from the soil.

"It's purple!" I exclaimed.

She grinned. "Those are my favorites. I plant several different varieties every year—purple, yellow, white. I always mix the seeds together when I plant, so that when I pull them, I never know what I'm going to get. Adds a little fun to the harvesting."

"Wow. Well, it's gorgeous." I laid the carrot aside and pulled the next one—yellow this time. We worked in silence for a while, and before long, we had a nice pile of carrots going. Fiona was right. There was something healing about the whole experience. It felt good to have my hands in the dirt, to smell the light scent of carrot as I pulled each one from the ground, and to work on something so *real.*

After a while, I broke the silence.

"You were right, Fiona. This was exactly what I needed."

She just smiled and gave me a wink.

"Can I ask you a question?"

"Anything."

"Can you think of any reason why Don Kistler would want to kill my mom?"

She looked up from the carrots, surprised. "Don? What makes you think it was him?"

"Nothing, really. I mean, I don't have any real reason to suspect him, other than his weird reaction when he saw me. He's just the only person I've met so far that seems to even be a possibility, and the more I learn about him, the shadier he seems to be. That's why I was wondering if you knew anything that might connect them."

"Hmmm..." She leaned back and put her hands on her thighs. Her face wrinkled up in thought as she contemplated the idea. "Other than them being neighbors, I can't think of any connection. Lonnie and Eileen didn't go to his church; they went to the Methodist church on the other side of town. I know Eileen felt about him the same way I do, but I don't remember any trouble between them."

"Okay." I didn't bother masking my disappointment.

"Don does have a nasty side to him," she admitted. "I've seen that myself. But I can't remember it ever having been directed at your mama. I don't know that he would ever go so far as to commit murder, either. But then I don't like to think about anyone in our community going that far. It happens, though. It's been happening ever since Cain and Abel, and it will keep happening until the end of time, I suppose."

"Yeah, I suppose so. You know, there's something else bothering me."

"What is it?"

"A feeling like I'm missing something. It's like alarm bells, but I don't know what for. It almost feels like if I'm not careful, I'm going to screw something up big time."

"What do you mean?"

"Well, yesterday, we ripped up all that carpet and made this giant mess. All because of something I thought I saw. And it turned out to be for nothing. What if I do the same thing, but to someone's life?"

"Well, I don't know that it was all for nothing. It got rid of that hideous carpet, didn't it? That's an improvement if nothing else!" She chuckled. "But what do you mean? Whose life are you worried about ruining? Don's?"

I swallowed hard again. "I don't know. It's just a feeling. I don't know how to explain it."

She nodded her head thoughtfully.

"Might be the sight," she said. She went back to pulling carrots, thinking things through. "In the old days, having the knowing was more curse than gift. It marked you, and people feared you. It was something to hide or try to get rid of. But nowadays, people are a lot more open to that thing. You're not likely to get burned at the stake anymore."

"True."

"But I wonder..." She frowned again, measuring her words. "What if the knowing had something to do with what happened to your mama? And *that*," she said slowly, "makes me wonder if you might be right about Don Kistler."

A troubled look passed over her face.

My heart felt like it was going to pound out of my chest.

"What do you mean?" I demanded.

Fiona sighed and brushed off her hands. "It's old history, and I don't like dragging it back up. You'd better come inside. We'll need some tea for this one."

We gathered up the carrots and carried them to the back porch of Fiona's stone cottage. She slipped off her garden boots before opening the door to the house. I followed suit, leaving my running shoes behind before walking into her living room.

It was tiny, but utterly charming. Botanical illustrations hung on every wall, and each corner was home to three or four potted plants. Every piece of furniture had a quilt or blanket strewn across the back. It was the kind of room that invited you to curl up with a cup of tea, to read, or simply watch the fire.

"I absolutely love your home," I said.

"I told you it was the prettiest one on the lane." She winked at me as she crossed through to her kitchen. It was tiny too, with an antique stove. Stepping into it felt like stepping back to another time and place. There were herbs strung up to dry and garlic braids hanging in a corner. The back wall was all open shelving covered with jars of dried herbs and hand-labeled bottles full of dark liquid. It was a room from storybooks. I was utterly enchanted. *This room is full of magic.* Not that I actually believed in magic. But here, in this moment, I felt ready to believe in anything. I could easily imagine Fiona being a dryad in human form, or maybe a crone with magic powers.

She rattled around the kitchen, putting on a kettle and pulling various jars from her shelf. She opened a few different ones and scooped out a small spoonful of dried herbs from each, combining them in a ceramic teapot. When the water came to a boil, she poured it over the herbs and put the top of the teapot in place to let them steep.

I loved watching her work. It was different, being in the kitchen with a woman. It was something I had never really experienced. Mom was the queen of takeout. I didn't have a single memory of us doing something like baking cookies together. We had never even had a home-cooked Thanksgiving meal. In these moments with Fiona, I started realizing how much I had missed, and it opened a deep ache in my soul.

Fiona pulled two cups from her cabinet, put a spoon of honey in each, then poured the hot herbal tea on top. When she handed me my cup, I inhaled deeply. The aroma was familiar.

"Chamomile?" I asked.

She nodded. "With a few things added, yes. Chamomile is one of my favorites. It's just plain soothing, and that's what we both need on a day like this."

I let her drink her tea in silence. I was eager to get back to the conversation, especially if she knew something that might connect Don to my mother's murder. But a dark mood had fallen on her. It was so unlike her that I didn't know how to proceed.

After a few minutes, she gathered herself and began her story.

"This is old history, you understand? Water under the bridge. Like I said, I don't like to even bring it up. But if Don had something to do with Eileen's passing..." Her voice trailed off.

"It was years ago, back when Don and his family first moved here from Harrisburg to start a new church. Church planting, they called it. Your mama was a teenager." She fell silent again, brooding over her teacup.

"Well, I tried to do the neighborly thing, you know? They were building that house and were going to be living on the lane. So, one day, when they were over there taking a look at the progress on their house, I walked over and invited them to dinner."

"That was nice of you," I said, encouraging her to keep going.

She sighed again. "Only it turned out to be a big mistake."

"How so?"

"Well, you'd have to know him to really understand how it all even happened. He was young, fiery, and charismatic. I may not have liked his style of preaching, but a lot of people sure did. They got all caught up in his spell. Practically thought he was God himself. I've never seen anyone swoop into a new town and have so much influence so quickly.

"Anyway, he apparently remembered that I had visited his church once but never returned. And when he came to dinner, he decided to ask me about it. And by ask, I mean confront me like."

I made a face. "Confront you? Over not going back to his church? I've never met a minister like that."

"He's a different breed, alright," she agreed. "Well, I made the same joke to him I made to you, about how if the god he worshiped was confined to the church building, then we must be worshiping two different gods. Only he didn't find that very funny. Oh, he took that and ran with it. Accused me of worshiping idols or something like that. Said I was a rebellious witch who didn't recognize the authority of the Lord on him. Told me I was going to burn in hell if I didn't repent."

My jaw dropped. "He didn't."

"He did. And when I didn't immediately fall to my knees begging him for forgiveness, he started trying to turn the whole town against me. Spread rumors about me. Told people that the herbal medicines I made were really potions, and that if they took them, they were using them to their own damnation. Told people that any child I delivered would have the mark of the devil on him."

I was in shock. "But surely nobody believed that. You had been part of the community for much longer than he had."

A look of pain crossed her face. "You know, that was the hardest thing of all? That some people did. Like I told you, I've never seen anyone gain influence over people so quickly. Most people knew he was full of it, that's for sure. But not everyone. I lost friends I thought would be there for a lifetime. My livelihood took a big hit, too, because people were scared to use me as a midwife or herbalist. Most of them were smart enough to know that what he was saying was malarky, but I think they were still worried about what other people might think of them for continuing to use old Fiona's tinctures. Or worried that their babies might always be looked at suspiciously, just because I delivered them."

"Fiona, that's awful," I said, reaching out and covering her hand with my own. "I am so sorry. I don't know how you've lived with him as a neighbor for so many years. How could he be so cruel?" My heart broke for her. She was one of the kindest, most giving people I had ever met. Thinking of her being blackballed in the community like that was just horrible.

"Religion is a funny thing," she said. "It brings out the best in some people. But it brings out the worst in others. I reckon Don's one of the latter."

I nodded.

"Well, things went on like that for a few months. Then it escalated. Some kids from town decided they'd better teach 'the witch' a lesson. They snuck out here in the middle of the night. Spray-painted awful things on my house. Destroyed my garden. Killed my chickens." At this, her eyes filled with tears.

"Oh, Fiona." How could people be so awful?

She wiped away the tears. "I was plumb scared to death. I called Sheriff Joe down the road, and he came, right in the middle of the night, and broke things up. Then he marched over to Don's house and banged on the door until Don got out of bed. He told Don he was holding him personally responsible for the damage to my house, and that he better do something to stop all of this nonsense, or else."

She paused for a moment, fiddling with the hem of her apron, before continuing. "That Sunday, Don changed his tone and scolded the people in his church for being hard on me. As if he wasn't the one who egged it on in the first place! He told them that while he appreciated their fervor, the way to win me back to the fold was with kindness. He also said that he had personally inspected my herbal goods and found them to *not* be evil potions after all, and that the person who started that rumor should be ashamed of themselves."

"But *he* started the rumor!" I protested.

"Exactly. But don't you know that not one of those people following him seemed to remember that? No, all they could do was praise him for setting such an example of graciousness." She rolled her eyes. "But I didn't care at that point. All I cared about was that the rumors stopped, and I got to get back to my livelihood. Joe also put the fear in those boys that night, and I haven't had any trouble since. There are a few people in town, even now, who will still call me a witch behind my back. But," she winked, "I've been called a lot worse in my life."

I laughed with her, glad to see the dark cloud dissipating.

"Anyway, we've all lived in relative peace with each other ever since. Like I said, that was years ago, before you were even born. We're not exactly what you would call friends, but I haven't had any more trouble from him."

"Wow." I let out an exhale. "What a story. But what does it have to do with my mother, other than proving that Don is a sorry human being?"

"Don't you see? Don's followers are downright terrified of anything they even suspect of being from the devil. What do you think they might do if they found out someone in the community had the second sight?"

The thought chilled me. "But surely that wouldn't give them cause to hurt someone. Like you said, it's a gift she was born with. It's not like she was practicing the dark arts or something."

Fiona shook her head. "To their minds, if it happens inside their church, it's a gift from God. But if it happens outside their church, then it's from the devil himself."

"Hmmm." I mulled it over. It made sense, in a terrifying sort of way. "Who all knew she had those abilities?"

Fiona thought about it. "Her parents, obviously. Me and Lonnie. Joe. She helped him out on some cases, but they kept that real quiet. As far as I know, that's it. She wasn't the type to go around putting on a show or trying to get attention from it. She kept it close to her chest."

I sat back, deflated. "Well, if none of them even knew about it, then it certainly wouldn't have given them reason to kill her. Wait. You said she helped Joe out on some cases? Like as an investigator?"

Fiona nodded. "Every now and then, she would see something related to a case he was working on. She came to me the first time, unsure what to do about it. I told her she could trust Joe. Took her to talk to him myself. He followed up on what she saw, and sure enough, it helped him crack the case. They worked together off and on after that."

"Wow. That's amazing." I was so impressed. I felt the now-familiar stab of grief at missing out on knowing my mother. She seemed incredible.

But knowing she had worked with law enforcement to solve some cases meant that Fiona was wrong about nobody having a motive.

If she had helped take down criminals, someone might have wanted revenge.

Chapter Fifteen

Fiona had given me a lot to think about, but unfortunately, digging into it all would have to wait. The movers were due to arrive the following morning, and I needed to somehow whip the house into shape.

First, I needed to deal with the carpet. I dragged it all on to the front porch, out of the way of the movers, until I could dispose of it permanently.

I had gotten lucky with the carpet pad. It was tacked down around the edges instead of glued. It had come up fairly easily, so Fiona and I had rolled up all the intact pieces. I dragged them out to the porch and added them to my carpet pile.

That just left the tacks and the few spots where the pad had been stuck down to the floor. If I could take care of those, I would feel pretty good about the movers coming. The floors would still need to be refinished someday, and I hadn't even started painting. But as long as I had clear floors for moving day, I would be happy.

It took hours longer than I expected, but by nightfall, I was finally finished and able to sweep up all the mess. Prying up the tacks on my hands and knees had been one of the hardest jobs of my life. But it was done, and I was ridiculously proud of the result. The floors weren't pristine, but they were in great shape, considering. Even without refinishing them, the cottage looked a thousand times better.

With that finished, I showered and changed into a sweatshirt and leggings. I would put away my camping furniture in the morning, but other than that, there wasn't anything left on my pre-mover list that was actually doable.

I had just heated the last of my clam chowder when I heard a knock on the door. I groaned. It was like the worst kind of *déjà vu*. If it turned out to be Don and Patricia, I swore I would never again eat clam chowder.

Preparing myself, I opened the door. Emerson was standing on the step in blue scrubs and a jacket.

"Oh! Hi!" I stammered, suddenly very aware of my faded sweatshirt, bare face, and damp hair.

"Hey, Daphne." He grinned and I melted. "Sorry I didn't get to pick up that carpet last night. I thought I would swing by after work and grab it for you. I see you've already done half the work for me."

"Oh, thank you. It's really nice that you remembered. Come on in, let me throw on some shoes and I'll help you carry it."

He looked down at my fuzzy socks and grinned again. I could feel my cheeks turning red. This was not exactly the version of Daphne I wanted him to see.

He stepped inside.

"Wow," he said, sounding genuinely impressed. "You did a fantastic job getting these floors cleaned up."

"Thank you. I'm pretty proud of it."

"You should be."

I blushed again, hiding my face as I laced up my running shoes.

"Shall we?" I asked.

"Let's get to it." His eyes met mine and for just a moment, it felt like time stood still. In all my life, I had never felt chemistry like this with anyone. I was drawn to him in a way I couldn't possibly explain.

"Here, you go around and grab that end, that way I'll be the one walking backward," he said.

He had backed up his truck to the porch and lowered the tailgate, so we didn't have far to carry the rolls. Together, we made quick work of it, and I felt even better about the movers coming.

"Do you mind if I wash my hands before I go?" he asked as we loaded the last one.

"Of course you can! In fact, I was just heating up some clam chowder from the market. Have you had dinner yet? I could throw together a salad, and I have an open bottle of red." It wasn't much of a dinner, especially for a second date, but I didn't want him to leave.

When I was with him, everything else faded. It gave me some sort of emotional distance from everything that had happened the last few months. With him, I felt more like the version of myself that I had been before Dad got sick, before everything got hard and sad and heavy.

It was nice.

"That sounds great, actually."

"Wonderful! The guest bath is just down the hall to the left."

"Back in a sec."

I headed to the kitchen to wash up, then poured glasses of wine and started putting together a simple salad. Dinner with Emerson two nights in a row. I felt almost giddy, until Katie's warning came back to me. Her words still confused me. Maybe she just didn't know him as well as I was starting to. Maybe she was wrong about whatever she thought she overheard.

I busied myself with dinner preparations, and locked thoughts of Katie and her warning away, far in the back of my mind.

Emerson came back a moment later. "Smells great," he commented.

"Sorry it's so simple. And, I don't actually have a table and chairs," I laughed. "I've already gotten so used to roughing it that I didn't even think about it before inviting you to stay. I owe you a better dinner than this when I get all set up here." I poured chowder into a bowl and handed it to him.

"This is great," he said. "But I know you'll be glad to get your things. Tomorrow, right?"

"Yes! First thing in the morning." I gestured for him to follow me into the living room. I put my wineglass and bowl on the hearth, using it as a makeshift table. It would require sitting on the floor, obviously, but I didn't mind. "I'll be right back with the salads."

When I returned, he had placed his glass and bowl beside mine, and was already on the floor, propped up against the hearth. I paused for a moment and leaned against the doorframe, just taking in the picture. It was cozy and warm, and despite the reasons for my being there, I felt the sudden reassurance that I was exactly where I belonged.

"What is it?" he asked, eyeing me curiously.

I shook my head, bringing myself out of my thoughts. "It's nothing. I guess this whole thing is just still so surreal. I can't believe I'm here." I crossed to the hearth and gently placed the salad plates down, before curling up cross-legged in the floor beside him.

"I've never done anything as impulsive or crazy as deciding to move up here," I confessed. "And it could have been a disaster. But instead, I'm, well, happy. You know, when I first moved to my apartment, I lived there for weeks before I met any of the neighbors. People just didn't really talk to each other. Myself included. I never even thought to introduce myself or try to form some sense of community. We were just all living our separate lives. I've only been here a few days, and I already feel connected. It's nice." I smiled, picking up my wineglass to take a sip.

"Small town life has its perks," he agreed. "But it also has its downsides."

"Such as?"

"Lack of privacy. Gossip. Everyone knows everyone. I thought I was moving out to the woods to have privacy and solitude. You'd be surprised at how hard that is to find here."

"I can see that. I actually haven't spent this much time around other people since living in a college dorm," I laughed.

"Where did you go to college?" he asked, in between spoonfuls of chowder.

"University of Arkansas. Fayetteville."

"Ahh," he said, cocking his head. "Decent football team."

"So I've heard." I laughed. "Although, honestly, I've never been able to get into football."

He chuckled. "What did you major in?"

"Elementary Education."

"Oh, a teacher, that's cool. The school here will be lucky to have you."

"Nope," I said. "It turns out I absolutely hate teaching. Shortly after finishing my degree, I decided to open my own business instead."

"What's your business?"

"I do all the post-processing for wedding photographers. They upload the raw photos, then I do the edits and create their client galleries."

"That's great. I never even realized that was a service."

"Yes, and more in demand than you would think. Full time wedding photographers usually shoot two weddings a weekend. That alone is a good 20 hours of work. On top of that, they do bridal sessions, engagement sessions, boudoir sessions—"

"Boudoir?" he interrupted, with a raised eyebrow.

My cheeks warmed as I tried to explain. "You know, when brides take pictures beforehand in their lingerie, as a gift to their husbands."

"Interesting," he said, grinning.

"Anyway," I said, still blushing, trying to get my thoughts back on track. "On top of the actual photography, managing client expectations is basically a full time job. Brides expect a huge amount of personal service these days. So, photographers spend a lot of time in one-on-one consultations, site visits, and answering questions. On top of all that, they still have to run their businesses. You know, websites, blogs, social media posting, et cetera. It's a time-consuming job. So more and more of them are outsourcing what they can. For some of them, that means hiring someone like me. I make sure galleries are turned over quickly, that the work is consistent and in their personal style, and take care of any extra editing requests."

"Wow. I had no idea. But it sounds like you found a needed service and carved yourself a place in it. That's great."

"Thanks. I love it. And it gives me a lot of freedom, as far as being able to work from home and set my own hours. It's been really great."

"So tell me more about these boudoir sessions." He wiggled his eyebrows at me.

"You're terrible!" I gave him a little shove on his upper arm, but left my hand there as our eyes met. Those magic butterflies returned, as he leaned forward and tucked my hair behind my ear. His fingertips grazed the side of my cheek, then gently tilted my chin up.

His lips met mine and the world went hazy. The kiss was soft, sweet. I lifted my hand to his, still on my cheek, and he deepened the kiss before finally breaking away. He smiled at me, and brushed my cheek with his thumb.

"I've been wanting to do that ever since the storm interrupted us the other night."

"Me too." I whispered the words, afraid to break the spell.

He picked up his chowder and went back to eating, as if the whole world hadn't just changed.

Chapter Sixteen

"So, tell me about your plans for the place," he said, his tone casual.

Still reeling from that kiss, I wasn't sure I could put a coherent sentence together.

"We've been talking about me all night," I said, jabbing him playfully. "I'd like to know more about you."

"What do you want to know?"

"Well, what did you do in the Air Force?"

"I started as a medic, then they put me through school and I became a trauma nurse."

"And you grew up in Wisconsin? Is your family still there?"

His grin grew wider. "Yeah, my parents are still there. They bought some land about an hour outside the city a couple of years ago. Opened a bed-and-breakfast. It was a dream of Mom's her entire life. They're great. My brother Alex still lives in the city. He's a fancy lawyer now."

His whole face seemed to light up as he talked about his family.

"It's nice that you have a brother. I always hated growing up as an only child."

His smile faded. "Yeah." He reached up and rubbed the scruff of his beard. "I had another one," he said after a moment. "Ken. My baby brother. We lost him in Afghanistan."

"Oh, Emerson." I reached out and put my hand on his arm.

"It is what it is," he said, but his voice had a gruff edge I hadn't heard before.

I rubbed his arm. I knew there was nothing I could say to make it better. At least, that had been my experience when I lost Dad. What I would have appreciated was someone just sitting in the silence with me. So that's what I did for Emerson. His loss may not have been a fresh one, but the pain of it was obvious.

After a few moments, he cleared his throat. "Sorry," he said. "It's been a long time since I've talked about Ken. It still isn't easy."

"I get it. I mean, I haven't lost a sibling, and certainly not like that. But losing my dad was awful. I hated talking about it. Hated hearing everyone say they were sorry for my loss. Then I found out about my mother, and it was another loss all over again. Only with her, I don't even feel like I have the right to grieve." I paused for a moment, gathering my thoughts. "It's such a strange grief. How do you grieve someone you can't even remember? Anyway, I didn't mean to make that about me. I was just trying to say that I know what it's like to lose someone, and you never have to apologize to me for getting hit with those feelings."

He reached up and clasped my hand as our eyes met. The connection was different this time. More than just chemistry, it was a deep understanding. Two hearts, both hurting in their own ways. Kindred spirits who both knew the pain of loss.

"I think it's amazing that you moved here to find out more about your mom. I wanted to ask you more about it last night, but you seemed so sad when you mentioned her. I didn't know if you felt okay talking about it."

"No, it's okay," I said. "It's just that the whole thing sounds crazy."

"I don't think so."

"Maybe that's because you don't know the whole story," I said, with a small laugh.

"Try me." He gazed at me intently.

"Well, it's true that I came here to learn more about her. But I'm also trying to find out what happened to her. Her death was ruled a suicide, but it doesn't fit."

"What do you mean?"

"It's hard to explain. It just doesn't feel right to me—or to Fiona."

"Are you saying you think she was murdered?" He rubbed his scruff again, contemplating.

"Yeah, I do."

"Whoa. That's heavy."

"Tell me about it." I sighed.

"So what exactly makes you think it was murder instead of suicide?"

"Are you sure you want to hear all of this?" I took a long sip of my wine. "We could put the past to bed for a while and talk about more pleasant things."

"If it's important enough for you to pack up your entire life and move out to the middle of nowhere, then yeah, I want to hear it. Besides, maybe I can help you."

"Well." I swallowed hard. "I have what Fiona calls the second sight." The words tumbled out quickly, and I braced myself for his reaction.

"The second sight?" It was obvious he didn't know what I was talking about.

I tried to explain it, but it felt so awkward. I stumbled over my words, knowing how it must sound.

He listened quietly until I finished. "So you've had some, um, visions that make you think she was murdered. But you don't have any proof?"

"No, not yet."

"Do you at least have a theory, or someone with a motive, or anything else to go on?" His skepticism was obvious. This wasn't going nearly as well as it did with Katie.

I could feel myself becoming defensive. "Nothing conclusive, no. But I've been getting a strange vibe from Don Kistler, and Fiona shared some things with me today that make me suspect it was him. Or that he is at least behind it."

Emerson raised his eyebrows. "Don. Huh."

"You don't believe me, do you?"

"I want to believe you." He spoke slowly, carefully, as if talking to a patient. "Really, I do," he said, reacting to the look on my face. "This is just a little out of my wheelhouse, so to speak. I guess I'm not sure what to think. You know, science has never been able to verify ESP. Quite the opposite, actually."

"Fiona says we don't have to understand something for it to be real."

"Fiona would say that, wouldn't she? But I guess what I'm trying to say is that Fiona and I have completely different worldviews. I mean, if someone came to her and asked what to do for an ear infection, she'd probably tell them to put some flower drops or essential oils or something in their ear canal. I'd tell them to go to their doctor for some antibiotics. Know what I mean?"

My heart began to fall. But what was I expecting? It was easy to talk to Fiona about these things, but Emerson had a point. Most people would consider her to be eccentric, at best. Katie had been unbelievably accepting, and I was grateful for it. But I was well aware of how this all sounded.

"Look," I said. "I know it sounds totally unbelievable. I'm still getting used to it myself. But this is just something I have to do. I have to follow up on this and find out if someone murdered my mother."

"That, I can understand," he said, with a raised brow and a cock to his head. I got the feeling he was thinking of his brother again.

He stretched out his legs and leaned back against the stone hearth, deep in thought. I sipped my wine, waiting for him to speak first.

"I've never liked Don," he said finally, in a contemplative tone. "Occupational hazard, working the job I do. But I've got to be honest with you. I don't see him as being capable of murder."

"Why not?"

"I don't know. At his core, he seems weak to me."

"That's not the impression I've been getting. From what I've heard, he seems to control everything and everyone around him."

"He has a lot of power, that's for sure," Emerson agreed. "But the way I see it, he's like the wizard in the Wizard of Oz. It's all a show. His power over people comes from what they believe about him. But at his core? I don't know. I just don't see him being willing to get his hands dirty like that."

"Maybe there's more to him than you've seen."

"Maybe you're right."

"Hey, what did you mean when you said that disliking him was an 'occupational hazard' in your job?"

Emerson turned back toward me, a clear look of disgust on his face. "I'm not sure I should tell you this."

"Please do."

He weighed it carefully. "Okay, but I can't give you names or anything, due to confidentiality."

"Okay." My heart quickened, wondering what I was about to hear.

"Once, I got a call to pick up a girl. She was barely eighteen years old. Had just graduated from high school. Was out hiking on the bluffs with some friends, on a camping trip to celebrate their graduation. She took a nasty fall. They were worried about potential internal injuries, so we picked her up to fly her to the trauma center out east. Anyway, she was desperate for us to call Don. Not her parents, who live right here in town, but Don. Of course, he didn't show up. He wasn't going to drive a couple hours for her." Emerson rolled his eyes.

"Well, that's not so bad," I said. "He probably can't drop everything for every single person in town."

"That's not the point," he continued. "She ended up getting transferred back to our local hospital. I went to check on her. I knocked, but walked in pretty quickly. Habit. Anyway, he was there. He jumped off her bed and looked like a deer caught in the headlights. It was pretty obvious what was going on."

"Gotcha," I said. "I already knew—or at least highly suspected—that he was having an affair, but I didn't realize he liked them so young."

Emerson stared at me with a trace of admiration in his eyes. "You've been here for what, three days? And you already knew he was having an affair? How? The rest of town seems to be in the dark about that."

I giggled. I was tempted to tease him, telling him it was the sight. But things were starting to feel normal between us again, and I didn't want to do anything that would mess that up. So I explained about running into Don at the motel, and how Katie said that Don had gotten into trouble for infidelity a few years ago.

Emerson was obviously shocked. "Wow. You've found out more

about him in a few days than I have in two years. I had no idea he almost lost the church over something like that."

"Crazy, isn't it? Unfortunately, having an affair isn't a crime, and it does nothing to tie him to my mother's murder."

"It's more than an affair," Emerson said, with a sudden flash of anger. "He's using his position of authority to sleep with someone less than half his age. She's a child compared to him. It's barely legal, and it's certainly not right." He drank the rest of his wine in a single swallow.

"It speaks volumes about his character," he continued. "And now —" he stopped suddenly.

"Now what?"

"Nothing. Forget it. I just don't like the guy. Even so, his philandering is miles away from murder. As much as I would love to see him locked up where he can't do any more damage, I still don't think he's the killing type."

"Yeah. Maybe not."

"But, hey." Emerson looked at me, his face grim. "If it was him, do us all a favor and take him down, ok? You would be doing a service for the entire community."

"I will," I said. It was a promise.

Chapter Seventeen

Tuesday was a beautiful whirlwind. The weather was perfect, and the movers arrived bright and early, seemingly energized by the crisp mountain air. In a few short hours, they did what I couldn't possibly have done on my own. Everything was unloaded and all my furniture was put into place. There were boxes everywhere, and it would take days for me to unpack and put everything away, but even so, it felt like a real home.

And more importantly, I was finally going to sleep in a real bed again.

I was so busy putting the house together that I worked right through lunch. I was starving by dinner time, but I had no desire to cook. Everything was a huge mess, and I was too exhausted to deal with it.

It was a night for eating in town, for sure.

I dressed quickly, discarding my work clothes for something more suitable. I grabbed my keys and headed out the door, but changed directions when I got to my car. Fiona had done so much for me these last few days. Why not invite her to go to dinner with me? I could treat, as a thank you.

It was simply too beautiful outside to drive to her cottage. The fall color had peaked, and the leaves were starting to rain down from the sky. They crunched beneath my feet as I walked. The sky appeared blustery and cold, but the earth seemed to have missed the memo. It was the warmest day I had experienced there yet, as if the earth was clinging to the last bit of summer. It had always felt like a magical time of year to me. Experiencing it here in the mountains was glorious.

When I knocked on her door and told her my idea, Fiona accepted my invitation.

"Marco's?" I suggested. Even though we had eaten there just days ago, it seemed a fitting place to celebrate.

"My favorite!" she answered. "I'll drive!"

It was a quieter night at Marco's, which was fine by me. It was nice to eat without someone popping over to the table every five minutes to say hello. Dinner was delicious, and after a nice meal and company, I felt like I had the energy to tackle my unpacking again. *And the weddings that are waiting for you,* I reminded myself with a grimace. I loved my job, sure. But it was going to be hard to concentrate on my work while the house was turned upside down. Sometimes, I wished I had gotten a little more of my dad's ability to just not see the clutter. He was always so focused on whatever he was doing that the world around him faded. I could use a little more of that.

For the first time, thinking of Dad brought a smile instead of tears. It was a turning point, I realized. The loss would always be there, and I knew enough to know there were still tears of grief in my future. But I also knew now that I would be okay.

When Fiona drove me back to my house, it was pitch black. I winced, once again regretting that I had forgotten to leave a light on.

"Whew! Your house is darker than the inside of a cow! I'll sit right here with my headlights on until you make it to the door and get it unlocked," Fiona said. "Might be a good idea to invest in some motion detector lights. Helps keep the critters away."

"That's a good idea. I need to remember to leave the porch light on when I leave, with it getting dark so early now. It made a big difference that first night."

"Yeah, that would help," she agreed. "But motion detector lights, too." She pointed her finger at me. "One of the best investments I've made."

"Got it." I smiled at her. "Thanks for coming to dinner with me. And, well, thanks for everything these last few days. I'm really, really glad to have found you."

Her eyes grew misty. "And I'm glad to have you back after all these years." She cleared her throat. "Now go on and get inside. Tomorrow, you wander down to my house if you want, and I'll send you home with some greens from the garden. I've got a feeling our first hard freeze is on the way this week. Got to get everything harvested first."

"A freeze?" I laughed. "It was seventy-three degrees today."

"Exactly," she said, tapping the side of her nose with one finger.

I shrugged. Fiona knew the mountain better than I did, that was for sure. If she said it was going to freeze, it likely would.

"Well, goodnight then," I said, climbing down out of her truck. "I'll see you tomorrow. It will probably be late afternoon before I stop by. I'm going to force myself to spend tomorrow morning catching up on work."

"That will be fine, I'll be there all day getting things ready for winter. Goodnight, dear!"

I was grateful for the light from Fiona's truck, but the headlights were so blinding in the dark that I had to squint. As I made my way up the porch steps, I tripped over something solid, something that hadn't been there before. As soon as I did, Fiona jumped out of her truck and shouted for me to stop.

I looked down and saw what she did.

Reaching out from underneath the front porch was a man's arm.

I screamed.

I STOOD PARALYZED UNTIL FIONA GENTLY MOVED ME BACK.

"There, there," she soothed, as if she saw dead bodies every day. "Stand back, don't touch anything. I'm just going to check."

She went to her truck and retrieved a flashlight, then went back to the steps and shined it underneath the porch where the headlights were blocked by the deck facing. She squatted slowly, showing her age for once, and reached her hand in.

She came back to me with a grim look on her face.

"I can't believe it," she said, shaking her head. "It's Don. I've got to call Joe."

Don. My heart thudded in my chest.

"Is he..." I couldn't bring myself to finish the sentence.

She nodded. "As a doornail."

I HAD NEVER BEEN SO GLAD TO HAVE A SHERIFF, RETIRED OR not, living so close. He arrived in less than five minutes, but even that felt like an eternity.

"Fiona." He acknowledged her with a nod, without even looking at me. "So, it's Don? And he's definitely dead?"

"Yep," Fiona answered. They exchanged a look, communicating something that neither one of them wanted to speak in front of me. "It's Don, alright. He's there, underneath the porch."

The man moved quickly to the steps, stooped down, and shined a flashlight, just like Fiona had done. He checked the wrist for a pulse, then came back to us.

"Terrible," he said. "Just terrible. I've already called the sheriff and the Rosemary Mountain police. The coroner's on the way."

He looked at me, as if noticing my presence for the first time.

"Joe, this is Daphne," Fiona explained. "Daphne Sullivan."

His eyes widened. "As in?"

She nodded. "Yep. Eileen's girl."

"Well, I've got about a million questions, but I guess they'll have to wait until we deal with this," he said, gesturing back toward the body. "Daphne Sullivan. My goodness. You were practically a baby last time I saw you. You look just like your momma."

"So I've heard," I said. I laughed and then felt horrible. How could I laugh when someone had just lost his life?

"You probably don't remember me. The name's Joe Hemsworth."

I reached out to shake his hand.

"How long have you been back, Daphne?"

"Just a few days. I moved in on Friday."

He frowned and stroked his chin. "Terrible timing, isn't it? You move in, and just a few days later, one of our longest residents is found dead on your property. Now that's an odd thing."

"Now, don't you be getting any ideas." Fiona interrupted. "Daphne and I have been eating at Marco's. You don't get to go pinning it on her just because she's new in town. She couldn't have done it. I'm her alibi!"

"Now, now, Fiona. Calm yourself down," he soothed. "You're getting a little ahead of yourself. First, let's not jump to conclusions about murder, unless you know something I don't. We won't know that for sure until we get him out from there and can see better what happened. Maybe this was an accident."

Don *accidentally* died underneath my porch? The look on my face must have been incredulous.

Joe noticed. "The man liked his fried catfish," he said, with a shake of his head. "For all we know, he was walking up your front steps and had a heart attack."

"A heart attack?" I said, disbelieving. "You're kidding, right?" I took Fiona's flashlight and scanned the ground in front of where Don lay. "I've never seen a heart attack cause so much blood loss."

Joe's face twitched, like he wanted to grin but was holding it back. "That's true, but you're also in the mountains where all sorts of wild animals will take advantage of someone who's down. Heck, even farm pigs will take advantage of a man down, and we've got some of those living here on the mountain, too. All I'm saying is let's not jump to conclusions. It's the coroner's job to determine the cause of death, not ours. And until we get him out of there, we don't know what happened."

"And the second thing?" I asked.

"Hm?"

"You said first, we have no reason to believe he was murdered. What's the second thing?"

He peered at me with sharp eyes, considering. "Well, if it *was* murder, who's to say it happened while you were at Marco's?"

"Well, obviously, Joe, his body wasn't there when she left the house. She would have seen it or tripped over it then." Fiona interjected.

"No, that would just mean his *arm* wasn't there when she left the house. What if he was wounded and hiding under the porch, but not dead yet? What if he was trying to crawl out when he took his last breath? Did you notice anything when you picked her up?"

"I didn't pick her up. She walked down to my place."

"Then you're making an even bigger assumption," he said.

"What assumption?" she demanded.

But I knew. I knew exactly what he was thinking. I could have left Don injured or dead and walked down to Fiona's in order to get myself an alibi. I suddenly felt sick.

He didn't say it. Just raised his eyebrows at Fiona and gave her a pointed look. I felt like there was an entire conversation happening that I wasn't part of, and it was terrifying.

Fiona huffed.

I stayed silent. The whole thing was so surreal that I half expected to wake up any minute. It felt like the kind of thing you laughed about later, surprised that your own subconscious could paint such a vivid dream for you.

Yet, it was real. There was a dead man underneath my front porch.

And, as a retired sheriff had just made clear, if it turned out to be murder, I would be the prime suspect.

CHAPTER EIGHTEEN

EVERYTHING THAT HAPPENED NEXT WAS A BLUR. THE current sheriff, Greg Morrison, arrived first, pulling up in his official car. I felt a wave of relief when I saw him. I remembered him from the night Emerson had walked me to my car. He had been kind. Surely, he would be reasonable and listen to me. He was friends with Emerson, after all.

Just as quickly, panic welled up within me again.

He was friends with Emerson.

The same Emerson that heard me promise to take Don down.

This could not be happening.

Joe's entire body stiffened as soon as Greg pulled up, and greetings were clipped on both sides. In a way, it made me feel better. If Greg disliked Joe, then maybe Joe's subtle accusations would fall on deaf ears.

Fiona and I moved back as the two men conferred by the porch. They were all business and didn't seem to notice us. We both seemed to have the same thought—stay quiet and out of the way, so we could keep an eye on what was happening. Not that I expected they would allow me to leave or even go inside my own house at this point.

A handsome older man arrived next, driving a shiny SUV.

"Who is that?" I whispered to Fiona.

"Dave Rogers."

So this was Katie's husband. I could see why Fiona was scandalized by the age difference. He was very attractive and reminded me a bit of Harrison Ford. I could understand how he and Katie had hit it off.

"I thought he was a family doctor. What's he doing here?"

"He is, but he's also the county coroner, and the only thing we have in the way of an official medical examiner." She spoke in hushed tones. "He still has his practice, but only sees a few patients these days."

More vehicles arrived. My driveway was turning into a parking lot.

"There's the deputy, and the funeral home," Fiona explained, as people unloaded from their vehicles. "And it looks like the entire police department came out! It's not every day something like this happens around here."

"Why is the funeral home here? Shouldn't there be a crime scene van or something?"

Fiona just laughed, quietly. We were still talking in whispers. Thankfully, the men seemed to have forgotten about us altogether.

"Honey, we don't have anything like that here. The funeral home transports anyone who passes."

I filed the information away for later. I hadn't considered how limited the investigation into my mother's death would have been.

After the officers took what seemed like a million photographs, Don's body was carefully removed from underneath the porch. The sight of it gave me chills. I didn't like the man, but I hadn't wished for him to die.

Dr. Rogers examined the body, then exchanged glances with Joe.

"Well, I'll do an autopsy to make it official," he said, directing his words to Joe. Annoyance flickered across Greg's face. "But it's fairly obvious that the cause of death was a gunshot wound to the chest."

So much for Joe's ridiculous heart attack theory.

Joe let out a long breath. "I was afraid of that."

Dr. Rogers looked grim. "Me too. But are you really surprised?"

Joe said nothing.

Greg began barking orders to secure the scene.

My new home.

A crime scene.

· · ·

WHILE GREG—SHERIFF MORRISON, I CORRECTED MYSELF— took Fiona's statement, his deputy began blocking off the front of my house with yellow crime scene tape. *I'm glad the movers came already.* I was struck by the insanity of the thought and giggled aloud. Not that it was funny. Nothing felt funny. Overwhelming, yes. Terrifying, yes. Surreal, yes. But not funny. Still, anxiety forced me to giggle. Then, of course, the inappropriateness of it all triggered even more anxiety. My breathing quickened, and I felt lightheaded.

"You alright?" Joe said. He had been watching me and I hadn't even noticed.

"Yes. No. I don't know." I lifted my hands in surrender. "I don't—" I didn't even have an ending to the sentence. I felt utterly lost, like someone drifting at sea without an anchor.

Until a familiar truck pulled into the driveway.

Emerson jumped out and ran over to me.

"What's going on?" he asked, his face filled with concern. "I was at the base and we heard your address come over the radio. They said there was a possible homicide?"

"Don." It was the only word I could get out. The panic continued to rise and swirl. I was drowning.

"Did he hurt you?" Emerson grabbed my arm.

I shook my head no. My teeth were chattering, from cold and fear.

He looked me over, then ran back to his truck and grabbed a blanket. When he came back, he wrapped me in it, and rubbed his hands over my arms, trying to warm me. I leaned against him, trying to sink into his comfort.

He scanned the area, trying to make sense of it all. Joe walked closer to us.

"Joe, what's going on?"

Joe sighed. "They found Don underneath her porch. Shot in the chest."

Emerson looked back at me, horror flooding his face. My teeth chattered harder.

"She needs to sit down," he said. "Hey Greg!" he called out.

Sheriff Morrison looked up from where he was talking to Fiona.

"I'm going to put her in my truck, ok?" Emerson called. "She's had a shock. She needs to get warm."

The Sheriff nodded his assent. "Don't go anywhere," he called back. "I'm coming to talk to her next."

Emerson practically picked me up and put me in the passenger seat of his truck, with the blanket still wrapped around my shoulders. He went around and hopped into the driver's side and started the engine to get the heat going.

After a minute in the warmth, my teeth stopped chattering, but I couldn't stop my hands from shaking. I pulled the blanket tighter.

"Emerson," I began.

"Don't tell me anything," he said, a warning in his voice. "You shouldn't say a word."

I couldn't blame him for his assumption, but it hurt just the same. "Emerson, it wasn't me. I didn't shoot him. I've never shot a gun in my life. I don't even know how. I have no idea what happened, but it wasn't me." The words came tumbling out, as I begged him to believe me.

He let out a breath and turned toward me. "Okay, okay," he soothed, running his hand up my arm again. "Tell me what happened."

I quickly caught him up on everything that had happened that night. He listened without interrupting, rubbing the scruff of his beard until I finished.

"Did you tell anyone other than me that you thought Don was involved in your mother's death?"

I nodded, slowly.

"Who?"

"Katie and Fiona."

He groaned. "If you told Fiona, then the whole town knows."

"Oh, I don't think so," I started.

"Trust me," he said. "There's a lot to love about Fiona, but she's a talker. And once her friends start talking, it circulates through the whole town faster than you can imagine."

I thought about the night I first met Fiona, and my initial impression of her as a gossip. I wanted to trust that she had kept the things I told her to herself, but I couldn't be sure. And Katie could have told her husband. Who knew how many people he might have told? The color drained from my face again.

"So someone who knew I suspected Don could have killed him at my house in order to throw suspicion on me," I said. The words came out slowly.

"That's what I'm thinking," he said grimly.

"But who would do that?"

"There's a lot of people in this town that don't like Don. *Didn't* like Don," he corrected himself. "And despite how quickly you hit it off here, most people in town don't care much for outsiders. You'd be an easy patsy."

"But I didn't do it!" My voice was almost hysterical.

"I know," he soothed. "Everything will be okay. Greg's a good guy. He's not the kind of sheriff who will go after you just because it's an easy way to close his case and keep his community intact. He'll find the truth. You'll be fine." He squeezed my hand.

I nodded numbly. It was bad enough that Joe had implied I would be a suspect. Worse, when Emerson assumed it. But worst of all was the realization that every private thing I had shared with Fiona, Emerson, and Katie was about to become public knowledge. I would almost volunteer to be locked up in a jail cell to avoid that. The panic began building again.

Sheriff Morrison chose that exact moment to knock on my window. I jumped.

"I need to take your statement," he said, when I rolled down the window.

"Can I stay with her?" Emerson asked.

Greg contemplated for a moment, then nodded assent. "Let's go over here and talk privately," he said, gesturing at the spot where he and Fiona had stood only moments before.

Emerson and I climbed out of the truck and followed him. "Now," he said, pulling out his pen and notepad. "Tell me what happened."

"Well," I paused and looked to Emerson for support. He just nodded and squeezed my shoulder.

"Well, Fiona and I went to dinner—"

"And that was your idea, correct?"

"Yes, Sheriff."

"Call me Greg." His smile was friendly. I relaxed the tiniest bit.

"Okay, Greg. Yes, I invited her. I didn't want to cook tonight, so I walked down to her house and invited her to dinner."

"Why didn't you take your car?" he asked, his tone casual.

"It was a beautiful day. I wanted to walk."

"Okay. So, you walked down to her house and invited her to dinner, and the two of you took her truck."

"Right. Yes. We went to Marco's and ate, then came back here. It was really dark. I had forgotten to leave a light on. Fiona said she would leave her headlights on while I walked inside, but I wasn't watching the ground. I tripped over—" I stopped, swallowing hard.

"Yes?"

"I tripped over his hand. It was on the bottom porch step. I should have seen it." My voice rose higher, frantic. "I should have been paying attention. The light was off. It was so dark. I should have watched where I was stepping. But I was just trying to get inside. It's so dark here—"

"It's alright," Greg interrupted, in a calming voice. "Just tell me what happened next."

I nodded and took a deep breath, willing myself to calm down again. Emerson's thumb kneaded circles on my shoulder, offering silent support.

"Fiona jumped out of the car and told me not to move. I saw his hand and screamed. She grabbed a flashlight and looked under the porch. She told me it was Don and that he was dead, and then she called Joe."

"Why didn't either of you call the sheriff's department? Or the police? Or 911?" He cocked his head and stared straight into my eyes, unnerving me.

"I-I don't know," I stammered. "Fiona just said she needed to call Joe. I wasn't thinking straight at all. When Joe got here, he said he had called you and that you were on the way."

"Hmm," he said, returning his gaze to his notebook. "And did any of you touch the body?"

"No. Well, maybe. I mean, I didn't. Other than my boot, when I tripped. But yeah, I think Fiona checked his pulse. I'm not sure if Joe touched him or not. He might have checked his pulse too."

"Hmm," he said again. "Now, Ms. Sullivan,"

"Daphne," I interrupted him. "You can call me Daphne."

He smiled. "Right. Daphne. Do you own a gun?"

"No. I don't."

"What were you doing today before you decided to walk down to Fiona's to invite her to dinner?"

"The movers came this morning. They were here for a few hours, then I spent the rest of the day unpacking."

"Alone at the house?"

"Yes, alone."

He proceeded to ask me what felt like a million more questions, wanting to know how long I had lived there and about my relationship with Don. I was able to answer honestly, if not fully. I managed to avoid talking about my mother, but I had to wonder if the omission would come back to bite me later.

"Okay," he said, tucking his notebook back into his pocket. "We're going to swab your hands for gun residue. That's all the questions I have for tonight. I may need to talk to you more tomorrow. I'm afraid your house here is off limits for the foreseeable future. Now, I'd like to take a look inside, if you don't mind."

I looked up at Emerson, questioningly. Something in his eyes felt like a warning.

I took a deep breath. "Obviously, I want to cooperate as much as possible, but I'm afraid if you want to search my home, you'll need to get a search warrant."

"I figured as much." Greg shrugged. "Hey Jackson," he called to his deputy. "Take Ms. Sullivan over to my car and swab her hands for GSR. I'm going to put a call in for a search warrant."

I followed the deputy to Greg's car, but barely even registered it when he swabbed my hands. I couldn't seem to grasp the reality of the situation. It still felt like a bad dream, one from which I desperately wanted to wake.

And it was about to get worse.

Emerson grasped my elbow tightly to get my attention.

"It's Luke and Patricia," he whispered, a warning in his voice.

I looked up and saw Patricia scurrying past the vehicles in my driveway. She was wide eyed and curious, but her demeanor suggested she had no idea we were gathered there on account of her husband.

Luke skulked behind her, head down and hands in his pockets. I knew he was older than I was, yet he reminded me of an overgrown sulky teenager.

"Well my goodness, Danielle, are you alright? I was just driving home, and I saw all the commotion and thought I better come and check on you," Patricia said. She spoke to me, but she never actually made eye contact. She was too busy taking in everything else, including my hands, still being swabbed meticulously by the deputy.

"It's Daphne," I snapped, followed by an immediate stab of guilt. Her husband was dead. Did it really matter that she got my name wrong?

"Oh, Daphne, yes, that's right. Sorry, I'm terrible with names," she said, her eyes still eagerly scanning the scene.

Luke shuffled up beside her and looked me over curiously. He never said a word. I shrank from his glance.

Greg's shoulders sagged when he spotted them. He walked over slowly, a pained look on his face. My heart sank. No matter what my personal feelings were about Patricia, she was still a woman about to find out she had lost her husband.

"Patricia. Luke," Greg said, nodding toward both of them.

"Sheriff Morrison. What's going on? I've never seen anything like it! Is everything okay?"

"Why don't we go back to your house and talk," he said gently, putting a hand on Patricia's elbow and attempting to turn her away from the scene.

"My house? Why would we go to my house to talk?" She was unwilling to leave. Even as he continued trying to shield her from the view, she twisted and looked behind him, mesmerized by it all.

"Patricia, I've got some things to tell you, and I'd feel a whole lot better if we could go talk about it somewhere private."

She finally looked at him, alarm registering on her face. "What? No.

If something's wrong, tell me now. Is it about Don?" Her eyes got big. "Where is he? What did he do?"

Greg sighed. His shoulders sagged again. "Luke, Patricia, I'm very sorry to inform you that Don was found deceased."

For a brief moment, Patricia looked utterly confused. Then, as she realized the meaning of his words, her face changed to one of horror.

"No!" she shrieked, crumbling to the ground. Greg grabbed her and supported her. "No, it can't be true!"

Her anguish pierced me. I felt compelled to hug her, to comfort her in some way. I stepped forward. "Patricia," I started.

She turned and looked at me, as if she was seeing me for the first time.

"You," she said, in a whisper. "I know who you are now. I should have seen it from the beginning. Sullivan." She spat out the word. "You're that nasty Eileen's daughter, aren't you? AREN'T YOU?" she demanded.

"Y-yes, I'm Eileen's daughter," I stammered.

"How could you? How COULD YOU? You-you WITCH!" She screamed the word, then buried her face in Greg's shirt, sobbing.

I stepped back, stunned.

Luke caught my eye. He was standing behind his mom, straighter than I had ever seen him stand. He was staring right at me.

And he was grinning.

Chapter Nineteen

Fiona marched to my rescue. "*Sheriff* Morrison," she said, glaring at him. "Are we free to leave?"

"That might be a good idea," he said, still holding a hysterical Patricia.

I turned my gaze to the cottage. My beautiful, cozy cottage was now a crime scene. I wanted to leave, yes. I wanted more than anything to be away from this. But I had nowhere to go.

I looked at Fiona questioningly.

"You're coming home with me," she said firmly. "We'll be good and out of the way while they finish up here."

I nodded, relieved. "Fiona, my car and your truck are both blocked in. How are we going to get to your house?"

She looked at me like I was crazy. "We'll walk, of course. If you want to cut through the woods, it will be faster."

"In the dark? After someone was murdered? Are you serious?" I shivered. Even the road felt threatening tonight.

"It's okay, I'll drive you both," Emerson offered. "I'm not blocked in, and I need to head home anyway."

I could have kissed him right then and there.

. . .

We pulled up to Fiona's well-lit house, and she hopped out to unlock the door. I turned to Emerson. I didn't even know where to begin.

"Thank you," I said. "For being here tonight. For helping me hold it together. I'm so sorry about all of this."

"Why should you be sorry? It's not your fault."

I swallowed hard. "And yet it is, isn't it? I may not have pulled the trigger, but I'm involved, somehow. If I hadn't come here..."

"If you hadn't come here, you think Don would still be alive," he stated.

"Yeah. Yeah, I do."

"I don't know if that's true. Someone wanted him dead. Maybe it's true they saw an opportunity when they heard the rumors. Maybe that sped things up. But if someone is determined to commit murder, they're going to do it one way or another. Maybe we're jumping to conclusions by thinking they're trying to throw suspicion on you at all. Maybe it's all a big coincidence that it happened on your property."

"I doubt it," I said skeptically.

"Me too," he admitted. "That would be a significant coincidence, considering."

"Yeah."

"Hey," he said. "It's all going to be okay." He squeezed my hand.

I nodded in agreement. But everything inside me said he was wrong. It most certainly was not going to be okay. It felt like storm clouds were gathering, and I had a feeling this was only the beginning.

I grabbed my bag and hopped out of the truck. Fiona was waiting for me in her doorway. It reminded me of the way Dad would wait for me. I walked to her and immediately burst into tears.

"Oh, honey," she said, embracing me and patting me on the back. "It's a shock for sure."

"I'm so scared," I confessed.

She pushed me back and looked at me with an odd expression on her face. "Scared about what?"

"Fiona, they think I did it."

"Who thinks you did it?"

"Joe. Maybe even Greg—Sheriff Morrison, I mean. Even Emerson assumed at first." Knowing that he had even briefly considered me capable of killing Don hurt worse than anyone else's suspicion possibly could.

"Well, what on earth makes you think that?" she said, looking bewildered. She ushered me inside and sat me down on the couch. "Oh, I know Joe was giving you a hard time at first, but that's just how he is. He likes to think out loud, you see. And they have to search the crime scene, but that's nothing personal against you. Just bad luck on your part, him being shot at your house."

I wasn't convinced.

"Greg didn't seem happy that we called Joe first."

"Well, that was probably a mistake on my part," Fiona admitted. "But Joe was sheriff for so long, plus he lives right here. And we're old friends. I just didn't think of calling anyone else."

"Why do he and Greg not like each other?"

"Well, I'd say because Greg has big shoes to fill and he knows it. Everyone loved Joe. And Greg's not from around here, see. He had only lived here for a year when he ran for sheriff. So folks weren't too happy to see him replacing Joe."

"But they voted for him."

She shrugged. "Sure, but that doesn't mean they were happy about it. He ran uncontested."

"Well, that explains why Greg is awkward around him, but Joe seemed tense, too."

"Men." Fiona dismissed it with a wave. "They think they have to turn everything into a pissing contest. Truth is, Sheriff Morrison is doing a fine job. But he changed things. Runs things his own way. Does things different than Joe. That rubs Joe wrong, you see? Not that he wanted him to fail, really, but you know. He'd have been happy to see him stumble a bit, at least."

"I guess that makes sense. But you really don't think either of them suspects me?"

"They're stupid if they do. I wouldn't let it worry you." She patted my hand. "I think what you need is a nice cup of tea. Something to calm your nerves and ease your mind."

"That sounds wonderful," I said gratefully.

"You go on and curl up with one of these blankets, and I'll bring you a nice cup."

I followed orders, slipping off my shoes and curling up in the corner of the sofa with one of her many throws. Between her and Emerson, I had never felt so taken care of in my whole life. Dad loved me with all his heart, I knew that. But he wasn't the nurturing, affectionate type. And Mom, well, she had never been particularly nurturing either. To say the least.

I would always remember this as one of the worst nights of my life. But I knew I would also remember it as a night when two people I cared about had been with me every step of the way. And that was worth something.

"Here you go," Fiona sang, carrying a beautifully painted teacup to me. I took it and inhaled the sweet, floral aroma of chamomile.

I took a long sip and let the familiar ritual soothe me to my soul. The tension in my body began to relax.

"Feeling better?" Fiona asked, putting her cup aside.

"Yes. I really am." I felt clear-headed for the first time all night. "Fiona..."

"Yes, dear?"

"Don's murder has to somehow be connected to my coming here. Right?"

She thought carefully. "I'd say that's a definite possibility."

"I have to figure out who killed him."

She nodded, her lips set in a thin line. "I figured you'd see it that way."

"You disagree?"

She took her time answering. "I don't know. Sheriff Morrison is a good man and a good sheriff. I think he'll find the truth without our help. And I don't think you have a responsibility to get yourself involved, especially if it puts you in danger."

"But?"

"But." She sighed. "While I think you're wrong about the sheriff and Joe thinking you were the one to shoot poor Don, I'd say it's pretty clear from that outburst out there that Patricia sure does. And Patricia has a lot of pull over a heck of a lot of people. If you're serious about settling down and making a place for yourself here, we've got to nip that in the bud as quickly as possible."

"She called me a witch."

"I heard."

"You know what that makes me think?"

"What, dear?"

"That you were right. That they knew about my mother's second sight."

The realization dawned on Fiona's face. "Yep, I'd say that confirms it."

"That gives us a legitimate motive for why Don would have gone after her."

She shook her head sadly. "If it turns out that he really did hurt your mama, I'll never forgive myself."

"For what?"

She raised her hands in frustration. "For living here all these years and never figuring it out. For never holding him accountable. Eileen deserves justice." Tears formed in her eyes.

I nodded. "We'll get it for her. If he was behind it, we'll find out. And if he was the one who hurt her, well, it seems like he did get justice in the end."

She nodded gravely.

"So," I said, with a small laugh. "That's just two seemingly impossible tasks. We need to prove that Don murdered my mother, even though there's no evidence she was murdered at all, and he's not even here to question. And on top of that, we need to figure out who killed Don."

Fiona wrinkled up her face. "Now there's an interesting thought."

"What?"

"Now that Don's not here, we can't question him about Eileen," she pointed out.

It hit me like a ton of bricks. Maybe he had an accomplice. Or maybe he wasn't my mother's murderer at all, but was involved somehow and knew who was. And maybe *that* person was threatened by my being here.

I let out a loud exhale. "Well, that complicates things." I thought for a minute. "Do you have a notebook?"

"I'm sure I have one around here somewhere. Why?"

"I feel like I need to write things down to keep everything straight."

She got up and went to the kitchen, pulling open drawers until she found a small notebook and pen. She brought them to me, and I started making notes.

"So let's brainstorm," I said. "Realistically, who else would have had a motive to hurt Eileen? And how would Don have found out about it?"

Fiona's face drew a blank. "I can't think of anyone specifically that would want to hurt your mama. Now, if word was out that she had the sight, there's probably a whole lot of people at Don's church who would start raising pitchforks. But I'd think we would have seen some harassment before it got all the way to murder, you know?"

"That's true," I said, tapping my chin with the top of the pencil. "What about Luke? He was grinning at me when Patricia had her meltdown."

"Something's not right with that boy, that's for sure. But he was just a kid back then."

"Kids commit murder, too," I pointed out. "But I can't imagine any scenario where a child could have gotten an adult to write a suicide note, and then either coerced her to take all those pills or forced them down her throat. That seems beyond the realm of possibility."

Fiona nodded.

"But what if," I went on, "Don really was the one who killed her, and *Luke's* the one who knew about it. Maybe knowing that his dad is a killer is what made him the way he is. I mean, that's childhood trauma for sure. Maybe when I moved here, it brought things back up for Luke. I'm about the age Eileen was when she died. If Don thought he had seen a ghost when I arrived, maybe Luke felt the same way. Maybe he wanted to go to the police, and Don was trying to stop him. Or maybe he just wanted to punish Don for his crime."

I smiled triumphantly. It made total sense.

"It's a good theory," Fiona admitted. "But we have the same problem we've had all along."

"I know. There's no proof."

Fiona nodded again. Her face was tired and weary, for once actually showing her age. She had been strong for me when I was falling apart, but now I could see the toll the night had taken on her. I put the notebook down on the table and picked up my bag.

"We're both exhausted," I said. "Maybe everything will look clearer in the morning. If you'll point me to the bathroom, I'm going to get ready to turn in."

She pointed me down the hall. When I came back, there were extra quilts, sheets, and a pillow stacked on the couch. I gave her a hug, then tucked myself in, knowing that sleep was unlikely to come that night.

Chapter Twenty

I awoke the next morning to sunlight streaming in through the windows and the sound of Fiona humming a tune under her breath in the kitchen. I could smell the life-giving aromas of fresh coffee and bacon.

I stretched lazily, wanting to bury myself back underneath the blankets. It was safe and warm under there, and I could almost forget that my house was now a crime scene. Everything would be okay as long as I could just stay beneath the covers.

If only.

Regretfully, I pushed aside the blankets and put my bare feet on the cold floor. At least there would be coffee and bacon as a reward for facing the day.

"Good morning," I said, making my way into the kitchen.

"Well, good morning to you, too!" Fiona sang out. She was bright and energetic, as if last night hadn't even happened. "Mugs are in that cabinet," she said, pointing. "Coffee's over there. Sugar's in the jar and cream's in the fridge. Breakfast is almost ready. I figured we could use something good and hearty after yesterday."

"That sounds great."

"How'd you sleep?"

I shrugged. "Okay." *Actually, I was awake most of the night imagining myself in prison, but I suppose it could have been worse.*

She gave me a skeptical look but didn't say a word.

At least the night had given me time to think. I had mulled over the situation repeatedly. It just didn't add up. I could come up with plenty of theories and wild speculation, but that's all I had. There was absolutely no proof of anything. I didn't even know which crazy theory to try investigating first. And even if I picked a theory at random, I didn't know where to look for "clues." That was as true about Don's murder as it was about my mother's.

Fiona's voice broke me out of my thoughts. "Do you want to hang around here today? I've got to get to work on that garden, but you're welcome to stay as long as you want."

"Thanks," I said. "I really appreciate it. But I need to go home—if they will allow me back in."

"Might not be a peaceful place to be today," she warned.

"I have to face it at some point."

"Then eat up," she said, placing a plate piled with bacon, fried eggs, and biscuits in front of me. "Always easier to face something with a full belly."

I dug in and immediately felt better.

FIONA WAS RIGHT. I WALKED DOWN THE LANE TO FIND MY home still decorated with glaring yellow tape blocking me from entering my own front door. Even though it was still quite early, the deputy who had swabbed my hands was already there snapping photographs and making notes. He nodded to me as I walked up the driveway.

"Ms. Sullivan," he acknowledged.

"It's Daphne."

"Jackson Ford," he said, walking over to shake my hand. "Sorry about all this mess. We completed the search of your home last night, so you're free to go back inside. I just came to look over things in the daylight. See if anything struck me, or if we missed anything. I'll be out of your hair soon." His tone was apologetic and he seemed genuinely friendly. I relaxed. Maybe not everyone assumed I was a killer.

"Don't worry about it. Do whatever you need to do. The sooner you figure out who did this, the better." I meant it. I didn't care how long they spent out there, as long as they found the truth.

"Do you mind if I ask you a few questions?"

"Sure, that's fine."

"I've already looked over the statement you gave Sheriff Morrison last night, but I was wondering if you've thought of anything else."

"Like what?"

"Have you noticed anything suspicious? Don was your closest neighbor. Have you noticed any loud arguments or anything else interesting when you've been outside?"

"No, I haven't. But I've only lived here for a few days. I wish I could think of something. Wait—" I hesitated.

"Yes?" His face was eager.

"Well, this was before I moved here, and it didn't happen here on the lane. But maybe it's important. The first time I saw him was actually a few weeks ago at the Sunset Motel. I had just made an offer on the house and was staying there for the night. I ran into him in the parking lot. It seemed like he didn't want anyone to know he was there."

"Did you already know him?"

"No."

"Then how are you sure it was him?"

"Honestly? He kind of scared me. Then, when he came over here to introduce himself, I recognized him."

Jackson frowned. "How did he scare you?"

I realized then I had stepped into murky waters. I didn't really want to bring up anything about Eileen. But I also wasn't going to lie to a deputy in the middle of an investigation.

So, I chose my words carefully. "He seemed startled to be seen. Stared at me without speaking. I said something to him about the sunset. He didn't reply. Just kept looking at me like he had seen a ghost. It gave me the creeps."

"Hmm." Jackson frowned again. "That's interesting. I don't know if it means anything, but at this point everything helps. Anything else?"

"No, not that I can think of. But if I do think of something, I'll let you know." I started to walk away, but he stopped me.

"I know you're new here, but I'm asking everyone. Do you know of anyone with anything against Don?"

I started to say no, but then I realized that wasn't really true. I hadn't met a single person who had anything nice to say about him. I had heard how beloved he was in the community, but I sure hadn't seen that reflected.

"Nothing specific against him," I said carefully.

"What do you mean by that?"

I clenched my jaw. I had really stuck my foot in it. Fiona had made it clear that she didn't want the past brought up and mentioning it to the deputy felt like a betrayal. I also didn't want to get Emerson in trouble for saying anything about his patient.

"I can't really say. I've only heard rumors of things long before my time here, so I don't know specifics. Perhaps Joe Hemsworth could be of some help? He was the sheriff back then. You might ask him for more details."

He nodded. I could feel him watching me until I disappeared behind the house.

THE POLICE SEARCH HAD LEFT MY HOUSE AN EVEN BIGGER mess than it already was. Boxes had been opened, drawers had been searched. I knew it was necessary, if only to help clear my name, but it was so violating. I hated it.

I immediately went to work, trying to put things in order. I needed it to feel like a safe haven again. The living room was halfway finished when I heard a soft rap on the back door. I nearly jumped out of my skin, still unnerved by Don's murder. I was contemplating pretending not to be home when I heard a familiar voice call out.

I sighed with relief and opened the door. "Katie. Hey." It was so good to see a friendly face.

"Oh my gosh, Daphne, Dave told me what happened. Are you okay?"

"Yeah. I'm okay. Come on in. I just made coffee, but I'm afraid it's not decaf. Would you like a cup anyway?"

She hesitated only briefly. "Maybe just this once. A small cup. Thanks. Do you have cream and sugar?"

"Actually, I do. I'll fix you up. Have a seat wherever you can find one." I let out a small laugh, gesturing at the boxes taking up space in my living room. One of these days, I would actually have my house put together for visitors. *Unless I'm in prison.*

I pushed the unwelcome thought away.

I grabbed my coffee and poured Katie a fresh one. When I came back to the living room, she was curled up in the sofa's corner, looking perfectly at ease despite the surrounding mess. I handed her the cup of coffee, which she took from me with what could only be described as reverence.

"Mmm." She closed her eyes as she savored a long sip. "Regular tastes so much better than decaf."

"It really does, doesn't it?" I laughed.

"So tell me. What happened last night?" she asked, leaning forward with wide eyes.

I quickly recapped the story for her.

"Wow," she said, shaking her head. "That's crazy. I can't believe I missed the whole thing. I wish I would have been here. Maybe I could have helped somehow. I can't believe Patricia said those things to you."

I shrugged. "It could have been worse, I guess. Grief is hard. You and I both know that. I really don't blame her for getting so upset."

"That's true. I imagine that even though Don wasn't a particularly great husband, it's still a loss for her. I honestly don't know what she'll do now. I can't imagine her being on her own."

I knew exactly what she meant. My initial impression of Patricia was that she was someone whose entire identity was wrapped up in her husband. It was impossible to imagine her by herself.

Katie grinned and put her coffee aside to pick up a gift bag sitting at her feet. "Well, I hate to change the subject, but in happier news, I bought you something yesterday."

"You did?"

"Yes! A housewarming gift. I drove over to Asheville to shop. I like to go once a month or so. I take the whole day to get my hair done, hit the outlet malls, and eat somewhere fabulous. And Dave doesn't like me driving home at night, so he has me stay at a nice hotel." She grinned again. "It's total girl time. You should go with me next month!"

"That sounds like a lot of fun, actually."

"It's wonderful. I always come back so rejuvenated. Anyway, I went yesterday, and while I was shopping, I found this." She handed me the bag. "I thought it would be perfect for you."

I opened it, touched that she would think of me while she was shopping. I was even more touched by the thoughtfulness of the gift itself. It was a book of photography, a compilation by various photographers in the state. Thumbing through just the first few pages made me want to curl up with it for hours.

"Thank you," I said. "Really. I absolutely love it. It's perfect."

She beamed. "I thought you might." She picked up her coffee cup and gazed at it regretfully. "Do you think it would really matter if I drank just a tiny bit more? I mean, I'm not even pregnant yet. How bad could one more cup be?"

I laughed at her. "I won't tell if you don't. Want me to fix you another?"

She held up her hand. "You sit. I can tell you're dying to flip through that. I can help myself."

I grinned and told her where she could find everything, then went back to the book.

It was exactly the kind of project I would love to be part of. Each photographer had highlighted a different town or region in the state, capturing both the landscape *and* the community. There were breathtaking pictures of mountain summits and sweeping views. But my favorite photographs were the ones that captured the spirit of daily life. A woman feeding chickens in the early morning hours, with fog rising off the mountain in the background. Children staring wide-eyed at a Christmas parade, their anticipation and joy practically leaping off the page. A lone man in a fishing boat, dwarfed by the rise of trees behind him, the only sign of human life in an otherwise pristine, rugged landscape.

It was amazing. I knew immediately that when I shot the images for my own book, I wanted to include the people of Rosemary Mountain.

They were part of the magic of this place, and a photographic tribute wouldn't be the same without them.

"Judging by your face, I'd say the book's a hit," Katie said, returning with her contraband.

"It's amazing. I think I just fell in love with photography all over again. I really do love it, thank you."

"You're wel—" She was cut off by the sound of her cell phone ringing. "Oops, it's Dave," she said before answering. After a quick chat, she hung up the phone with a sigh. "I'm sorry. His receptionist called in sick today, so he needs me to come in and cover for her. I'm going to have to run."

"That doesn't sound fun."

She grinned wickedly. "You might be surprised. Sometimes it can be *very* fun playing secretary." She gave me a wink, and I blushed as I realized her meaning.

"Oh. Well. Have a great time then."

She giggled and grabbed her purse. "I'll see you later, Daphne. Let's do coffee again soon."

I let her out the back door and locked up behind her. Her visit had done more to lift my spirits than anything else so far. And once this whole crazy investigation was finished, an overnight shopping and spa trip would be a perfect way to celebrate.

Chapter Twenty-One

The photography book was just what I needed to motivate myself to get back to work. I settled down at the laptop and put in a marathon editing session, stopping only to stretch and walk a lap around the house every hour or so. By the time my stomach growled, alerting me that lunch time had long passed, I was feeling much better about the state of my job.

Since work had gone so well, I gave myself permission to spend a couple of hours unpacking. The physical act of putting things away was oddly soothing. It felt good to create order and logic in my life in a tangible way. More than ever, I wanted my little cottage to become a haven.

I was able to knock out the rest of the living room boxes fairly quickly. I would eventually get around to painting and refinishing the floors, but until then, the room was complete. And I loved it. Dad's book collection looked perfectly at home on the back wall of the living room. Some of those books had probably lived here before, when I was a baby. It felt right to bring a piece of him back here.

I angled the couch in front of the fireplace and dressed it in throw pillows and a soft blanket. A few candles and the photography book Katie had given me looked perfect on the coffee table. It was a cozy room, made so much warmer with the dark walnut bookcases and cognac leather furniture. I couldn't believe it was mine.

I sank into the couch, debating the merits of a late afternoon nap. A bit of rest might recharge me, enabling me to put in one more late-night work session. I might even be able to catch up completely, which would be great, because I knew I had a boudoir session scheduled for edit the next day. Boudoir shoots were always labor-intensive edits. It would be wonderful if it were the only thing on the docket.

An aggressive knock on the back door made me jump. It wasn't Fiona's normal rap, and it wasn't Katie's soft knock. Emerson? Maybe.

The knock rang out again, followed by a voice. "Daphne? It's Joe Hemsworth."

I frowned and walked to the door, opening it for him. "Come on in," I said.

He walked inside, looking around the room with sharp eyes before turning to me. "I'll cut right to the point. Daphne, do you have the same, um, skills as your mother?"

I hesitated. Fiona had mentioned that Eileen had helped him out on some cases. So, he obviously knew, and the fact that he had come to Fiona's rescue all those years ago said a lot. But I was also very aware that he had looked at me like a suspect last night. I wasn't sure how wise it was to be open with him.

"Well?" He was impatient.

"To which skills are you referring?" I asked, buying myself a little more time.

He sighed and pinched the bridge of his nose. "I feel crazy even saying this. Do you have the ability to, you know, sense things? Know things? See things that have already happened? That kind of thing."

"A little," I said slowly. "Sometimes, anyway. Not as much as her though, from what I've heard at least."

He walked past me and took a seat on my couch.

"Um. Make yourself at home." I didn't bother to keep the sarcasm out of my voice.

"We need to talk." His tone was serious.

"Okay." I took a seat across from him, on the fireplace hearth.

"Why did you come here?" he demanded. "Why did you buy this house?"

"The truth?" I asked.

"I'd prefer it."

I struggled internally. I didn't fully trust him, but Fiona did, and that meant a lot. I decided to tell him the whole story.

When I finished, he sat quietly for what felt like an eternity.

"I knew your mom real well," he said finally. "She was a sweet girl. Fiona doted on her like a daughter. Those two were like two peas in a pod. It broke Fi's heart when she died."

I had to ask. "You knew her personally. You must have investigated her death. Do you honestly believe she committed suicide?"

A look of anguish briefly crossed his face before disappearing again behind a wall. "There was never any evidence to the contrary," he said. "Everything pointed to suicide."

"I didn't ask about evidence. I asked what you believe." My heart pounded in my chest.

"Daphne, a sheriff can only go where the evidence points. You understand that, right?"

"But you don't believe it." I could feel it, could see it. My voice dropped to a whisper. "You never believed it, did you?"

The look of anguish returned, lingering longer this time. He was silent, but I was too. I held his gaze, refusing to back down from the question.

He finally let out a defeated sigh. "No. No, I didn't believe it."

I knew it.

"Then tell me. Please. What do you think happened?"

"I don't know." He shook his head. "Honestly, I was hoping you could tell me, if you were anything like your mom. I never could figure it out. It seemed to me that someone must have forced Eileen to write that note and take those pills. But why? Who would have that kind of power over her? And if something was wrong, why wouldn't she come to me for help? I've gone over it a million times. But there just wasn't any evidence that things didn't happen exactly the way they looked. It was only my gut saying different. And who knows? Maybe I was just an old man who didn't want to believe his young friend could have done something like that."

"I think your gut was right," I said. "Mine says the same thing."

"Did you kill Don Kistler because you thought he murdered your mother?" He asked the question calmly.

"No." I matched his tone. Firm, but calm. "I did not kill him. I don't know who did, or why, but it wasn't me."

"Okay." He nodded. "But you do think he was involved, don't you?"

I nodded slowly. "I do."

"Why?"

I shrugged. "My gut, I guess."

He sighed. "I'm not going to tell you to stay out of this. If you're anything like your ma, and I suspect you are, I know that would be a waste of breath. But be careful. And if you find out anything about either of these murders, you come to me first, okay? Not Sheriff Morrison. Not your boyfriend. Not even Fiona. Okay?"

"Now, it's my turn to ask *you* why." Internally, alarm bells were ringing.

"Because there's at least one killer who has you on his radar," Joe said, exasperated. "Maybe two. We don't know yet what all is going on. I don't know who you can trust one hundred percent except me."

"I trust Fiona."

He nodded. "I trust Fiona too. I know her well enough to know she'd never do anything to hurt you. You're basically the only family she has left. I'm not telling you to keep her out of it because I think she might be involved. I'm telling you to keep her out of it because I don't want Fiona on a killer's radar either."

And suddenly, I could see it. He cared for Fiona more deeply than I had realized.

"Okay," I agreed. "I'll come to you first."

He slapped his hands down on his knees. "Maybe between the two of us we can figure this thing out. Brings back memories, you know. Working cases with your mom." He shook his head. "Time's a funny thing."

"I wish I could have known her."

"I reckon that's hard on you."

I nodded, silently, swallowing the lump in my throat.

He stood up to leave. "Well, I best be going. But before I go, let's trade cell phone numbers. I want you to be able to get in touch with me quickly."

"Good idea." I looked around me. "I must have left my phone upstairs. I'll go grab it and you can text yourself from my number."

I ran upstairs to get it, then waited silently while he sent the text.

"Keep your phone with you," he warned. "And lock the door behind me. You can't be too careful out here."

CHAPTER TWENTY-TWO

Despite my promise to Joe, I had no intention of leaving Emerson or Fiona out of things. They were the two people I trusted most in this, more than Joe himself. I didn't want to put Fiona in any danger. But I felt certain that Emerson could take care of himself.

I texted him the minute Joe left. *Hey E, are you busy?*

He replied quickly. *Not busy, but on shift. Everything ok?*

Everything's fine. Just wanted to talk about what happened last night.

I'm here until midnight, he typed back. *Lunch tomorrow?*

I smiled. *That sounds great.*

I'll pick you up at 11.

I got up early the next morning to squeeze in a few hours of work before Emerson arrived, but I struggled to focus. The stress was probably getting to me. I shook it off and pushed through the morning, alternating between unpacking and catching up on work tasks.

By the time Emerson arrived, I was feeling more like myself and had made a nice dent in my to-do list.

"Hey." He smiled at me when I opened the door. His dark jeans and olive green flannel shirt, framed by the golden woods behind him, gave off a real woodsman vibe. I liked it. A lot.

"Hey, yourself," I said. "Make yourself comfortable. I just need to run upstairs to grab a coat real quick, then we can head out. I'm starving."

"Me too," he said, stepping inside. The bookshelves immediately caught his attention. He went straight to them and began reading the titles with a look of awe on his face. "Man. You have a killer library."

"It was my dad's." I paused for just a moment, taking in the mental picture. Something felt so right about him being there. Somehow, even though we had really just met, it felt like I had known him forever.

On the drive into town, I caught him up on my conversations with Fiona and Joe.

"Do you really think it's a good idea to investigate this on your own?" he asked, skepticism in his voice. "Greg is good at what he does. I think you can leave it to him."

"I like Greg. Really. And I'm sure he's great at what he does. But, Emerson, this is personal. We're talking about two murders here, and I'm connected to both somehow. I can't just sit back and wait for answers. My mother was killed twenty years ago, and nobody dug deep enough to find the truth, despite supposedly caring so much about her." I bit my lip and turned my gaze to the window, but barely noticed the scenery flying by.

"I'm sorry," I said, in a voice suggesting the opposite. "But I can't just hope that Greg comes through this time. Besides, I may be able to get answers he can't."

"How?"

"You know." I fiddled nervously with the sleeve of my coat. "With the sight."

"Right." His voice was uncertain, and I immediately regretted bringing it up.

"Also," I continued, trying to bridge the gap quickly, "people might be more likely to talk to us than to official law enforcement. Less intimidating, you know."

He glanced back at me and raised one side of his mouth in a half smile. "Okay," he said simply. "What do you need from me?"

I pulled out the notebook I had started at Fiona's. "I've been brainstorming about who might have had a motive to kill Don. Patricia and Luke are obvious ones. Hypothetically, my mother's killer—assuming that wasn't Don—could be one. But I was also thinking about the story you told me, about the girl in the ER who was having an affair with him. What about her? Or her parents? You said she was young. Could her father have found out and decided to punish Don for it?"

Emerson shifted in his seat and cleared his throat. "Daphne, I want to help you, but there are rules about patient confidentiality. I probably shouldn't have told you that story at all, and I definitely can't give you her name. I seriously doubt she was involved, though."

"But she might have been," I insisted. "Or she might know something. If she was having an affair with him, then there's no telling what else she might know."

He sat silent for a moment. "I'm sorry, Daphne, I can't give you her name."

"Okay, but can you at least tell Greg? Surely that's not breaking any rules, right?"

"Actually, I can't really tell him either unless he asks during the course of the investigation, which he wouldn't even know to do."

I sat back in my seat, momentarily defeated. But there were other possibilities to explore. And I might be able to figure out who the girlfriend was by going to the motel where I had seen Don.

"Hey, is Marco's okay for lunch?" Emerson asked, breaking me out of my thoughts.

"Yeah, fine," I said absently, before scratching a few ideas in my notebook about how to figure out who Don's girlfriend was.

Marco greeted us himself and led us to his most private table in the back. He squeezed my shoulder before leaving us. I thought I detected a trace of sympathy in his eyes when they met mine. He had obviously heard about what happened.

"He's a nice guy," Emerson commented as he perused the samplings of bread in the basket Marco had placed on our table.

"He's wonderful," I agreed. "And this place beats every other Italian restaurant I've ever been to."

"Welcome to Marco's, what can I—"

As I looked up and smiled at the waitress from my first night there, she stopped suddenly.

"You," she said, her face reddening. "How can you show your face here?" Her voice cracked.

I froze, my breadstick midair. Her hands were shaking, and tears welled up in her eyes. My mind blanked, as I tried to think of something —anything—to say.

Before I could come up with anything, she spun on her heels and walked away from the table. I looked at Emerson helplessly. He gave me a pointed look.

"Oh." I let out an exhale as I realized why he had brought me here. "I get it."

Marco quickly came back to our table.

"I'm so very sorry. Our waitress suddenly felt ill and needed to rest. It will be my pleasure to take care of you myself. And I'll bring you something extra special," he said smoothly.

Emerson took over and ordered drinks and an appetizer for both of us. Marco squeezed my shoulder again before disappearing, the sympathy unmistakable this time.

"So she's the one I need to talk to," I said. "Man. That's awful. So young and pregnant, and now this. I can't even imagine. Unfortunately, she seems to assume that I'm the one who killed him. I guess that means she didn't."

"Hey, I didn't say a word. But, hypothetically speaking, if she were having an affair with him, I really don't think she's the type to kill."

"No. But she still may know something. I need to talk to her."

"I don't think she's going to talk to you."

"I still have to try. Wait here a minute."

I got up and found Marco. "I need to talk to Christie. Is she still here?"

He hesitated. "I'm not sure that's a good idea."

"I'm not trying to upset her. I think I can help."

He looked at me for a moment, judging. "Okay. You can try. She's in the back office." He pointed down the hallway to a closed door on the right. "But listen, pregnant women, hormones, you know." He raised his hands helplessly and let his voice trail off.

"We'll be fine. Thanks, Marco."

I walked down the hallway and knocked softly on the door.

"Come in," Christie said with a sniffle, likely assuming it was Marco or his wife knocking.

"Hey Christie," I said quietly, opening the door slightly. "Can we talk?"

"You!" Her face reddened again. "I don't want to talk to you."

"Please," I begged. "Just for a minute."

She let out a breath and glared at me. "What do you want?"

I let myself in and pulled the door closed, wanting to keep our conversation private. I walked over and took the empty chair across the desk from her. She eyed me warily and glanced around as if checking to see if anything nearby could be used as a weapon. She was angry, but she was also obviously scared. I tried hard to project as non-threatening a posture and tone as possible.

"Christie, I know you've heard what happened, and you think I killed Don. I didn't, I promise. I would never do anything like that." I spoke slowly, reassuringly, in the same tone I would use if I were speaking to an injured animal. "I don't expect you to believe that just because I said it. But I'm here because I want to find the real killer. I want to find out what really happened to Don and bring whoever hurt him to justice. And I think you might be able to help me do that."

She eyed me suspiciously, but her body relaxed slightly. She sniffed and blew her nose on the tissue wadded up in her hands. "Even if I believed you, what makes you think I could help do that? It happened at *your* house," she said accusingly. "Plus, you're the only new person in town, and everyone knows you were spreading rumors about him. Nobody here would ever say things like that about him, and nobody here would ever hurt him. Everyone here loves Don. *Loved* Don." Her voice cracked, and fresh tears sprang up as she corrected herself.

"Christie, your baby... It's Don's, isn't it?"

Her eyes flashed with fear, like a cornered cat. "What makes you say that?"

"You told Fiona you were with a married man. You refused to give his name. I know Don was having an affair. I saw him meeting someone at the Sunset Motel. That was you, wasn't it?" I was glad that I could give out reasons for my suspicion that had nothing to do with Emerson.

Her face confirmed it. "Please, you can't tell anyone," she choked. "People wouldn't understand."

"I'm not here to judge or to get anyone in trouble," I said, choosing my words carefully. I couldn't promise not to tell anyone. Not if she had information that would lead to arresting the real murderer.

"We were in love," she said, tears welling again. "His wife was awful to him, but he couldn't leave her. Not yet, anyway. You know how it is."

Oh, I think I do.

"The baby was an accident. A surprise," she said, tenderly cradling her bump. "We had to be even more careful after that. But he was going to take care of me. Of us."

Sure he was. I had to fight the urge to roll my eyes. I clamped my lips shut and forced a sympathetic look on my face, nodding in encouragement for her to continue.

"He was going to leave Patricia and marry me, just as soon as his son could take over the church. You know the denomination leaders wouldn't let him keep leading it if he divorced his wife. He was going to give up *everything* for me. But Matthew wasn't ready for that level of responsibility. So you see, we had to wait, just a little while. But we were going to move away from here to somewhere just wonderful. Maybe California, he said! I've always wanted to see it. But now he's gone, and I don't know what I'm going to do." Her voice quivered. I feared she was going to break down completely on me.

My heart broke for her. Obviously, I didn't believe one word of Don's promises, but she had. Now, it was clear she was overwhelmed and terrified. She seemed so young, so fragile, and so very alone.

"Do you have family here?" I asked.

"Not really. Not anymore. My parents disowned me when I got pregnant. They called me a whore and told me to get out." She sniffed.

My heart sank even farther. "Oh, honey. I am so sorry. Where are you living? How are you making it?"

"When Marco and Sophia heard about my parents, they turned the room above their garage into a little apartment for me. They really saved me. I was living in my car before that," she admitted. "They don't even let me pay rent, and they still give me my full wages for waitressing. They are the nicest people."

"Yes, they are," I said. Inwardly, I was fuming at Don. How could he have allowed his so-called lover—his *pregnant* lover—to be homeless in her car? It was unbelievable to me, especially knowing the house he lived in and the car he drove. He was a lousy person in just about every way I could think of.

"Christie, you obviously knew Don well. Do you know of anyone who would want to hurt him? Anyone who was angry at him?"

"No!" she said earnestly. "He was just the best man. Everyone loved him." Her cheeks pinked. "I still can't believe he picked *me.*"

I bit my lip again and forced a smile, even though it felt like a grimace.

"What about your parents? If they were angry enough to kick you out, is there any chance they found out who the father was and did something about it?"

"Oh, no! First of all, I don't think there's any way they could have known who it was. We were really, really careful. And they loved him too. That's how I met him, actually. They've been faithful members of his church from the beginning. I still see them there every service. They don't talk to me..." She faltered. "But they were at the prayer vigil last night, and I can tell they're devastated, too."

My rage grew. If they had been members of the church from the beginning, that meant that Don had known Christie since she was a baby. It was absolutely disgusting. It also meant that he was her parents' pastor. Knowing that they had kicked her out of the house, he could have used his influence to talk to them about forgiveness and encouraged them to support her during her pregnancy. The fact that he apparently hadn't made me hope he had suffered just a bit before he died.

"What about an ex-boyfriend?" I asked. "Someone else who may have found out and was jealous that, um, Don chose you?"

She nodded and seemed to weigh this question seriously. "Well, there's no ex-boyfriend. Don was my first." She blushed. "But if Patricia found out, well, there's no telling what she would have done. She's *awful.*"

"What about other parishioners? Or maybe someone he was in business with?"

"Everyone at the church loved him," she insisted. "But, well..." She hesitated.

"Yes?"

"I don't know if I should say."

I sat up straighter, feeling a surge of hope. "If it might help bring his killer to justice, then you absolutely should tell me. We don't want Don's murder to go unsolved, do we?"

"Well, no," she said. "I didn't say anything to anyone because, well, I thought it was you. But now that I know you're trying to help Don, I guess I'll tell you. But if you tell them, can you leave my name out of it? I don't want anyone knowing."

"I'll try my best," I promised.

She lowered her voice and glanced around as if to make sure no one was listening, even though we were the only two people in the room.

"There's a man who calls him sometimes," she whispered. "Don would always get flustered and would go outside or to his car to talk so that I couldn't hear. But one time, he thought I was asleep, so he just went into the next room. I pretended to stay asleep so that I could listen."

She glanced around again, obviously nervous.

"The man was angry. He was so loud that I could hear some of what he was saying, even though the phone wasn't on speaker."

"What was he saying?"

"He said that Don needed to keep his promises." She blushed furiously. "He also said, well..."

"Yes?" I prodded her.

"Well, he said that Don needed to stop spending so much time with his 'cheap whore' and get to work." Her voice cracked, and she blinked furiously.

"Oh, honey," I said, squeezing her hand. My heart just kept breaking for her. She was so very young to bear the weight of the words that were placed on her.

"Anyway," she said, embarrassed, "Don was never himself after he got one of those phone calls. He would always get stressed, you know, kind of broody like. If the man called, our date was usually over real quick."

"How often did the man call?"

"It used to only be every now and then. Maybe once a month or so. But lately, it had been more often. It was so frustrating because I didn't like the way Don treated me after one of those calls. And it was happening more and more." She blushed again. "Not that I should have been thinking of me, of course. He's an important man, you know. Or, well, *was* an important man. I don't know how I'll get used to him being gone." The tears started again.

I hated to keep pushing her to talk about things that obviously hurt her, and inwardly I cursed Don for what he had turned her into. No young girl should have lost so much over a man who didn't seem to care about her at all. It was infuriating, and I made up my mind that I would help her if possible. But for now, I needed answers, which meant I had to keep pushing.

"Did you recognize the man's voice? Did Don ever say his name or tell you who he was?"

"No," she shook her head emphatically, but something in her eyes made me think I should press the issue.

"Do you have any idea who he was? Did you ever see his name pop up on caller ID or anything?" Ah. Bingo. A micro expression on her face told me she definitely knew something she hadn't told me.

"Christie, anything you know might be the key to solving this. I know how much you cared about Don and that you want to bring his murderer to justice. It would be so awful if the person who took him from you walked free."

This time, the expression on her face was as clear as day—fear. She knew something she wanted to tell me, but she was afraid. She sat silently, fidgeting with the tissue in her hands and avoiding my eyes.

"Christie," I said gently, reaching out to touch her hand again. "I'm getting the feeling that whatever you aren't telling me is something that scares you."

She nodded, almost imperceptibly.

"Here's the thing. I don't want to get you in trouble. I definitely don't want to put you in danger. But if you're afraid of the man on the phone, you might already be there. It sounds like he knew who you were and what your relationship with Don was. If he murdered Don, he might be worried that Don told you who he was or whatever they were up to." I chose my words carefully, not wanting to scare her unnecessarily, but also wanting to make the stakes clear. "We might need to go to the sheriff with whatever you know—not just for my sake, but for yours."

She looked up at me with wide eyes. "You're saying he might hurt me just for *knowing* something? Even if I keep my mouth shut?"

"I don't know," I said honestly. "I have no idea what Don was mixed up with, who this guy is, or what he may be thinking. He may not even be the person who killed Don. But I'd say he's high on the suspect list, wouldn't you? And if he thinks you might ID him, then yeah, I'd say you could be in danger."

Her hands shook slightly as she cradled her bump for comfort. "But I really don't know anything," she insisted.

"I think you do. Christie, please trust me. I promise to do whatever I can to protect you and help you."

She looked up at my eyes, deliberating. "I really don't know much. But one night, while Don was in the shower, I got his phone and looked through it. I had watched one day while he put the password in," she explained, with a sheepish look. "I was being silly. Jealous. I thought I had seen some sort of connection between him and this other woman at church, and I just wanted to make sure, well, you know."

I nodded, encouraging her to continue.

"Anyway. There were texts from someone he had named 'Mr. Boddy.' B-O-D-D-Y," she spelled out.

"Mr. Boddy?" I was bewildered.

"You know, like the old movie."

"What old movie?" I had no idea what she was talking about.

"*Clue,*" she said impatiently. "Like the board game. It was one of Don's favorite movies. I don't know why. But anyway, we watched it one night at the motel. Mr. Boddy was the millionaire who was blackmailing everyone. You know, Colonel Mustard, Mrs. Peacock, all that."

"Okay," I said, trying to make sure I was following. "So he named the man on the phone Mr. Boddy after his favorite movie. And in the movie, Mr. Boddy was blackmailing everyone?"

"Right," she said eagerly. "So that made me wonder if this man who kept calling was blackmailing Don."

"It makes sense," I said. "Especially knowing that if anyone found out about you, he wouldn't have been allowed to keep pastoring the church. Did you read any of the text messages?"

She blushed again. "Only a few."

"What did they say?"

"I don't really know. I couldn't really understand them," she confessed. "It's like they were talking in code."

"What do you mean? Try to remember everything you can."

"There were a lot of numbers. Like, strings of numbers. That's what most of them were. Just numbers and sometimes letters. It didn't make any sense to me. There was a message about birds in a nest or something, and another one about psychics. *That* was weird."

My heart pounded. "Psychics? What do you mean? What did it say?"

"It was something like 'Be on guard, the psychic's back from the dead.' Don's not superstitious at all, so I knew it had to be some kind of code or something."

Or something. "Okay. Can you think of anything else?"

"No," she said, and this time I believed her. She looked visibly relieved to have unburdened herself of the information she had been carrying. I only wish I felt the same. I was more confused than ever.

"I think we should go to the sheriff with this," I said.

"No." She immediately shook her head. "Everyone would know! I can't tell them without explaining everything." Her voice cracked as she pleaded with me. "It's bad enough being pregnant out of wedlock in this town. The looks I get. The snide remarks. Can you imagine if people found out I was having an affair? And it would ruin Don in the eyes of his church. I couldn't do that to him."

"You told Fiona the father was a married man," I pointed out. "She didn't judge you."

"Fiona's different from just about everyone here. You can tell her things, you know?"

Yes, I knew. I sighed. "Christie, I'm serious that you could be in danger. Going to the sheriff is the best shot we have at keeping you safe. We could ask him to be discreet."

"No. I won't do that to Don." It was obvious from her tone that she had made up her mind. I wanted to shake some sense into the poor girl.

"Christie, we *have* to tell him about Mr. Boddy."

"Then you'll have to figure out a way to tell him without bringing me into it."

"Fine," I said, exasperated. "I'll figure something out."

Chapter Twenty-Three

As I left the room, I found Marco pacing the hallway down from us. He looked up, obviously relieved.

"Everything's okay?" he asked.

"Yes, but—" I glanced around to make sure we were alone. "Listen, I can't explain, but Christie may be in danger."

"Danger?" His eyes widened.

"Yes. Please don't ask me any questions. Not yet. Just keep a close eye on her, okay? Keep her safe. Don't let her go off anywhere alone or anything."

His face was serious as he nodded. "Is this about Don?" he asked in a whisper.

"I really can't say anything more."

"We know he's the father." He whispered again, ensuring that Christie couldn't hear, even if she opened the office door unexpectedly.

"You do?" I asked, surprised.

He rolled his eyes. "Of course. Christie thinks it's a big secret, but it's obvious to anyone who's paying attention."

"Who else knows? What about her parents?"

He gave me a sympathetic look. "I said it was obvious to anyone who's paying attention. They didn't."

"That's so sad."

He nodded his agreement. "I don't know who else knows. It was obvious to me and Sophia from the beginning, but we're around her more than most. We tried to talk some sense into her when it first started up, without coming right out and saying what we suspected. But"—he shrugged—"young people who think they are in love. There is no reasoning with them."

As if saying her name had summoned her, Sophia appeared around the corner.

"Marco! We have customers waiting. What are you doing back here?" she scolded.

He put a finger in front of his mouth, warning her to be quiet, and motioned for her to come closer.

"We were talking about Christie," he explained. "Daphne knows Don is the father. She thinks Christie may be in danger. We need to keep an eye on her."

Sophia's eyes widened. "Why would she be in danger?" she demanded.

"If whoever killed Don thinks that Christie could somehow identify him, he might go after her," I explained in a whisper. "Keep her close, just to be safe."

Sophia nodded, her lips set in a thin line.

"Listen, Marco said it was obvious to you both that Don was the father. Who else do you think knew?"

Sophia shook her head in disgust. "They weren't nearly as discreet as Christie thinks. He would come in here to eat, and her face would light up. Any woman watching would have seen that something was going on. He would wink at her when she served him. She would linger at his table. They would whisper. He would hang around until her shift was over, then leave. She would follow just a minute or two later. Most people are on their phones these days, but anyone watching them could have realized something was up."

"Well, that definitely doesn't narrow it down." I groaned. "What about Patricia?"

Sophia snorted. "I don't think Patricia cared."

"What do you mean?"

"If you ask me, Patricia was relieved that Don had somewhere else to be. I'd probably feel the same if I were married to such a man. Now don't you go getting any ideas," she said, wagging a finger at Marco. "I happen to like you a little bit."

He grinned at her affectionately. I had liked them from the beginning, but my respect for them had only grown today.

"Listen, I'd better get back to Emerson. But if you have something I can write my number down on, I'd like for you to call me if you think of something else, or if Christie starts acting strange or anything. Anything at all. Okay?"

"Of course," said Sophia, handing me the order pad and pen she carried in her apron. I jotted down my number, then headed back to the booth.

"Well?" Emerson asked as I slid in across from him.

"Not here." I glanced around the restaurant, which was quickly filling up. "I'll fill you in when we leave."

"I guess that means we get to put all this aside for a few minutes and enjoy our third date."

My lips rose in a playful smile. "Hmm. I'm not sure this counts as our third date."

"Why not?" he said in mock protest.

"I don't know that interviewing a crying pregnant woman really sets the right tone for a date," I said, laughing.

"Good point," he admitted. "It's not exactly romantic, is it? But, Daphne, I'll tell you one thing." He stopped and twirled his spaghetti on his fork, leaving me hanging.

"What?"

He swallowed his bite before shooting me a grin. "Not one of our dates has been boring."

"That's true. Let's see. We had flash floods for our first."

"You told me you're investigating a murder on the second," he added.

"Date two point five was a murder at my house."

"And date number three finds us investigating said murders together," he finished. "Nope, definitely not boring. In fact, I'd say you're about the most interesting person I've ever met."

He gazed at me intensely, and heat rose to my cheeks. I suddenly lost interest in my food.

"Ready to get out of here?" he asked, his voice thick.

"Yes." The answer left my lips the moment he asked. He dropped cash on the table, enough to cover our food and leave a nice tip besides. We both slid out of the booth, and his hand came to the small of my back, his thumb tracing light circles on my spine. The sensations made my mouth go dry.

He walked me to the passenger side of his truck and opened the door for me, but before I climbed in, he grabbed me by my waist and turned me toward him. He kissed me, deep, his hand slipping under my shirt to meet skin. I kissed him back, hungry and needy. I had never felt like this. Had never *wanted* like this.

He pulled away and sighed, bringing his forehead to mine.

"I guess you'd better tell me what you found out now."

"What? Oh. Yes. Okay." I shook myself, coming back to earth. He helped me into the truck and walked around to his own door.

I hoped he felt as frustrated as I did.

"So catch me up," he said, starting the truck.

I quickly gave him the highlights of my conversation with Christie.

His face turned serious. "Hmm. Well, I guess you were right that she might know something. A Mr. Boddy, hmm? That's interesting. What now?"

"I don't know," I answered. "I think Greg should know, but I need to come up with a way to tell him that keeps her name out of it. And I haven't figured out how to do that yet. It at least gives us another lead, though. Can you think of anyone who might be blackmailing him? Or any specific reason they would?"

He thought for a minute. "Well, like you said, if anyone found out about the affair with Christie, that could be the end of his career as a pastor. But as far as I know, nobody else knew about it."

"Marco and Sophia knew," I mused. "But I don't see them as the blackmailing type."

"I doubt it," he agreed. "But you never know about people."

Something was nagging at me, like there was something important I had missed somewhere along the way. But whatever it was, I couldn't quite place it.

BEFORE I KNEW IT, WE WERE BACK AT MY COTTAGE.

"Do you want to come in?" I asked, feeling suddenly shy.

"I'd better not," he said, his voice thick again.

"Why not?" I regretted the words as soon as I asked them.

He ran his hand through his hair and leaned against his door. "I really like you."

"Well, that's good, because I like you too. Obviously."

He put his hand over mine and rubbed his thumb over my wrist.

"I feel like there's a 'but' coming," I said, my heart sinking.

"I just don't think we should rush things. No matter how much it kills me to say that. But the truth is, we don't know each other very well. You don't know *me* very well."

I didn't know what to say. Katie's words ran through my mind.

"Also," he continued, "This whole Don thing, your second sight thing, the murder investigation...well, it's complicated. And to be honest with you, the whole reason I moved here was to get away from complicated." He smiled a sad sort of smile. "Then I met you and that kind of went out the window."

"So what are you saying?"

"All I'm saying is I don't think I should come in right now, because we both know if I do, we're going to make things even more, well—"

"Complicated?" I finished for him.

He shrugged a yes, then leaned over and kissed me, softly this time, his fingers brushing lightly across my chin.

"How about we go for a walk tomorrow?" he asked, his lips still close to mine. "I'll show you some of my favorite spots on the mountain here."

"That sounds nice," I murmured.

He kissed me again, then pulled away.

"Go on in," he said roughly. "Before I change my mind."

"Is that a promise?" I giggled.

He kissed me again in reply.

Chapter Twenty-Four

I awoke the next morning, weary from a strangely restless night. After Emerson had dropped me off, the rest of the day had felt like a waste. I hadn't been able to stop thinking about Emerson, Christie, or Mr. Boddy. I had felt tired and cranky, completely out of sorts and unable to focus. I had made a fresh pot of coffee, but had fallen asleep at my desk shortly after drinking it. Worse, the caffeine that failed to help me focus still managed to keep me tossing and turning all night.

On top of that, the feeling I'd had yesterday lingered. Something was nagging at the back of my brain, something I had missed. It felt as if the answers I was looking for had come to me in dreams—dreams that were sitting just on the edge of my memory, unable to be retrieved.

Unfortunately, even my morning cup of coffee couldn't put me to rights. I somehow felt even more tired after drinking it.

I breathed a sigh of relief after reading an email from the boudoir photographer telling me that the session hadn't gone well and they were going to reshoot later. That was a huge red flag for an editor. If a boudoir client was unhappy before even seeing the final product, then odds were she would be someone with a million extra editing requests.

But at least that was a problem for another day. I could afford to take a day off. And I needed it.

I just needed to clear my head and figure out what I was missing.

Since coffee hadn't done the trick, I decided to try exercise and fresh air. Fiona had been right, as always. The temperature had dropped significantly that week. I added a hat and scarf to my normal ensemble and headed outside for a walk, hoping the mountain would work its magic.

Unfortunately, that was not to be.

I could feel that something was wrong the minute I stepped outside.

Someone had ripped down the crime scene tape. But even worse, they had taken a can of spray paint to the front of my house.

The words *I did it* and *I'm crazy, please help me* were spray-painted in red across the front. My jaw dropped. How could someone do this? *Who* would do this?

My mind immediately went to Patricia. Or Luke.

With a shaking hand, I pulled my cell phone from my pocket and dialed.

"Daphne?" Emerson answered out of breath, and I realized I was likely interrupting his morning jog. "What's up?"

"I-I came outside for a walk, and someone... Someone vandalized my house." My voice was shaking.

"I'll be there in three minutes." His tone immediately became serious. "Go inside and lock the door."

"Okay."

I hung up, but instead of following his instructions, I snapped pictures of the vandalism. I stayed back so that I wouldn't contaminate the area with my own footprints, mindful that it was still a crime scene as well. I hoped the deputy had finished processing everything yesterday. What a mess.

My initial fear subsided, having been overtaken by anger that someone would do this. They weren't just hurting me. They were hurting the investigation.

Then it hit me that maybe that was the point.

. . .

I was still outside when Emerson pulled up in his truck.

"I told you to go inside and lock the door," he admonished, before turning to survey the scene. His face changed when he saw the words written on my cottage.

He looked at me, then looked back at the house, his expression unreadable.

"I called Greg. He's on his way." His tone of voice felt different somehow. Like it was putting distance between me and him.

"Thanks." I moved toward him, seeking comfort. He put his arm around me, but kept staring at the house.

"Any idea who did this?" he asked, still in that strange tone.

"I immediately thought of Patricia. She was furious the other night."

"Yeah, but can you really see her doing this?" His brows furrowed. "I don't think Patricia has it in her. Honestly, it shocked me when she screamed at you. She's always been so meek when I've been around her. Luke, maybe. I could see him doing this. I just don't know why he would."

"Maybe he's angry because he thinks I killed his father." It seemed clear to me.

"Eh..." Emerson's face was still skeptical. "I've never gotten the impression that he was very fond of Don, and he didn't seem torn up the other night, did he?"

"Well, no," I admitted. "He didn't. But he was grinning when Patricia did her thing and screamed at me. Maybe he just likes the drama."

"Maybe." He gave me a long look, his brows still knit in concentration. "I guess we'll see what Greg thinks. Meanwhile, let's get you inside. There's nothing we can do out here until he arrives."

"Yeah. Okay." I rubbed my eyes and massaged my temples.

"You okay?"

"Yeah. This whole thing has just given me a massive tension headache."

"Hang on, I've got some meds in my truck." He reached into a medical bag in the back and pulled out a bottle of pills. "Here. Take two."

I took the bottle gratefully and popped three instead, knowing it would take that many to knock out a headache this bad. He just raised his eyebrows.

"Keep it," he said when I tried to hand the bottle back to him. "Something tells me this won't be the last headache before all this is said and done."

I nodded. "I'm afraid you're right."

We walked back to the house to wait for Greg.

Greg announced his arrival with a firm knock on the back door.

"Thanks for coming," I said, gesturing for him to come inside.

"That's my job." He exchanged glances with Emerson. "That's some nasty business out there, Daphne. What time did you notice it?"

"When I went out for a morning walk. I wanted to clear my head. Unfortunately, I saw that instead."

He nodded. "Did you hear anything unusual this morning? Or last night?"

"No, I really didn't. I didn't sleep well. Maybe it's because someone was here in the middle of the night. I don't know, though. I can't say I noticed anything in particular."

"Has anyone harassed you since the other night?"

"You mean Patricia," I said flatly. "No, she hasn't. I haven't heard from her or seen her."

"Patricia or anyone else." He shrugged. "Don had a lot of fans in the community."

"No. Nothing like that. Everything's been quiet until this morning."

"Okay," he said. "I took a quick look before coming in, and I'll take a closer one before I leave. But it's unlikely I'll find anything that would help us identify who did it. I'll ask around with your neighbors, but—"

"But Patricia and Luke are the only ones likely to have seen or heard anything, and they are the most *unlikely* to tell you who it was," I finished for him.

"Right."

I sighed. "Can I at least clean it up? Or does it have to stay until you're finished with the crime scene?"

"You can go ahead and clean it up. We're done with the scene, and it would be contaminated now, anyway."

"I thought about that. Do you think that's the reason behind it?"

He shrugged. "It's possible. But if so, it was pointless. We had already gone over it with a fine-tooth comb. I'd say it's more likely directly about you."

Oddly, that made me feel better. The idea of Patricia or Luke, or even a stranger, acting out of anger was much less terrifying than the idea of a murderer coming back to my home while I was sleeping.

"Well," he said. "I'm going to take another look and then ask around. I'll come back and let you know if I find any answers for you." He exchanged glances with Emerson again. Their wordless communication made me more than a little uncomfortable.

"Thank you. Really. I appreciate it."

"That's my job," he repeated.

I let him out and locked up behind him, then sank into the corner of the couch, wrapping myself in a blanket. Now that the adrenaline had faded, I was even more exhausted and cloudy than before.

Emerson watched me from the other side of the sofa.

"How are you doing with all this?" he asked quietly. He propped an elbow on the arm of the couch and looked at me with that odd expression.

"I'm okay. Mostly, anyway. I don't know."

"You look like you haven't slept at all."

"I did. It just wasn't restful. I tossed and turned all night."

"You've been through a lot of stress. Not even just this. First, your dad, then finding out about your mom. Moving is also considered a major life stressor, medically speaking. It all takes a toll on you. Physically *and* mentally. Anyone would have a hard time with all this. I just want to make sure you're really okay. You can talk to me, you know, if you're struggling."

I frowned. "*And* mentally? What are you getting at, Emerson?"

"Just that you seem worn down and stressed," he soothed.

"Huh," I said, sarcasm creeping into my voice. "Worn down and stressed, or crazy?"

"I didn't say that."

"No, but you implied it."

"I didn't imply anything, Daphne," he said, obviously exasperated. "But have you looked in the mirror today? You look like hell."

"Thanks." I rolled my eyes.

"You know what I mean. You're pale, you've got bags under your eyes, and you obviously didn't sleep. And the words out there..." He softened his tone. "Look, this kind of thing would get to anyone."

It *was* getting to me. I knew I looked awful, and I felt even worse. The pills hadn't touched my headache. It was pounding harder than ever, and all I wanted was to curl up and sleep until this whole thing was over.

But fair or not, I didn't like his insinuation—or being spoken to like I was his patient.

"Like I told you," I said, forcing myself to keep my tone even. "I'm tired. I have a headache. And yes, this is a lot of stress. But I'm fine. Great, actually. Why don't you just be honest with me and tell me what you're really thinking?"

"What am I really thinking?"

"That I'm crazy. You've thought so ever since I told you about the second sight, haven't you? Things changed between us that night. And they changed again this morning. You believe I painted those words on the front of my house myself."

"Did you?" he asked, watching me carefully.

"Of course not," I snapped. The tone of my voice surprised me. I willed myself to get it back under control. "I can't believe you would even ask me that."

"You're the one who brought it up," he pointed out. "Look, I believe you. But that doesn't change the fact that I'm worried about you. I know what stress can do to a person."

"Well, you don't have to worry about me. I can handle it. I just need to get a little rest and knock out this headache."

"Okay," he said, his mouth set in a firm line. "I'll take off then. You should definitely get some rest, though."

Don't tell me what to do. I knew my anger was out of place. But knowing that didn't make it go away.

"Okay, I'll be sure to do that," I said, my voice dripping with sarcasm.

His face registered surprise at my tone, then—was that hurt? Yes. I had hurt his feelings.

Part of me, buried deep beneath the growing layer of irritation, wanted to apologize and make things right. But that part of me couldn't seem to claw herself to the surface.

The part of me that was tired, hurt, and frankly pissed off was just so much bigger.

"Okay. Take care of yourself, Daphne." He rose from the couch and walked to the back door. He turned to me like he wanted to say something else, but then clamped his mouth shut and shook his head.

I wanted to tell him to come back, to stay with me. To just let me get a little sleep. Then everything would be better, and we could talk again and take that walk.

But I didn't.

I gave him a two-fingered salute, then sank deeper into the couch cushions, closed my eyes, and went to sleep.

Chapter Twenty-Five

I slept deeply for hours. When I finally woke, Emerson was gone. My memories of our conversation were hazy, but I was aware enough to know that I had overreacted.

He was a genuinely nice guy whose entire profession was about taking care of people. Why had I gotten so irritated when he was trying to take care of me?

The truth was that his questions had hit too close to home. My mental state that morning had scared me. I had never felt so foggy. That's the only way I could describe it. It was hard to even remember what had happened the night before, and when I saw the vandalism, I couldn't help but wonder.

Emerson asking about my mental state had simply confirmed my own fears.

I hadn't been irritated with him.

I had been terrified of myself.

I immediately picked up the phone to call him. When he answered, his voice was short. Distant.

"Emerson? Hey. I just wanted to call and apologize for the way I acted earlier. I wasn't myself at all. You're right, I felt terrible, and I shouldn't have reacted that way when you were just trying to make sure I was okay."

"It's fine," he said, still in that short tone. "Don't worry about it."

"It's not fine. I don't know how to explain it. I just wasn't myself."

Silence.

"Listen, do you want to come over tonight?" I asked. "I'm going to head to the grocery store in a bit. I thought I might pick up something nice for dinner."

There was a brief pause before he answered. "Thanks for the invitation, but I don't think that's a good idea."

"Okay." I squeezed my eyes shut and steadied my voice, unwilling to let him hear the quiver threatening to break through. "Well, I'll talk to you later, I guess?"

"Yep."

"Okay... Bye."

"Bye."

The tears welled up before I hit the disconnect button. So I really had ruined things. He didn't want complicated, and boy, had I gone and made things more complicated. It hurt much more than it should have for a relationship that wasn't even a week old.

I pulled my knees into my chest and rocked back and forth. I barely knew him. We had only been on three dates. I was being ridiculous.

But knowing that didn't make it hurt any less.

First, I had lost my dad. Then, I had lost the mother I couldn't even remember. Now, I had lost a man who made me feel things I had never felt before. Loss, loss, loss. I didn't think I could bear another hit.

Unfortunately, I didn't have a choice.

GREG WAS SOON BACK TO GIVE ME A REPORT.

I steeled myself, not knowing what to expect. He had been friendly earlier, but I remembered the glances between him and Emerson. I invited him to come in and sit down. He did so, his face unreadable. It was clear that something had changed in the few hours since he had been here before.

"Well, Daphne, I've been talking to your neighbors," he said.

"And? Do you know who did this?"

"I'm not certain yet. But, Daphne, some of your neighbors are worried about you."

I played dumb. "Worried? About me? Do you think I'm in danger? Harassment doesn't always lead to violence, right?"

"That's not what I mean when I say they're worried about you." He cleared his throat and stretched his legs awkwardly before continuing. "See, there's some concern that maybe you're not handling things too well right now. There's no shame in that. We all struggle from time to time, and from what I hear, you've been through quite a lot this year."

I immediately regretted apologizing to Emerson.

"I'm fine," I said, my voice clipped.

"The thing is, I'm not sure you are. One of the phrases written out there was 'Please help me.' Was this a cry for help, Daphne? Because if it was, I'll try to get you the help you need."

I dug my fingernails into my palms and forced myself to stay calm. "Sheriff, I can assure you that I did not vandalize my own home. Whoever did so was obviously trying to make me look unstable, and is likely the same person who shot Don Kistler in my yard in order to throw suspicion on me. I hope that instead of continuing down this line of inquiry, you will put your efforts into finding the real culprit." I was incredibly proud of my little speech—and for how steady I kept my voice while making it.

Unfortunately, it didn't seem to faze Greg.

"I understand your perspective on things," he said, nodding. "But regardless of what happened with Don, or even what happened on your front porch there, I'm saying that you have some people in this community that care about you. They're worried about you, and rightly so. Daphne, I know about your mother."

"What about my mother?" I asked tightly.

"I read the reports. No one wants to see something like that happen again. That's why I'm here, not just as a sheriff, but as a friend, offering you help. Now, why don't you talk to me? Tell me what's going on."

I was shaking all over. Whether from fear or rage, I wasn't sure.

"Let me be very clear." I said the words forcefully, emphasizing each one. "I did not vandalize my own house."

"Daphne, I'm not your enemy. Let me give you a piece of friendly advice. All this will go better for you if you cooperate. Okay? I'm trying to be gentle with you, but here's the facts. Right now, you're the number one suspect in a murder investigation. You need to understand that. You've got a lot of people in this town who are already convinced you're guilty. And now the general consensus is that you painted those things on your house yourself. More than one person has told me they're worried you're losing your marbles. Now, I could play this hard with you, and it's going to get to that point real soon if you don't cooperate. But right now I'm trying to give you a chance. Like I said, there's people in this community who care about you. If you're ill, we want you to get help. But let *me* be clear. This is still a murder investigation. And if you're involved in that in any way, your window of doing this the easy way is going to close soon."

I clamped my lips tightly and fought to control my shaking. Two breaths and I could speak with a steady voice. "Am I under arrest?"

"Not yet." He sat back and watched me, gauging my reaction.

"Then you need to leave. I won't be speaking to you again without an attorney."

He sighed. "So that's how it's going to be? Daphne, I'm trying to help you here, whether you see that or not."

I didn't say another word. I simply walked to the door, held it open, and gestured for him to leave. He shook his head and sighed again, then walked to me.

"Don't leave town," he said. "That's a warning. You can expect to be hearing from me." He left without a look back, walking with purposeful strides. I knew even without him saying it that he would be back soon, and next time it would be to arrest me. He may have come here as a friend, but I had made him an enemy. And all I had done was tell the truth.

I closed the door behind him and fell against it, shaking. I was terrified to my very core. He had said that "multiple people" were worried about me. Emerson had already made it clear that he was concerned, so that was no surprise. But multiple people?

It was the worst kind of betrayal.

Stupid Daphne. Always being ridiculous. You just thought you had found a home in this community, but look how quickly they turned against you.

My cheeks flushed and hot tears sprang forth.

I wanted to run away from it all. Just stop unpacking boxes, call the movers back, and go home to Dad's house. It hadn't sold yet. I could do it. I could pretend this whole thing had been one giant nightmare and start over again somewhere safe.

Don't leave town. That's a warning. The sheriff's words echoed in my mind. They formed their own kind of jail cell, a prison trapping me in this community I suddenly wanted to run away from.

I picked up my phone again, this time to make the last call I wanted to make.

"Hello? Daphne?"

"Hi, Mom." My voice crumbled.

"What's wrong?"

"I-I need your help. I need you to help me find an attorney."

"An attorney? What in the world? What's going on?"

"Nothing. It's just..." I broke into muffled sobs.

"Good grief, Daphne, what is it?"

When I could finally speak, I spilled it all in one long, incoherent mess. "Everything is awful. Murder. My front porch. People think I did it. Someone spray-painted my house. And I met someone. But it's over." I sobbed harder before choking out my final words.

"I want to come home, Mom."

There was dead silence on the other end of the line for a good minute.

"Daphne," she finally spoke, her words deliberate. "Let me make sure I'm understanding you. Are you telling me that someone was murdered on your front porch and that you are a suspect in the investigation?"

"Yes." One more sob.

More silence. "Okay. Text me your address. I'm on my way. I'll get in touch with an attorney. Don't do anything stupid."

"Like when I moved here?" The words spilled out, surprising me.

"Well, I wasn't going to rub it in, but yes. I told you it was a bad idea. Moving back to the town where your father's worst nightmare happened? A town he chose to take you away from to spare you the memories and grief of it all. It was a terrible idea. And now this."

"Not just the town," I said before I could stop myself.

"What do you mean?"

"I didn't just move to the town. I bought their old house."

Silence hung between us before she spoke again, using the same deliberate voice as before. "You mean to tell me you're living in the exact same house where your mother went crazy and committed suicide?"

I didn't say anything. I wanted to tell her she was wrong, that my mother wasn't crazy, and that she absolutely didn't kill herself. I wanted to scream at her for even speaking about my mother in that tone of voice. But I didn't. Because the truth was that I didn't even know what to believe anymore. And as much as I hated to admit it, I needed her. I needed her to come help me put my life back together because I had proven that all I was good at was destroying it.

"Just hang tight," she said in a softer voice. "I'll take care of everything. I'm going to look into flights versus drive times. I'll let you know when I have a plan."

"Okay."

We hung up.

I wasn't sure if I felt better or worse.

I busied myself with unpacking. If Mom was on her way, I needed to get the guest room in shape. More than that, I needed a distraction, something physical and mundane. *I should have listened to Mom. I never should have come here.* It hurt, knowing that was true.

I needed something to steady myself. Some comfort. I thought longingly about the bottle of Malbec sitting on the pantry shelf. *Oh, what I would give to just lose myself in that right now.* Drink until everything felt fuzzy and hilarious instead of depressing and terrifying.

But I knew that was a terrible idea.

Coffee. Stick with coffee.

Tea kettle on. Two scoops in the French Press.

There was a tremor in my hands that I had never seen before.

Pour the water. Careful, it's hot. Steep for three minutes.

Why wouldn't my hands stop shaking?

I paced the kitchen, watching the clock. Three minutes seemed to drag on forever. I finally pressed it, poured a cup, then went to the pantry for sugar.

When I flicked on the pantry light, my heart nearly stopped.

Sitting on the shelf, right by the sugar, was a can of red spray paint.

Chapter Twenty-Six

I rocked back and forth on the couch, my mind racing. Was it possible? No. Surely not. Despite whatever fear and doubt I had about my own mental state, I had not spray-painted my own house. Right? I wasn't that kind of person. I wouldn't do something like that.

But was it *possible?*

"*No.*" I spoke it aloud, as if the word were a talisman that could break through the confusion surrounding me. *No.*

I am not crazy.

I breathed deeply, bringing to mind everything reassuring that Fiona had said about my mother. This was not some hereditary mental illness. I wasn't fated to lose my mind simply by living in this house. Something else was going on here. The person who had killed Don was more committed to seeing me go down for it than I had realized. And that person had been in my house.

So think.

If Greg found out the paint was in my home, it would confirm everything he had suggested earlier. I had to get rid of it. But there were two major problems with that. One, if I got caught, it would look even worse. Two, it might be the only clue to who the real vandal—and likely the real killer—was. Getting rid of it was probably a crime. Not to mention the fact that I desperately needed evidence that pointed to someone else.

Suddenly, it hit me. If someone planted the paint, why not plant the murder weapon too? It could be here in my home, even now. And it was one thing for Greg to find the paint, but finding the murder weapon would be another thing altogether.

I started shaking again. I felt sick and lightheaded. Who would do this to me?

"Hold it together," I spoke aloud. Hearing my own voice felt like an anchor. I still felt sick, but I somehow felt a little stronger.

THINK. It was a command this time.

Suddenly, I knew I needed to do what I should have done that morning.

I picked up my phone and dialed Joe's number.

Joe arrived within minutes. I hadn't told him what was going on, just asked him to come quickly. I breathed a sigh of relief when I heard his knock.

His face was grim when I opened the door for him.

"I don't like this at all, Daphne," he said gruffly. "What someone did out there to your house reminds me too much of some things that happened a long time ago."

"I don't like it either. But it gets worse."

"Worse?" His eyes narrowed. "Are you okay? Did someone hurt you?"

"No, no, nothing like that. Come in and sit down. I'll tell you everything."

I went over everything that had happened that morning, then asked my real question. "So what do we do about the paint? I have to get rid of it, right?"

He squeezed the bridge of his nose with a pained expression. "Daphne, are you seriously talking to a former sheriff about getting rid of evidence that might be connected to a murder investigation?"

"Then tell me what to do, Joe." I was pleading at this point. "I'm scared out of my mind. Do you get that? I'm being framed for murder. I'm being made out to look insane."

"Well, at least you'll have an insanity defense," he said with a smirk.

"Not funny. Not funny at all."

"Sorry." He sobered and pinched the bridge of his nose again. "Look, don't do anything yet. Let me talk to Greg. I'll get a feel for where his head is at."

"So I'm just supposed to sit here and wait for Greg to show up and arrest me?" Panic started rising in me.

"Well, you could. But I'd recommend you start scrubbing that paint off the front of your house."

I snorted. "That's kind of the least of my worries right now, but thanks."

"You sure about that? You know, when I was working with your ma, she always liked to get her hands on things. Something about physically touching objects seemed to give her more insight, so to speak. Maybe that's what you need to do, too."

He was right, and I was annoyed I hadn't thought of it myself.

"Okay. I can do that. But if Greg shows up?"

"Call me and I'll come."

"Okay."

"Now, before I go, we need to check your windows."

"My windows?" I gave him a blank look.

"I'm just wondering if your vandal was someone you invited into your house, or if they had another way to get in. If there was a window or something unlocked, maybe they climbed in that way to put the spray paint on your shelf."

It was something I hadn't even considered, and it chilled me to the bones.

"The paint wasn't there this morning, unless I just completely overlooked it. But I guess it's possible someone did that while I was napping this afternoon. I was out pretty deep."

We walked around together, checking all the windows. Joe's hunch was right. One of the larger kitchen windows was unlocked. Someone could have climbed in easily and been right next to the pantry.

"You were right," I said, shaking my head. "I can't believe I didn't even think to check. I feel so stupid."

"You're new to this. You'll learn." He leaned back against the kitchen counter, deep in thought. "You and Emerson have been spending some time together, right?"

"Yes. We have."

"So, I'm assuming he's been to your house a few times."

"Yes, he has." I didn't like where this was going.

Joe frowned. "Maybe we should take a look at him. He's ex-military. Nobody in town knows him that well. Could be something I need to check into."

"No way," I said, feeling the need to defend him no matter what my personal feelings were at the moment. "He's a really nice guy. One of the nicest I've ever met, honestly. And I get the feeling he has a really strong sense of ethics. I can't imagine him killing anyone."

Joe gave me a pointed look. "What do they do in the military?"

"This is different. And he's not the kind of person who would play mind games."

Joe just shrugged. "Maybe not. I'm still going to look into him. I spent over forty years in law enforcement, and I'd say at least half the killers I met were nice guys. Upstanding citizens, even. You just never know."

"I guess that's true." I could feel the worry etched on my face.

He studied me for a moment. "Daphne, you don't have to investigate, you know. I promise to do my best for you, for your ma's sake. It's plain as day this is getting to you. You're about as pale and worn out looking as anyone I've ever seen."

"Thanks," I said sarcastically. "I'll be sure to work on reducing stress while I'm trying to figure out who's framing me for murder."

"Funny." He chuckled. "That's good. Laughter is good for you. Alright, well, I'm going to do a little digging. You get to work on that porch. Remember, you call me right away if you get anything. Anything at all, no matter how small."

"Will do." We started walking to the back door.

"And Daphne, be careful. Don't trust anyone, ok?"

I shivered. "You make it sound like the whole town could be dangerous."

He smiled sadly. "Like I said. You just never know." He paused, as if deliberating about saying what he was really thinking. Finally, he spoke.

"I think your ma's mistake was being too trusting. It was hard for her to believe that anyone could really hurt another human being. You'd think she'd know better, working with me. But she always saw the best in people. Always thought they were good in their core, even when they showed her otherwise."

I nodded. "I don't really remember her, but I could see that being true. I won't make the same mistake."

He smiled that sad smile again and started to say something else, then stopped. He just shook his head and left.

I had the overwhelming feeling that he knew more about my mother's murder than he was telling me.

CHAPTER TWENTY-SEVEN

I DECIDED TO FOLLOW JOE'S ADVICE AND PRIORITIZE scrubbing the front of the house. I hoped he was right, that if I got out there and put my hands to work, I would get something that might actually help.

First, though, I hid the spray paint deep in a closet where it wouldn't be seen by anyone who dropped by. Joe might not approve, but he hadn't given me a better option. Next, I called Mom to check in on her travel plans.

"You sure picked a far enough away place to live," she said, an edge to her voice. "I found a flight to Asheville, North Carolina, tonight. I'm packing now. I'll have to rent a car there and drive to you. If everything goes according to plan, I'll be there by nine."

"Okay. Do you want me to meet you in town so you can follow me up the mountain? It gets dark here at night, and you're not familiar with the roads."

"I'm sure I'll be fine." The edge remained. "I've also contacted a defense attorney in Asheville. He'll be meeting with us tomorrow morning."

"Thanks. I don't know what I would do without your help."

"I just hope that when all of this is over, you'll come to your senses and move back home."

It stung even though I knew she was right. I forced myself to swallow my pride. "I've already been thinking about that. I think I'll move back to Dad's place." I forced a chuckle. "I guess I'll become a crazy cat lady or something and fill the place up with cats and books to keep me company."

"Hmm. Well, if nothing else, I'm glad this whole thing has made you realize what a terrible idea moving out to the boonies was to begin with. I need to go now so I can finish packing. I'll see you tonight."

I hung up and pushed away the negative taste the conversation had left in my mouth. It was clear I was in for more than one lecture when she arrived. But I would just have to endure it. It would be my penance.

A QUICK INTERNET SEARCH TOLD ME I WOULD LIKELY HAVE to make a trip to the hardware store for some chemicals and a pressure washer if I wanted to get rid of the spray paint. But I had no intention of putting it off that long. I would do what I could with a bucket of soapy water and a scrub brush.

I started at the beginning of the text, which happened to be right by the kitchen window. I let the work take over and cleared my mind, focusing instead on the feel of the warm water when I plunged my hand into the soap bucket, and the rhythmic motion of scrubbing the paint. It wasn't quite as soothing as a yoga class, but I often found that tasks like these offered their own form of meditation.

I relaxed into it. The more I relaxed, the more impressions I started getting. There was sadness here. Grief for Don? Maybe, but I wasn't sure that was right. Definite sadness though. It felt so heavy and solid that I wondered how I possibly could have missed it earlier. But this, at least, I knew the answer to. It was easy to simply not notice the energy around me if I was focused on something else, the way a teenager buried in her cell phone could completely miss a glorious sunset. It had always seemed to me that we humans left traces of ourselves wherever we went. Physical traces, yes, as we quite literally shed our own skins as we walked

—this was what search and rescue dogs picked up on, and what enabled them to trace a path with such remarkable accuracy. But we left traces of our emotions, too, like perfume lingering in a room long after the wearer was gone. I may have had a bit of the second sight, but I was certain that anyone who was really tuned into it could feel energy. That's why we had sayings like "you could cut the tension with a knife." It was there for anyone to feel, and people often did, whether they realized it or not.

But it was also just way too easy to ignore.

Soon, I became aware of a new sensation: the feeling of being watched. It came out of nowhere and sent icy dread up my spine. I carefully lowered my brush into the bucket and turned around to the driveway.

No one.

The feeling didn't go away, though.

I scanned the woods and caught a glimpse of movement.

"Come out from there!" I commanded, making my voice much more confident than I actually felt. I immediately regretted it. I was standing here on my porch with a mere scrub brush as a weapon.

A scrub brush wouldn't do much good if Don's killer was waiting in the woods for me.

A figure slowly stepped out from behind the tree, and my belly cramped with fear.

It was Luke.

Luke Kistler had been hiding in the woods, watching me.

I slowly moved sideways toward the door, thinking that if he threatened me, I could at least make it inside and bolt it before he got there. Hopefully. If he wasn't lightning fast.

He slowly walked toward me, hands in his pockets, in his shuffling way.

"Don't come any closer!" I commanded again. There was only a slight tremor in my voice, thankfully.

He stopped and looked up at me.

I realized he wasn't here out of anger or malice. In fact, I got the distinct impression that he was simply lonely.

I relaxed, if only slightly.

"What were you doing watching me?" I demanded. This time, my confidence was more real.

"I'm sorry about your house," he said, ignoring my question.

"Did you do it?"

He shook his head.

"Do you know who did?"

He shook his head again, but this time there was a brief hesitation. He knew something. I was sure of it.

"Do you want some help?" he asked.

I was the one hesitating now. I didn't fully trust him, and the idea of being close to him felt oddly repulsive. But he knew something, and I was desperate for information.

"Okay. Sure. Thanks."

He shuffled up to the porch and surveyed the damage. I thought I saw a little grin playing at the corner of his mouth, and I tensed up in response.

He dipped his hand in the soapy bucket and pulled out the scrub brush, then started working on the paint with quick motions. His efficiency surprised me. For someone who seemed to shuffle around slowly all the time, he was surprisingly adept.

"I hope you get away with it," he said out of the blue.

"Get away with what?"

"You know." He gave me a sideways glance. "My dad. I hope you get away with it." He paused for a minute, as if he was thinking. "I could lie for you, you know. Help you."

I was flabbergasted. "Luke, I didn't kill your dad."

"Uh huh."

"Seriously. I didn't."

He turned to look at me head-on. "Really?"

"Really."

He actually seemed disappointed. "Oh. Well, it sure looks like you're going down for it. Maybe I'll still lie for you."

"What do you mean it looks like I'm going down for it? Why would you need to lie?"

He turned back to the wall and resumed his work. "I listen to things. People don't always know I'm there. I heard the sheriff talking to my mother."

My heart sped up. "What did he say?"

"That Doc could determine the time of death, and you had an alibi for that. But Doc said it was impossible to know exactly when my father was shot. Said Dad probably didn't die right away. Said you could have shot him, then left him there to die alone. Sheriff said he would be asking around to see if anyone heard a gunshot so they would know for sure what time it happened." He gave me another sideways glance, as if watching to see if I was going to continue claiming innocence.

"I'm sorry, Luke. I'm really sorry he suffered. But it wasn't me."

He shrugged and continued scrubbing. His lack of emotion over his own father was downright chilling.

"Anyway. He hasn't talked to me yet. I was thinking I could tell him I heard the shot. I go for walks around our house a lot at night. I could tell him I heard it clear as day during the time you were gone. Give you an alibi, see?"

"Why would you want to help me?"

This time, he avoided eye contact. "I figure if you killed him, you had a good reason for it."

"Well, I'm sorry to disappoint you, I guess." I had no idea what else to say. This was the strangest conversation of my life. "But listen, I don't want you to lie. I'm innocent. We'll find out what really happened, okay? But the right way, with the truth."

"The truth shall set you free," he quoted. "That's from the Bible." He gave me another sideways glance.

"I know."

"I remember you," he said, changing the subject.

"From where?"

"From when you were a baby. Living here."

"Really?" I found that surprising.

"Yeah. I was a kid. Your mom was always nice to me. Sometimes I would imagine I was your brother and that she was my mom too." His voice got thick.

My heart broke for him. "It sounds like your childhood was rough."

He shrugged. "It's alright. Things will be better now."

A thought occurred to me. "What will happen to the church?"

"It will go to my brother, Matthew. He's been the associate pastor for a few years." There was a sense of satisfaction in his voice.

"I'm guessing that's a good thing?"

"Yeah. He's good. Not like Dad. Not like me." This time, there was definite pride in his voice. It was apparent he loved his brother. "And it's about time, anyway. He's been doing most of the real work for the last few years, and Dad barely paid him a dime. Said he should be in it for the ministry. Never mind the fact that he has a wife and kids crammed into a tiny apartment and needs to put food on the table." He snorted again.

And never mind the fact that Don drove an incredibly nice vehicle and had a gorgeous home. It made me wonder if Matthew had a motive to get rid of Don. Luke seemed to think highly of his brother, but I wasn't sure he was a good judge of character.

"Luke, can I ask you something else?"

"Go for it."

I hesitated, choosing my words carefully. I didn't want to say too much. "Does the name Mr. Boddy mean anything to you?"

He looked at me curiously. "Like in that old movie?"

"Right."

"I've seen it," he said. "Why?"

"Is there anyone that your dad called by that name?"

"Not that I heard. Why?"

"Just wondering. Was your dad involved with anyone who seemed shady or scary? Is it possible that he was being blackmailed over something?"

Whatever I said shut him down. He kicked the porch with his foot, his eyes downcast again. "I don't know anything about that. I should get back to the house. Mom will be wondering where I am. Lots to do, you know, with arrangements and everything."

"Luke, if you know something, it might really help me."

"I don't know anything," he mumbled. "Really." He looked up at me with a pained expression.

"Okay," I said gently, feeling like I shouldn't push him. "Thanks for your help. I really appreciate it."

His cheeks pinked, and a hint of a smile appeared. I got the impression that he had been starved for affection his whole life. It seemed more and more clear that Don had left a path of victims in his wake.

Maybe it was karma that he had finally suffered a bit before he died.

Chapter Twenty-Eight

By the time nine o'clock rolled around, I was exhausted. I had made very little progress getting the graffiti off the porch, but if nothing else, the conversation with Luke felt like valuable insight. I had a new lead and felt like I could mark Luke off the suspect list. He obviously had emotional issues, but the fact that he had been convinced I was the killer meant that he wasn't. That, or he was a much better actor than I was giving him credit for.

I had gotten the guest room to a place where I felt Mom would be comfortable, and I had managed a trip to town to grab groceries. On my first trip to the store, barely a week prior, I had been anonymous. This time, it felt as if everyone was staring at me, trying to get a look at the woman they assumed was a cold-blooded killer. I got in and out as quickly as possible and drove straight back to the cottage.

I paced my living room, checking the time on my cell phone every few minutes. My stomach was in knots. I wasn't sure if I was worried about Mom driving through the mountains or just dreading the confrontation that would take place when she arrived. I would have to swallow my pride no matter what. I needed her help more than ever. If that meant agreeing that she was always right and should oversee my life choices, well, then that's what I would do.

Even if a tiny part of me would rather go to jail.

WITH EVERY MINUTE THAT TICKED BY, THE FEELING IN THE pit of my stomach worsened. I should have insisted on meeting her. She wasn't used to mountain driving or how dark this area was at night.

Making matters worse, cell phone reception was spotty at best until you got to Rosemary Mountain. Fiona had explained that our surprisingly good coverage was due to Bill Brinkley's influence. He had insisted on the tower being built where it would benefit our side of the mountain, and he had apparently gotten his way. But there was a whole stretch of winding mountain roads between Asheville and town where Mom wouldn't be able to call for help if anything happened.

By nine thirty-eight, I still hadn't heard from her. I grabbed my purse and threw on a coat. I stepped out onto the porch just in time to hear the rumble of a car climbing slowly up the gravel lane. A few moments later, the car turned into my driveway, nearly blinding me with its headlights. I breathed a sigh of relief.

But the relief was short-lived. Mom began griping before she even got out of the car.

"I knew this place was in the middle of nowhere, but this is truly ridiculous," she called out as she climbed out of the driver's seat of her rental.

I ignored the comment and jogged down to help with her bags. "I'm glad you made it safe. I was getting worried."

She waved it off. "I was perfectly fine. I just had to drive slower than usual. You have an inordinate number of deer in this area that like to jump out in front of moving vehicles for some reason. After watching a semi in front of me hit one, I realized I should proceed with utmost caution."

She popped the trunk, and I grabbed her suitcase. I recognized it as the largest one she owned, a giant rolling leather case that she had purchased years ago for an extended business trip. I felt a mild stab of panic when I saw it. Just how long were we going to be stuck here together?

I followed her to the porch, stifling a giggle as I watched her navigate the gravel driveway in her stiletto heels. Mom still believed in dressing for travel. You would never catch her showing up at the airport in something that was actually comfortable.

"Really, Daphne," she lectured as she climbed the porch steps. "You've moved out to the land of moonshiners!"

"Well, I haven't met any yet, so I can't offer you the local favorite, but I have a decent bottle of red waiting for you if you're interested," I responded drily.

"Thank goodness." She breathed a dramatic sigh of relief. "You'd better make it a large pour."

I opened the front door and motioned for her to go first, following her with the enormous bag. She stopped at the front entrance and took it all in.

"Well," she said. "It's almost pretty. In a rustic sort of way."

I rolled my eyes behind her back. "The guest room is upstairs," I said. "Which means I'm probably going to need your help to carry this thing up there. It must weigh more than the fifty-pound limit."

She turned toward me with a raised eyebrow. "Well, who knows how long this thing is going to take to wrap up? Best be prepared. Lead the way."

I rolled the case to the stairs and grabbed the top while she deftly lifted the bottom. She was stronger than she looked. The money she spent on her personal training had benefits.

After managing the stairs, I rolled the case into the guest room. I felt suddenly nervous about showing it to her. I genuinely wanted her to like it. It felt important somehow.

"This is your room," I said, standing back against the door so that she could enter first.

She walked in and gazed around. It was neat and clean, I had made sure of that. And while I knew it wasn't her style, I hoped that the "rustic elegance" I was going for would win her over. I had chosen a quilt in soft yellows and creams, and had put plenty of pillows on the bed. Gauzy curtains hung over the windows, and I had picked up a vanilla-scented candle and fresh flowers at the grocery store for the bedside table. It wasn't the Ritz, but it was a sweet, comfortable room.

Which, now that I thought about it, was probably the exact opposite of how I should have decorated it for her.

She glanced around but didn't say a word. She simply tossed her purse and coat on the bed, then asked if it was time for that wine yet.

"Sure," I said, deflated. I led the way back down the stairs.

"So, tell me everything," she commanded, placing her already empty glass on the coffee table and looking at me expectantly.

I leaned over to pour her a second. "Well, I guess I need to start at the very beginning."

So, I did. I started with the visions I'd had as a young girl. I could see the skepticism on her face, but I pushed forward anyway. I knew it would be a lot for her to overcome. She had always believed Dad's version of what happened to Eileen. I knew, even as I kept going, that she was assuming the same about me right now.

She started to interrupt, but I put up a hand and stopped her.

"Please, let me finish," I said, surprised by how steady my voice was. "I know what you must think. But please. Just listen."

"Okay," she said simply.

I continued, explaining what happened when I found the box of my mother's things, the real reason I had moved here, and how Don's murder was likely connected to Eileen's.

She was visibly pale by the time I wrapped up the story.

"Well," she said shakily. "I think we might need something stronger than wine."

"It's a lot to take in, I know."

"Daphne, please don't hate me for this. But would you be willing to sit down with a doctor? Just to get evaluated. There's a genetic component to things like schizophrenia, you know. It wouldn't hurt to just make sure."

I pressed my lips together and took a deep breath to keep from responding in anger. "Mom, I know we're not close. I know you haven't been around me that much for the past few years. But you raised me. Did you ever once think that I was delusional?"

"No, Daphne, that's not what I'm saying."

"Think about it. Really." Then suddenly, a memory came back to me. It was something I hadn't thought about in years. "Remember that time when you were supposed to go on a business trip to Jackson?"

Her face wrinkled up. "Vaguely."

"It was a big deal. You were packed and already loaded into the car. Do you remember what happened next?"

She answered slowly. "You went into hysterics. Begged me not to go."

"Right. Do you remember why?"

She shrugged. "You were young. Separation anxiety is normal at that age."

"It wasn't separation anxiety," I said firmly. "You remember. What was it?"

She sighed. "You told me I couldn't go. That I would get into a terrible car accident if I did. That I had to stay home."

"That's right. And do you remember how Dad reacted?"

Her gaze drifted off, and her face became sad. "It scared him." She spoke softly, almost in a whisper. "He said I should stay home, just in case."

"That's right. He didn't tell you everything would be fine or that it was just separation anxiety. He told you to stay home. Because he *knew.* And what happened that night?"

She looked directly at me, her face the palest I had ever seen it. "That night, on the news, we saw that the weather had taken an unexpected turn and the roads had become icy. There was a massive pileup on the interstate, pretty much exactly where I would have been during that time. Several people died."

"Exactly. And no matter what Dad may have told you about Eileen, when I saw you getting hurt, he believed it. He stopped you from going. I don't know why he said the things he did about her. But he knew the truth." And now, I knew it too. Remembering that story put to rest the final doubts I had carried.

She put her hands together and pressed them to her lips, rocking herself back and forth. It was apparent she was having some sort of internal debate, so I sat back and waited for her to speak.

"I don't know that I can fully believe all of this right now," she finally said. "But I'll try."

"That's all I ask," I said. "Trust me, I know how it sounds. But, Mom, I'm not crazy. This is real. And somehow, Don's murder is related to all of it. I have to find out the truth."

Chapter Twenty-Nine

The next morning was surreal. We woke early in order to drive to Asheville to meet with the attorney Mom had hired. We stopped for coffee and donuts on the way, neither one of us feeling up to putting breakfast together.

The attorney maintained a poker face during the entire meeting, which felt unnerving. I was hoping he would reassure me that there was no case, that my innocence was clear, and that he would work tirelessly to clear my name. But he simply jotted down the key information, barely even making eye contact. If anything, I actually felt worse when the meeting was over.

We decided to stay in the city for a real lunch, which went a long way toward helping me feel normal again.

"You're pale," Mom commented as we waited for our salads.

"Wouldn't you be?"

She patted my hand in sympathy. "I don't really think you have anything to worry about. The gun residue test alone should clear you, right?"

"I would have thought so, but it can't take long to get those results back, can it? So, they should already know I didn't have any gun residue on my hands. Maybe they're assuming I wore gloves or something. And you didn't hear the sheriff," I reminded her. "If the town has decided I'm guilty, the facts don't really matter, do they? There won't be a place for me there, even if I manage to stay out of jail."

She nodded. "You may be right on that one. But if they don't have a case, they don't have a case. Besides, Anthony is good. His interpersonal skills may be lacking, but he's exceptional at what he does. And let's be honest, moving back home won't be the worst thing in the world, now will it?"

I hesitated.

"Daphne!" Her eyes got wide. "You can't tell me you actually want to stay there?"

"I don't know," I said honestly. "The truth is, before all of this happened, I was really..." I trailed off, not sure how to say it. "Happy, I guess. Content. I felt like I belonged."

"You? Belonged in the land of moonshiners and deer hunters and *murderers*, apparently?"

"I know it sounds odd," I said quietly. "But I liked it there. It felt like home."

I looked up to find her staring as if she didn't even recognize me.

"Don't get me wrong," I said, reassuring her, "I know now that I can't stay. Even if I'm cleared, it's obvious what people will think of me. But it hurts that the real murderer took that from me. He took Don's life, but he also took mine in a way. It's not the same thing, I know. But it still hurts."

And it did. It hurt more than I could ever have imagined. I had only lived in Rosemary Mountain for a week, but the thought of leaving broke my heart. When I left, I would leave a piece of myself there forever.

Mom continued to stare at me, her face unreadable. I wanted to know what she was thinking, but I also didn't want to ask.

"On the phone, you said you had met someone but had ruined it," she said. "Tell me about that. I noticed you left that part out of your explanations last night."

"Oh. Yes, him." It was true I had deliberately left Emerson out of the conversation. It embarrassed me how quickly I had fallen for him, and how quickly I had screwed everything up.

My initial instinct was to downplay everything. Mom had never been my confidant. It had always been easier to talk to Dad, even about dating.

But I wanted a mom. And I felt that, despite our differences, Janet was truly trying.

"His name is Emerson," I began. I told her everything, from that first meeting at the fish house to when everything fell apart.

"The chemistry between us is unlike anything I've ever experienced before," I confessed. "Everything seemed amazing until I told him about the second sight. Then I could feel things change." I didn't know how to explain what I was trying to say. "There was so much potential between us. But I guess it doesn't matter now. He was clear that he doesn't want anything complicated, and obviously, I'm complicated. Plus, I'll be leaving soon."

I went back to twirling my spaghetti, swallowing the lump in my throat.

Mom was silent for a few moments, seemingly deep in thought.

"You know, I can understand him having a hard time with all of this second sight stuff. It's hard for me too, and like you pointed out, I've known you your whole life. He just met you. *And* he's a medical professional. You can't blame him for questioning."

I nodded. "I get that. I really do. But I wish he would have just trusted me, you know? It felt like he immediately assumed the worst."

"Even so, he showed up for you. Not just on the night of the murder, but also as soon as you called him about the vandalism. Even when he thought you had done those things, he stayed and supported you. He didn't have to do that, you know."

"I know."

"All I'm saying is don't write him off yet."

I glanced up and saw that her face had softened. It reminded me of the love she had for Dad, love that was never fully returned. There were ghosts and hurts in her past as well.

"Thanks for the talk, Mom," I said. And I meant it.

CHAPTER THIRTY

It was late afternoon when we got back to the cottage, and I could feel a headache brewing. I immediately made a cup of coffee, hoping the caffeine would help, and popped two of the painkillers Emerson had given me. As I put the bottle back into the medicine cabinet, my fingers lingered on it, and tears sprang into my eyes. I missed him. I wanted him here.

I closed my eyes and leaned my head against the bathroom mirror, feeling the cool glass against my aching head.

Then, as if my longings had somehow magically summoned him, I heard Mom call up the stairs.

"Daphne! There's a young man named Emerson here to see you."

My heart immediately gave a little leap. I looked at my reflection in the mirror. It wasn't great. I gave my cheeks a little pinch to bring some color to them. It didn't help.

With a sigh and a shrug, I headed down.

Emerson was waiting at the foot of the stairs. "Hey Daphne," he said, clearing his throat. "Can we go for a walk?"

"Sure. Let me grab my coat. Also, I just made coffee. Do you want some?"

"No, thanks, I'm good."

"Give me just a minute."

I went to the kitchen and refilled my cup. Neither the caffeine nor the pills had even touched my headache so far, but I hoped they would kick in soon. I slipped on my coat and boots and told Mom goodbye. She gave me a meaningful look, as if to say, "See? I told you not to give up."

WHEN THE DOOR CLOSED BEHIND US, WE BOTH STOOD ON the porch awkwardly, as if neither of us was sure where to start. He put his hands into his pockets and rocked back on his heels.

I took a deep breath and spoke first. "Emerson, I really want to apologize. I am so sorry about the way I acted the last time you were over. I was being ridiculous. You were just worried about me."

He reached out and put a hand on my arm. "I get it. I *am* worried about you. I can't help that. But that was a rough morning for you. I think I came across wrong that day, like I was doubting you. And, well, I guess I was," he admitted, running a hand through his hair. "We haven't known each other very long, and when I saw what looked like a cry for help, I wondered..." His voice trailed off.

"It's okay," I said. "If I were in your place, I would probably wonder the same thing. I don't blame you. It hurt, yeah. It hurt that you would think I would do that. It also hurt that you immediately assumed I killed Don when you showed up that night. But you're right. We don't actually know each other that well. It's not like you have any real reason to believe me."

A pained expression crossed his face. "I'm sorry I hurt you."

"It's okay. You don't have to apologize."

He ran a hand through his hair again. "Look, I don't fully understand what's going on here. I still don't know what to think about this whole second sight deal. Like I said before, that just doesn't fit into the way I've always seen the world. But my gut tells me to trust you. About all of it. And my gut hasn't let me down yet. So from here on out, I'm on team Daphne. And I hope you'll give me the chance to get to know you better."

I didn't say anything—I couldn't. His trust meant something, something more than I could put into words.

"Also," he went on, "I wanted to apologize for being so short with you on the phone. I was meeting with Greg right then, so it was awkward to talk to you. I shouldn't have answered at all, not in front of him." His face was grim.

My stomach immediately knotted. "What is it?"

"Let's walk," he said, avoiding my eyes. The fear grew.

He started down the front steps, and I followed him. He waited until we were out on the lane before finally speaking.

"Daphne, I hate telling you this, but he's starting to seriously wonder if you killed Don," he said flatly. "He's a good man. He's my friend, probably the best one I've got here. I don't want you to think badly of him. And honestly, I shouldn't even be talking to you about this. But I figure you deserve to know what's going on."

"I got that impression when he came back to talk to me. It didn't go well. But there's no evidence linking me to the murder. Right?" I could feel the pitch of my voice rise, despite my efforts to keep it calm.

"He's not telling me much. He knows you and I are, well, friends, and that I believe you're innocent. So he's keeping it close to his chest. But he came over to basically warn me off." He shot me a sideways glance.

"Warn you off? Of me?"

"Yeah." He chuckled. "Basically, he thinks you concocted a story in your head about Don killing your mother. The way he sees it, your dad's death, followed immediately by finding out about your mom's suicide, sent you over the edge. He feels bad for you and wants to get you help. He's a protective sort of guy, you know? He doesn't see you as some cold-blooded killer; he sees you more as a broken, hurting woman who needs help. But either way—"

"He thinks I'm guilty," I finished.

"Well, yeah. Oddly enough, though, it was hearing him say those things that made me realize I didn't believe it."

"What do you mean?"

"Well, obviously, I was wondering all those same things when you and I had that fight." He glanced at me awkwardly, as if judging my reaction. "But when I heard him voice them, it's like, I knew. I knew that wasn't you. I knew I believed you. And I told him so."

"Well, I appreciate that."

He reached over and took my hand, squeezing it in solidarity. "I know him well enough to know that someone else is feeding him this story. He didn't come up with it on his own. I asked him where he's getting this, but he refused to tell me. And like I said, he's a good man and a good law enforcement officer. But unfortunately"—he shot me another sideways glance—"the story makes more sense to him than any alternatives."

I let out a sigh. "That's what I was afraid of, based on my own conversation with him. He said that people in the community were worried about me. He offered to get me help. Honestly? I thought he was talking about you."

He squeezed my hand again. "Not me. I had told him I was worried about you being under so much stress, yes. I mean, I know this is a sensitive subject, but you really don't look healthy, Daphne. You're so pale and tired-looking compared to when I met you. You've been through a lot. I mentioned that to him. But I've always told him there's no way you would have killed Don."

I believed him.

We walked on in silence, and I found myself grateful for it. The throbbing in my head was growing with each step, and I was starting to feel nauseous and dizzy. Each step sent a jolt through my body, all the way from my feet to what felt like a tiny man using a jackhammer behind my eye. The pain became so severe that I couldn't take it anymore. I stopped suddenly on the road. I dropped my coffee without thinking and held my aching head in my hands.

"Emerson," I said weakly.

"What is it? Are you okay?" He gently pulled my hands away from my face. "Whoa, you're as white as a ghost. What's wrong?"

"Headache," I managed to get out. "Like a jackhammer. And I'm so tired. I need to lie down."

"Do you have migraines? You keep closing your eyes. Are you experiencing sensitivity to the light?" he asked.

I could tell he had slipped into nurse mode and was assessing me automatically. It was the kind of thing I might have thought was cute if I hadn't been fighting back the urge to vomit all over him.

"Never before," I said. "But maybe that's what this is. And yes, the light feels really bright, but I'm also just so tired. Emerson, I really need to get home."

"Yes, you do," he said. He reached down and grabbed the mug I had dropped, handing it to me before scooping me up in his arms as if I were weightless. "You can close your eyes if you need. The bright sunlight is probably making the migraine worse."

I wrapped my arms around his neck and closed my eyes, sinking into the comfort as he carried me home. It felt like a mile, even though I knew we hadn't gone nearly that far.

When we reached the house, he knocked on the door with his foot, still holding me.

Mom opened the door and gasped.

"What's wrong with her?" she demanded, alarm obvious in her voice.

"Migraine," he said simply. "Can you point me toward her room? She needs to lie down."

"She's never had migraines before."

"Stress may have triggered them, but we can talk about that in a minute," Emerson said. "Right now, we need to get her in a dark room where she can lie down and sleep this off."

"It's up the stairs," I mumbled. "Last room on the left."

I closed my eyes again as he carried me up the stairs and placed me on my bed. He gently removed my shoes and tucked me in.

"This isn't at all what I imagined for the first time I brought you into my bedroom," I mumbled, half asleep already.

He chuckled in a low tone. "Me either. Where do you keep your medicine? I'll grab you some ibuprofen."

"Bathroom cabinet," I said, pointing.

He disappeared for a few minutes and returned with a glass of water and the bottle of pills he had given me before.

"I already took those, right before you got here," I said.

"How many did you take?"

"Two."

"It's fine. You can take two more. Then rest and give it time to work. I'm going downstairs to talk to your mom."

I nodded and swallowed the pills quickly, then closed my eyes and let sleep overtake me.

Chapter Thirty-One

The moon was high in the night sky when I finally woke. I could see it shining above the tree line through my window.

"If the light's on the right, it's going to get bright," I whispered to myself out of habit. The moon was close to full. I shivered at the thought. It felt like a warning, a foreboding. Of what? I didn't know.

I rolled to my other side so that I couldn't see it. The headache was gone, thankfully, but my brain still felt foggy and muddled. I couldn't focus or make sense of my own thoughts, so I listened to my body instead, going on instinct. I slid my legs over the edge of the bed, then immediately pulled them back when my feet hit the cold floor. The temperature outside must have dropped even more.

I forced myself to try again. This time, I welcomed the cold, allowing it to snake up my body and wake my senses. I turned back toward the window and forced myself to gaze at the moon once more. Yes, something was coming. I could feel it.

I grabbed a thin blanket and wrapped it around me, then slipped my feet into the slippers tucked underneath my bed. I headed downstairs, carefully and slowly, still feeling dizzy and disoriented.

Mom was curled up in a chair, reading a book from my shelf.

"Daphne!" she exclaimed. "Thank goodness. I was starting to think you were going to sleep straight through the night."

"What time is it?" I asked, wincing at the brightness of the overhead lights.

She glanced at her phone. "Just after nine. I kept dinner warm for you. Want me to make you a plate?"

My stomach rolled at the thought of food—nausea lingered quietly in the background—but I knew that getting something in my stomach would help.

"Yes. Thank you," I said, crossing to the couch. I sat cross-legged in the corner of it with the blanket still wrapped around me. Even here, I could see the moon, glowing as she rose ever higher. I shrank underneath it.

"Here you go." Mom returned with a bowl of beef stew.

I held the bowl in my hands and stared at it for a moment. "You made my favorite," I said, looking up at her.

She shrugged like it was nothing.

"I can't believe you remembered." Her homemade beef stew had been my favorite dinner as a kid, one of the only things she actually made from scratch, but I hadn't had it since before she and Dad divorced.

"Of course I remembered," she said quietly. "I am your mom, after all. One of them, anyway."

My eyes met hers, and it was as if I was seeing her, really, for the first time.

"I always thought you didn't want me." The words slipped out of me before I knew they were coming.

She stared at me with a strange expression on her face. "Of course I wanted you. Whatever would have made you think that?"

I raised an eyebrow. *Oh, I don't know. Your constant disapproval?*

"We're just so different," I said lamely. "I felt like I was a disappointment to you. And when you and Dad divorced, you didn't even want shared custody. I felt like, well, like you were glad to get rid of me so that you could live your real life." The pain of it made my heart physically ache, even all these years later.

She continued staring at me, dumbfounded. "Oh, Daphne. Is that really what you thought?"

I nodded, not trusting myself to speak. I regretted bringing it up at all. I hated feeling like this, as if I had reverted to my childhood self, insecure and desperate for her love.

"I wanted you." Her voice was thick with emotion. "You *were* my real life. You were the only real gift that marriage ever gave me. But you were his. Daphne, shared custody was never even an option. Can't you see that now, knowing what you know? He never let me adopt you. I asked more than once. He was adamantly against it. He was your only legal parent."

She lowered her eyes and picked at invisible fuzz on the blanket draped across her body. "Frankly, that's the only reason I stayed as long as I did. I thought if I waited until you were older to leave him, you might insist on seeing me more. He would never say no to you. But," she went on, smiling sadly. "You weren't just his legally. Your heart was his, too. And when I left, I lifted right out, didn't I?"

I didn't know what to say. The custody issue made sense now. There were two sides to every story, and I had never considered hers. But at the same time, knowing the truth about the custody issue didn't change everything else. It didn't magically fix our relationship or the strained dynamic that had existed between us even before the divorce.

"I'm sorry about the custody issue. I didn't know. But it was more than that." I took a deep breath and gathered the courage to go on.

"Even as a kid, I felt like a disappointment to you. I spent more time with Dad because, well, he actually liked me. He was proud of me. All I ever felt with you was that you wished I was someone different. You pointed out every mistake I ever made, but never gave me credit for what I did right. Being around you was exhausting, because I was always just waiting for whatever flaw you were going to point out next." The pain still hit me in the chest, a literal heartache. I had been so hungry for a mother's unconditional love as a child. I still was.

"Daphne, I am so sorry. You're wrong about how I felt about you." Her voice was soft. "But no matter how I felt, I can see I did a terrible job of expressing it. I hurt you, and I'm sorry. Lonnie's lack of love broke me in some ways. I'm not trying to make excuses for myself. But I took some of that pain out on you. I know that now."

She picked nervously at the hem of her sleeve. "I was jealous of how he felt about you—and your mother. How connected you were with him. I felt unwanted, and I handled it badly. I thought that if I was perfect, and if I pointed out the ways in which you weren't, maybe he would see my value," she admitted. "It was ridiculous, competing with a child for attention. I wish I could do things differently. I hope you'll give me the chance now."

Her tone was genuine. It was possibly the first apology I had ever had from her, and it meant something. It didn't change the past. But it meant something.

I nodded and gave her a half smile. I couldn't say it was all okay. I couldn't even honestly say that I forgave her. Not yet. But I understood her better. And it was a step forward.

Chapter Thirty-Two

I tossed and turned most of the night, reviewing everything in my mind. Minutes before the sun would begin painting the mountain pink with morning light, I slipped out of bed wanting to talk to Fiona.

After dressing quickly, I tiptoed down the stairs, avoiding the ones I remembered as extra creaky. I stifled a giggle at the absurdity. I had never snuck out of the house as a teenager. No, I had waited until I was an adult homeowner. Apparently, when it came to rebellion, I was a late bloomer.

I put on my coat and left through the back, closing the door as quietly as possible.

Mist rose from the mountain as the rising sun cast sunbeams through the trees, illuminating a frost that sparkled like diamonds. The sheer magic of it all took my breath away. The world was still. But the earth itself was awakening with a beauty I had never before witnessed. This alone was worth getting up before dawn.

I wrapped my scarf up higher and tucked my hands into my pockets, grateful that the sky was getting brighter by the minute. The woods already felt more comfortable than they had a week ago, but the darkness still scared me. *I hope that after decades of living here, I'm as comfortable as Fiona is traipsing through the trails in the woods without fear.* The thought surprised me. I had decided to go back home to Little Rock. Hadn't I?

I was relieved to see Fiona's kitchen light through her window, as well as the lazy drift of smoke from her chimney. I stepped up to the porch and lifted my hand to knock. Before my knuckles touched the wood, the door swung open.

"Daphne! Feels like it's been ages. Come on in."

I smiled. There was something so comforting, so welcoming about Fiona.

"Good morning, Fiona. I'm sorry to bother you so early."

"Nonsense! It's never a bother. Come on in and warm up by the fire. I'm just making some sausage and grits. Do you want some?"

"That sounds delicious."

I warmed my hands by the fire while Fiona went back into her kitchen, humming and stirring. My heart suddenly ached as I realized how badly I would miss her when I moved home.

"It's ready!" she sang out, placing plates down on the table. "Come on in here and tell me what's bothering you."

"How could you tell?" I asked, giving her a rueful smile.

"Oh, Fiona always knows," she said, chuckling.

In between bites, I caught her up on everything that had happened over the last few days. I left Christie's name out of it, despite feeling like Fiona should know. As Christie's midwife, she, more than anyone, needed to know what Christie was going through. But I wanted to keep my word, so I stayed silent on that, just saying I had found Don's mistress and what she revealed about Mr. Boddy.

I was worried about how Fiona would take the news about the vandalism, remembering her own troubles years ago. But thankfully, she already knew. Of course she did. This was Fiona, after all.

"Yeah, Joe told me," she said, shaking her head in disgust. "I hate it for you. It feels so, well, violating when someone does something like that. Home is supposed to be a safe haven, a sanctuary. Worse than the actual damage is the feeling that someone could touch that so easily."

"That's exactly how I feel." I took another sip of coffee, then shared what was really on my mind. "I have this weird feeling that time is running out. We have to figure out who killed Don fast."

"Are you asking me to play detective with you?"She had a bemused smile on her face.

"Maybe," I said with a small laugh. "Actually, I plan on poking around a bit later. And you could be of some help there. Luke mentioned that his brother would inherit the church, and it sounds like it will be a big relief financially. I'd like to find out more about that, and get a general feeling of what people think of Matthew and his wife. Either of them could have a motive."

Fiona nodded. "I can do that. Matthew was real quiet as a kid. Respectful. But I haven't seen much of him since he got married and moved to town. I do know Don worked him like a dog, and Don was never what you would call nice to him. It's hard to picture quiet Matthew as having done something like that, but you never know. I'll see what I can find out."

"Good," I said, feeling relieved already. "What do you know about Matthew's wife?"

"Not as much as you would think," Fiona admitted. "She's not from around here. They met at some church camp thing when they were both teenagers. She's real quiet, too. Keeps to herself. People who go to their church probably know her better. I'll ask around."

"See what you can find out, and I'll do the same." My voice rose in urgency. "I can't explain it, Fiona, but it feels like something's coming."

She nodded solemnly. "I know exactly what you mean. There's a feeling in the air..." Her voice trailed off as her eyes moved to the window. "I always feel a bit like that when the moon is on its way to being full," she admitted. "But it's stronger this time. I think you're right about running out of time."

"So you'll help me?"

She nodded. "I'll do what I can."

"Thanks." Having her on my side made me feel stronger somehow, like I could face whatever was coming.

"How about a cup of tea?" she suggested. "Then you can help me say my morning prayers. Maybe the Good Lord will be of some help to us."

I nodded in agreement.

Fiona put a teakettle on the stove and began pulling various herb jars from her shelving. She added a little of this and a little of that, mixing the herbs together in a fresh jar, sometimes stopping to inhale their aroma before adding a bit more of something else. It was fascinating. I felt as if I had been swept off to Ireland, hidden away in some woodland witch's cottage, watching her concoct a potion.

Still humming, Fiona poured the hot water over the herbs in her strainer and put a little saucer on top of the teacup.

"What's the saucer for?" I asked.

"To keep the volatile oils inside," she replied. "When the aromatics get hot, they try to fly away. I want to keep them in the cup until you're ready to drink it. Now, let me get my prayer book." She disappeared for a few moments, returning with it. She sat across from me and thumbed through it. "Ah, yes, this will be just the thing."

She turned the book around and spun it toward me, tapping the header on the page with her long finger. I looked curiously. The title was *Invocation for Justice.*

"A prayer for justice," she said. "That should serve us well today, don't you think?"

"What is this book?" I asked. I held the page open with my finger, but closed the cover so I could read it. "The *Carmina Gadelica?*" I stumbled over the unfamiliar words.

"One of my favorites," she said, reverently laying a hand on the cover. "It's a book of prayers, hymns, and poems that were passed down over the ages. The kinds of prayers my own grandmother and hers would say. These were gathered up in Scotland in the 1800s, but they're close enough to what my own would have prayed in Ireland."

I flipped through the book, which was an odd assortment. There were Christian prayers for every sort of event, from baptism to kindling the morning fire. But right alongside them were stories of fairies and prayers to counteract the "evil eye." It was certainly unlike any prayer book I had ever seen before.

I turned back to the prayer for justice. I wasn't sure how praying for "love to be my countenance" and the ability to "travel in the name of God, in likeness of deer" would be helpful for this situation. But the words were beautiful. And who knew? Maybe God really would hear the prayer and lend aid.

"Tea's ready," Fiona announced. She removed the saucer from the top of the mug and pulled out the strainer of herbs, setting them aside. She stirred a spoonful of honey into the cup, then handed it to me. "Let's go sit by the fire," she suggested.

I carried the warm mug into the living room and made myself at home in one of the cozy, worn chairs she kept on either side of the fireplace. She followed me, tossing a handful of herbs into the fire before taking the seat across from me.

"Now,"—she held out the book to where we could both lean forward and see it—"we pray our prayer for justice."

Together we prayed the prayer, falling into the natural rhythm of the Celtic hymn. As I lingered over the unfamiliar words, a newfound feeling of courage stirred within me. I realized that finding Don's killer wasn't just about protecting myself. It was so much larger than that. It was about justice for his family, and restoring a sense of safety to this mountain and these people I had grown to love.

My voice caught as we finished the prayer. Fiona reached out a hand and squeezed mine. I squeezed back and nodded, giving her a small smile.

She stood up, pulled the quilt from the back of her own chair, and brought it to me, tucking it around my shoulders. Then she quietly withdrew from the room, leaving me to think.

I settled my gaze on the fire and let my mind drift as I sipped the honey-sweetened tea. The scent of smoked herbs still lingering in the air, combined with the dancing flames, was nothing less than hypnotic. My mind simply refused to focus, and before long, I drifted into that subliminal stage in between worlds; not quite asleep, but also, most certainly, not awake.

I found myself startled by images arising unbidden. They were so unexpected that they threatened to lift me right back into the world of the living, but I sensed that if I paid too much attention to them, they would disappear. So I forced myself, somehow, to continue drifting lazily through this not-quite-dream world, allowing the images to come as they would.

I could never have predicted what I saw during that time. The scenes that came to me weren't from the time of Don's murder at all. They were much older than that. I knew, somehow, that they were from my mother's time—perhaps even scenes she had witnessed with her own eyes.

The sound of shattering glass brought me back to the waking world. I had dropped Fiona's teacup. She sat across from me, concern written all over her face.

"What is it?" she asked.

"Oh, Fiona," I said. My heart shattered into a thousand pieces, just like the cup on the floor.

"What?" she asked again.

"Fiona, it's Joe."

Chapter Thirty-Three

"Joe?" she repeated, with a look of disbelief on her face. "What on earth do you mean? You're telling me that *Joe* killed Don?"

"No. Let me explain." I gathered my thoughts, trying to make sense of them. "I had a vision, but not about Don's death. It might be related, but I'm not sure. In the vision, I was walking through the woods. Only it wasn't me. I think I was seeing through my mother's eyes. I don't know for sure, and I don't know how to explain it. But that's what I think was happening."

"Go on," she said slowly.

"I heard sounds. Voices. Two men. They were coming my way. For some reason, it scared me. I could feel my heart pounding harder. I stepped off the trail and hid behind some bushes. The men kept walking. Arguing." I swallowed hard. "They were younger, obviously. But I'm almost certain it was Joe and Don. Joe was telling him that things had gone too far. Don said *he* would be the one to decide when things had gone too far, and to remember that Joe was on *his* payroll and not the other way around. That if Don went down, Joe would go down too and lose everything he had ever worked for. Don said Joe needed to remember that and stay out of it, that what had to be done had to be done."

Fiona's face filled with horror.

"I couldn't hear anything after that, because they had passed out of earshot. But what I felt, in the dream, was fear. Fear for my life. I sensed that I—she—knew exactly what they were talking about. Fiona, I think Joe was a dirty cop, and he and Don were involved in something illegal together. I think my mother knew about it." I swallowed hard. "And I think that's why she was killed."

Fiona couldn't hide the tears. "Not Joe. Surely not Joe. Joe loved her, too. And he knew what she meant to me." Her voice was raw with grief.

A sudden thought chilled me to the bones. "Fiona, when he came to me, he told me to not trust anyone except him. He didn't even want me talking to you about anything I discovered. He said if I felt anything, saw anything, to come straight to him first. I thought he was trying to help me, but—"

"He may have been protecting himself," she finished.

"It looks that way."

I was more hurt than I had a right to be. I hadn't known Joe for long, not really. And hadn't I felt a distrust of him from the beginning? But that had changed. Like Fiona, as I had gotten to know him better, it had felt like I had known him my whole life. And the truth was, I had been enamored by the idea of working side by side with him the same way my mother had. My face flushed just thinking about it. How part of me had dared to imagine that was why I had come here. That not only was I going to solve her murder, I was also going to continue her legacy by helping law enforcement with my "gifts." The thought was humiliating now, especially knowing that the one who had triggered those ideas in me was nothing more than a dirty cop who was likely involved in the very murders I was trying to solve. I was angry at him for what happened to my mother. But if I was being honest, I was even more angry that he had made me a joke.

My face burned as I thought about it all.

And of course he knew the window was unlocked. He had probably been the one to unlock it.

I had been so very stupid.

"Do you think Joe is this Mr. Boddy?" Fiona's voice interrupted my thoughts.

I thought it over for a minute. "I don't think so. Not unless the dynamic between them changed drastically over time. The way Don's mistress described it, it seemed that Mr. Boddy oversaw Don. But in my vision, Don was the one in control. I'm thinking Mr. Boddy is a third person altogether. I don't know though. A lot of things can change in twenty years."

"What are you going to do?"

"I don't know, Fiona," I said, slowly. "I think I need to go to the sheriff with all of this. That's probably the right move. But on the other hand, I don't have any credibility with him. He's already made it clear he thinks I need help. Telling him I had a vision about Joe isn't likely to help that, is it?"

"I'll back you up," she said staunchly.

I smiled, despite myself. "Thanks. But honestly, I'm not sure that will help."

I mused for a bit. I might not have any credibility with him, but Emerson did. Maybe he would have a good idea about how to handle it.

Fiona's old-fashioned cuckoo clock chirped and I jumped, realizing how long I had been there. Somehow, sitting in front of the fire, hours had passed. Mom would be worried sick.

"I've got to go, Fiona. Mom's probably pacing the house, if she hasn't already called the police to find me. Listen, don't say anything to anyone. And if you see Joe, just act normal."

"I don't know if I can," she confessed. "I've never felt so betrayed in my whole life."

"Try," I said, squeezing her hands. "I couldn't bear it if anything happened to you, and if he was the one who killed Don, then there's no telling what he's capable of. So promise me. Keep yourself safe."

She squeezed my hands back. "You promise me the same, Eileen's daughter." Her voice was soft, and she looked at me as if she was seeing my mother. "I don't like this feeling of trouble coming that I can't quite see."

"Me either. But it will be over soon." Somehow, I knew in my heart that I was speaking the truth. One way or another, it would end.

She squeezed my hand again, before I turned and headed out the door.

Chapter Thirty-Four

My mind was a jumbled mess as I left Fiona. I trusted the vision I had seen. I believed it was real, and I was certain it held key information about what had happened to Eileen. But I wasn't at all convinced it was the answer to Don's murder. It left too many nagging questions.

Could Joe have killed Don to cover up what had happened so long ago? Possibly. But nothing about my brief interactions with Don suggested he had any intention of confessing anything to me. And frankly, it would be a stupid move on Joe's part. He had worked with my mother. He knew her gifts and he knew enough to suspect I had the same ones. Committing a murder in my front yard would be a reckless, idiotic decision. And nothing about Joe seemed reckless.

No, it didn't make sense.

I was so caught up in my thoughts that I nearly walked right into Katie as I turned the corner onto the lane.

"Whoa!" she laughed, putting her hands out in front of her in a pretend block. She pulled out her ear buds and gave me a friendly smile as she jogged in place.

"Sorry," I said, shaking my head. "I was in my own little world."

"I can tell." A look of concern crossed her face and she stopped her jog. "Daphne, are you okay? You look terrible."

"Thanks," I mumbled.

"I'm not trying to be mean. But you really don't look well. Are you okay?"

I tried to crack a smile, but my lips quivered and I couldn't. I just shrugged and kept silent as the tears threatened to spill.

"Oh, honey," she said, reaching out to put a hand on my arm.

"I'm sorry," I said, attempting to explain. "I'm just so stressed out about the murder investigation. It's really overwhelming. And Mom is here to help, and—"

"Say no more. I get it. It's a lot happening all at once. Can I do anything for you?"

"No, but thanks for asking. It means a lot. Really. When all of this is over, I'm going to take you up on that girl's weekend in Asheville."

"Absolutely," she said. But there was a glimmer of doubt in her eyes, suggesting she wasn't at all sure that this was going to be over soon.

"What is it?" I asked.

"Nothing!" she stammered. "We'll definitely do that. As soon as you've been vindicated, and have had time to rest, and to, you know, destress and get well..."

Her voice trailed off, and I realized what she meant. Of course. If there were concerns in the community about my mental health, then they certainly would have reached her husband and he would have passed them on to her. With as protective as he seemed to be, he wasn't likely to allow her to go away with me for a girls' weekend.

"Yeah," I said, swallowing hard. As much as I wanted to defend myself, I knew it was pointless. Simply saying I was fine wouldn't prove it. Getting drawn up into another emotional conversation right now might even make things worse, as far as our friendship was concerned.

It stung again, to realize how much the killer had taken from me. Even if I wanted to stay, there might never be a place for me here in Rosemary Mountain. I would always be marked with the stain of what happened.

"Well," I said, ending an awkward pause. "I should get back to Mom. We have some things we need to do today."

"Okay! Yeah. Have a great day, and I'll see you later, okay? When all this settles down."

Yep. That's looking less and less likely.

"Yeah! Later. We'll have coffee or something."

"Take care of yourself," she said, reaching out unexpectedly and giving me a quick hug.

I just nodded and swallowed back the hurt. She stuck her ear pods back in her ears, then jogged off with a little wave. I stood and watched her for a moment before turning toward home with a sigh.

Chapter Thirty-Five

Mom was literally pacing the floor when I arrived.

"Daphne! You about gave me a heart attack!" she scolded. "I had no idea what happened to you. Your car was in the driveway, you didn't leave a note. I called, and you didn't answer. I was calculating how long I should wait before calling a search party. Why did you leave like that without telling me?"

"Sorry, Mom," I said, feeling guilty. "I didn't expect to be gone long. I walked down to a neighbor's house and thought I would be back before you even woke. Time sort of got away from me."

Her face changed to interest. "A neighbor as in *Emerson,* perhaps?"

I briefly considered lying, as it would be easier to explain than the truth. "No, not Emerson. My elderly neighbor, Fiona. I wanted to talk to her about the case."

"Oh." Mom frowned. "Well, I was hoping the whole time that you were with Emerson and were just too distracted to look at your phone."

I pulled it out of my pocket and looked at it. Six missed calls and a dozen frantic texts. I felt another stab of guilt. "I'm sorry. It was on silent."

"Well, don't disappear on me like that again. But just in case you do, give me Emerson's number. And this Fiona's number, for that matter. I don't like being out here with no one to call and no way to even check on you. I felt completely helpless."

"I'm sorry, Mom. Really. It was thoughtless."

She opened her mouth as if to say more, then stopped. She let out her breath and shook her head. The next thing I knew, she had enveloped me in a tight embrace. I stood there awkwardly before patting her on the back in return. She had never been the hugging type, and I didn't know what to do with her unexpected emotion.

She finally let go, and I gave her an awkward smile.

"I finished unpacking your kitchen," she said. "And I baked muffins."

"You *baked?*"

"Stress," she said, waving a hand in the air. "It makes me do strange things."

I laughed and shook my head. "Well, I do love a good muffin. I was going to suggest that we head into town for lunch, but you're probably not hungry if you've been stress eating muffins."

"I said nothing about *eating* them," she corrected. "I baked them, but I was too worried to actually eat one. Now that you're home safe, I feel famished."

As if to back up her statement, her stomach growled audibly.

"In that case, let's head into town," I said. "There's a cute little Irish pub I want to take you to. I'll catch you up on the case while we drive. Then after lunch, I thought we might do a bit of snooping."

"Snooping?" She raised a finely arched brow.

"Snooping, investigating, whatever you want to call it." My mood grew dark again as my thoughts returned to Don's murder. "I have a new lead, but I don't think he's the killer. It's big, though. I have to find out what happened, and I feel like time is running out."

Mom frowned. "What do you mean?"

"I wish I knew. It's just a feeling. A heavy feeling that something is coming, and fast. It feels like a warning. All I know is that I have to figure out what happened before it's too late."

"Too late for what?"

I shrugged helplessly. "I don't know. I can't see it."

"And that's why you ran off to Fiona's this morning to talk about the case?"

"Yes, I needed her help."

Mom's stomach growled again.

"Grab your coat," I said. "I'll fill you in on the way."

I gave Mom the rundown as we drove into town. It felt more than a little awkward to explain about the vision. To her credit, she didn't say a word. But it was obvious from her facial expressions that she was skeptical, to say the least.

"So you think this Joe had something to do with your mother's murder, but not Don's?" she clarified.

"That's what my gut says, yeah. I've always assumed the two murders were connected, but now I'm not sure. Joe's definitely hiding something about his connection to Don, though, and I think somehow that's connected to Eileen's murder. But the idea of him killing Don doesn't make sense. What would be his motive? If he wanted the past to stay dead and buried, then why would he resurrect it with another murder right in my front yard?"

"Maybe he didn't actually want it to stay dead and buried," Mom suggested. "Think about it. He's struggled with guilt for years, and when you came back, he decided to punish Don—and himself. Maybe that's why he encouraged you to investigate. Maybe he wants to get caught and admit what happened so long ago."

"Hmm." I mulled it over. "That's possible," I admitted. "It's a theory we'll have to keep in mind, but I don't know. It just doesn't feel right to me. *He* doesn't feel right to me. Don't get me wrong, if he had anything to do with Eileen's death, then nothing would make me happier than to see him go down for Don's murder, too. But it feels off. I feel like I'm missing something."

"So, what are you thinking? You mentioned snooping around. Where are you going to snoop?"

I quickly explained my plan for trying to figure out who Mr. Boddy was and for having Fiona find out more about Matthew.

"Those are good ideas," she said. "But why are you having Fiona do that?"

"Because based on the visible reactions I got the last time I was in town, I don't think anyone would actually talk to me."

"Maybe not *you*. But nobody knows me. I'm a stranger with no connection to any of it. If we came up with a plausible excuse for me to ask questions, maybe I could get somewhere with it."

I looked at her in surprise. "You would do that?"

"Of course I would. I'll do whatever I need to do to make sure you're okay."

I was momentarily speechless.

"I'm glad you're here, Mom." And for the first time, I really meant it.

We had a quick lunch in a corner booth at the pub. The waitress from before snubbed me, no doubt remembering that I was last there as Emerson's date, but no one else seemed to even notice us. While we ate, we brainstormed ideas for finding Mr. Boddy.

"What if we could get Don's phone?" I suggested.

Mom looked at me like I was crazy. "And just how are we supposed to do that?"

"Don wasn't an idiot. If he was involved in something shady, he probably had a separate phone for it. Heck, his affairs alone probably meant that he had a second line. Burners are incredibly easy to get these days."

She continued to stare at me. "And just how would you know that?"

I laughed. "I do watch TV sometimes. Anyway, let's just speculate for a minute. If he had a separate phone that he was hiding from, say, his wife, where do you think he would keep it?"

She shrugged. "His office, or maybe his car. A briefcase. A safe. The possibilities are almost endless."

I tossed the idea around a bit. "His car is probably the most likely, especially if he was taking it with him on his rendezvous with Christie. But then again, Patricia might be more likely to find it in the car. I don't know how often they shared vehicles or rode together. The easiest thing to search is probably his office. I'm doubting the church has security. And even if a burner phone doesn't exist, we might find something else to prove the existence of Mr. Boddy."

"You cannot be serious." She leaned forward and hissed. "You want to break into a church office?"

I shook my head. "I seriously doubt it would require any breaking in. Churches are usually open to the public, right? I mean, ours back home always was. Nobody would recognize you if you went in to pray and light a candle. You could text me if the coast is clear so I could come in and go to the offices. And you could text me if you see anyone coming."

She looked skeptical. "What if it's not the kind of church where people go to pray and light candles? What's my excuse then?"

"You're quick on your feet. You'll think of something."

"Fine. Let's get it over with."

Mom's jaw dropped as we pulled up to the church. "Wow," she commented. "It's hard to believe such a small town has a church this size."

"I know," I said. "It reminds me of that gigantic one—"

"On the interstate?"

"Yeah." I giggled as we exchanged a look.

She looked back at the church, the smile dropping from her face. She let out a long sigh. "Okay. Be careful. Please."

"It will be fine," I reassured her. "There are only two other cars in the parking lot. Nobody is going to see me."

She nodded, got out of the car, gave me one last uncertain look, then strolled to the front door of the church.

I stayed in the car, per our plan, while she went in. A couple of minutes later, a text flashed on my screen.

The front doors open to a lobby. There's a receptionist there, but I have a plan to get her away for a couple of minutes. Wait until my next text, then head in and go to the right. Offices are that way.

I quickly typed back an acknowledgement and waited. The next text came quickly.

Now.

I slipped out of the car and headed for the front door.

I had every confidence that Mom could keep the receptionist away long enough for me to slip in. Janet had a way of getting people to do whatever she wanted. Still, I felt a quick wave of nerves run through me as I opened the door. I didn't want any more confrontations.

I peeked my head in, then breathed a sigh of relief. The lobby was empty. I quickly headed down the hallway to the right. The first conference room was empty, but I could hear a woman's voice coming from the second. I groaned inwardly, but decided to keep walking with my head angled away from the doorway, hoping she wouldn't see me. Or if she did, that at least she wouldn't stop me. I knew that simply acting like I belonged there could be enough to get me through.

I didn't dare turn my head to look into the office, but by the sound of it, the woman was on the phone making funeral arrangements, and didn't even notice me. I felt a quick pang of empathy. Don was a terrible person, but he still had people who loved him and would grieve his death.

I passed a few empty Sunday School rooms and a small kitchen before coming to a large door with an ostentatious black and gold plaque that read *The Holy Reverend Donald Kistler*. I allowed myself one eye roll before trying the doorknob. It was locked, but I was prepared for that. Dad had taught me well. Lock picking was a valuable skill for an antique collector who loved unique cases and chests, as pieces were frequently found without their keys. Dad had taught himself to pick the locks and then had taught me.

A minute or two of effort and I was in.

The office was beautiful and impressive. The mahogany desk gleamed, and the leather furniture looked brand new. It was rich, beautiful, and yet felt oppressive at the same time. I couldn't help but contrast it mentally with Dad's office. He had nice things, but his office felt lived in and welcoming. This one made me feel afraid to even touch anything. I tried to imagine myself coming here for comfort or pastoral counsel. The idea felt impossible. It was as if everything in the room was deliberately chosen in order to make a visitor feel small and intimidated.

I walked around to Don's side of the desk and started opening drawers, looking for anything that might be a clue as to the identity of Mr. Boddy, or whatever Don was caught up in. Everything seemed completely innocuous. He had a drawer of meticulously organized sermon notes, as well as a drawer of personal hygiene effects—a comb, hairspray, nail clippers, et cetera. There was a desk calendar tucked away on the keyboard pull-out. I scanned the entries carefully, but nothing stood out as suspicious. It was all board meetings, hospital visits, counseling appointments, and a couple of weddings.

The computer was password-protected, unsurprisingly, and my attempts at guessing correctly were fruitless.

There was a wall of bookshelves behind the desk. I scanned them to see if there was perhaps a notebook or diary hidden among the rest of the books. Time was passing quickly, I knew, but I didn't want to give up without finding something.

I glanced over every book on the shelf, hoping something would stand out. If not a journal, then maybe even a hollow book containing secrets—*anything*. But there was nothing. Not one thing stood out of place.

I slumped back into Don's desk chair and put my head in my hands.

Despair quickly turned to panic when the door swung open.

"What the hell?" The man's voice filled me with dread.

"Um, hi, Sheriff Morrison."

"And just what do you think you're doing in Don's private office?"

"Investigating," I mumbled lamely.

"Investigating *what* exactly?"

From the furious look on his face and the clipped tone of his voice, I knew I was in trouble. I went with the truth. Most of it, anyway.

"I have reason to believe that Don was mixed up in something shady with someone he called Mr. Boddy."

As soon as I said the words, I knew it was a mistake. Greg's face went from furious to something else entirely, something closer to pity mixed with exhaustion.

"I see. A Mr. Body."

"Yes," I pressed on, despite the warning bells in my head telling me to shut up. "I know it sounds crazy. But that's the name he used for the contact on his phone. I'm not sure what they were involved in, but I get the impression that the man is dangerous. He's probably your killer. And since some people seem to want to blame *me*, I'm trying to find him to clear my name."

Greg rubbed his face in his hands. "And just how do you know that's the name he used on his phone?"

"Um, what?"

"I said, how do you know that's the name he used for the contact on the phone?" He spoke each word slowly and deliberately, as if speaking to a child.

"I just do." I wasn't ready to give up Christie. "Someone told me. I can't tell you who, so please don't ask." A thought occurred that gave me a moment of hope. "But was the phone on him when he died? You could see for yourself and maybe find out who it was!"

"His phone is missing," he said flatly.

"Oh."

At that moment, Mom popped up behind Greg. "Daphne!" she said, out of breath.

Greg turned around. "And just who are you?"

"Janet Sullivan. Daphne's mom."

He turned back to me with a strange look on his face. "I thought your mom was—"

"Stepmom," she corrected.

"Hmm. Nice to meet you," he said, shaking her hand. "Listen, Janet, could I have a word with you privately?"

"Of course." She shot me a guilty look.

Greg looked over at me pointedly.

"Oh, um, I'll just wait in the hallway." I got up from the desk and walked past them, giving them the room.

"Stop," Greg said, a clear order. "Stand there at the doorway where I can see you. Don't go slipping off."

I nodded assent as he took Mom by the elbow and led her across the room. He spoke in low tones, and even though I strained to hear, I couldn't make out what he said. I could pick up enough from the body language and Mom's reactions, though. It was clear that he was expressing the same concerns to her that he had expressed to me.

Initially, Mom was clearly defending me. But toward the end of the conversation, I saw a change on her face that frightened me. She seemed to be acquiescing a bit, even nodding in agreement. I swallowed the bitter feeling of betrayal, reminding myself to give her the benefit of the doubt. She had, after all, truly been supporting me these last couple of days.

After several minutes had passed, they motioned for me to join them.

"Daphne," Mom began tentatively, "Sheriff Morrison here will ask the church to not press charges for breaking and entering, if you will agree to see a psychiatrist for an evaluation."

"What?" I spit the word out in disbelief.

"It's for your own good," Greg added.

"Daphne." Mom cut me off as soon as I opened my mouth. "There's no downside here. You get to avoid a charge on your record. And since you and I both know that you're fine, this will simply prove it to Sheriff Morrison and the rest."

"The downside is that it's unnecessary and ridiculous. Frankly, I'd rather have the breaking and entering charge! Although who says it was breaking and entering, anyway? This is a church building. It's open to the public."

Greg crossed his arms. "Churches are private property, and you didn't just enter a church building, did you? You picked the lock—no, don't interrupt, it's all on the security camera. That's why they called me."

"Oh." The sheepish feeling returned.

"You broke in and were searching a private office that you didn't have permission to enter. The private office of a man that half the community is convinced you killed."

"And what about you?" I demanded. "Tell me the truth. Do you honestly believe I killed Don? If you do, then why not just arrest me now?"

"Daphne!" Mom said, putting a hand on my arm. "I think you need to calm down."

"No. I want an answer." I looked Greg square in the eye. "Do you honestly believe I killed Don?"

He let out a sigh and stayed silent for what felt like half an hour. Finally, he spoke, acting as if it killed him to do so. "No. No, I don't."

I could see Mom exhale in visible relief.

"Then why do you keep treating me like a suspect?"

"Like I said. Half the community is convinced you did it. Frankly, our investigation hasn't turned up any better suspects. And while I'm not convinced you did it, I *do* take very seriously the concerns in the community about your mental health. You may not be a murderer, but you're making plenty of other bad decisions. Like breaking into Don's office, for one example. Vandalism for another. That's why I'm insisting you get some help. If you refuse, I'll ask for a court order."

"I've already told you I didn't spray paint my own house!"

"Yeah, you said that." He nodded. "But I have a witness who saw you doing it."

My mouth dropped open. "Who on earth?"

He shook his head. "That's confidential."

"Sheriff," Mom spoke hesitantly.

"Yes?"

"I wasn't going to say anything." She looked at me with an apology in her eyes. "But I found a can of red spray paint hidden in the top of Daphne's coat closet. Daphne, maybe you really do need to talk to someone."

I stared at her in disbelief. I was practically shaking. "I cannot believe this."

"Oh, Daphne," she reached out to touch my arm.

"No. Don't touch me." I shrugged her off and looked Greg in the eye again. "Am I under arrest?"

"If that's the way it's going to be, then yes."

"Fine." I held out my hands.

He sighed and slapped a pair of cuffs on me with an apologetic look at Mom.

"Ma'am, I'm going to take her in for processing. I expect that bail will be set pretty quickly."

Mom nodded. I bit my tongue to keep from telling her not to bother. I was so furious that I wanted to tell her to pack up and leave.

But I had enough sense left to know that I needed to get out of jail as quickly as possible. After all, I had no intention of dropping my investigation into Don's murder and the mysterious Mr. Boddy.

CHAPTER THIRTY-SIX

A few miserable hours later, I was informed that my bail had been paid and that I was being released until my upcoming court date. An apologetic-looking Janet was waiting for me.

I passed her without a word and headed straight toward the car.

"Daphne," she said, following after me.

"Save it," I snapped.

"No." Her voice was firm. It was an order, and I automatically obeyed, turning to face her.

"Daphne Sullivan, you do not get to do this to me. You do not get to shut me out. I know you're angry. But so am I. I've supported you through this whole thing, but I'm worried about you. I didn't know what to think when I found that spray paint, but I gave you the benefit of the doubt. Then, when Sheriff Morrison said a witness saw you, what was I supposed to think? On top of that, you came home this morning telling me you had a supposed *vision*..."

"You should believe in me," I said, my voice breaking. "Believe in *me*. Your daughter. Not some unnamed witness."

"But the spray paint—"

"Was planted in my house. Someone is obviously trying to frame me for Don's murder. But *I'm* telling you I didn't do it. So believe in *me."* I was begging, not just for this situation, but for my whole life, really. The pain of years of rejection and criticism ripped through me all at once.

She sighed. "I don't know what to believe."

My heart sank. "Well then, there's nothing left to talk about, is there?" I turned around and walked away.

WE DROVE HOME IN SILENCE. WHEN WE REACHED THE house, Mom spoke without making eye contact.

"I think I should pack my things and head back home. I called the attorney and told him about the recent developments. He'll be in touch prior to your court date. I'm sure the two of you can handle things from here."

"That's probably best," I agreed. But instead of relief, I felt disappointment. Either she believed my mental status was fine, and yet hadn't stood up for me, or she believed I was ill, but was leaving me alone anyway. Either scenario hurt.

WITH HER TUCKED AWAY IN THE GUEST ROOM, I WENT TO the kitchen to make a much-needed pot of coffee. The muffins she had made were still untouched. When I saw them, I felt a pang of regret as I thought about how different things had been between us only a few hours ago.

I drank a cup of coffee, followed by a second, but I didn't feel any better. Exhaustion was threatening to overtake me, and one of those massive headaches was beginning. I knew enough about the nervous system to know that it was likely the post-effects of a fight-or-flight system gone haywire earlier in the day. But knowing why I felt so bad didn't make it better. I popped a couple of pain pills and poured a third cup of coffee, hoping it would bring me back to life. I didn't have time to sleep away what was left of the day. The walls were closing in on me. I was almost out of time. I had to solve Don's murder before something else happened.

My mind raced as I tried to sort through the details of the case. The more I thought about it, the more it seemed that everyone involved could be a bad guy.

Joe had been involved with Don. He had access to my home. He had been a threatening, suspicious person from the beginning.

Sheriff Morrison. What if he's actually out to get me? Maybe he's trying to frame me, but is reluctant to push forward because he wants to look like a good guy. Could he be Mr. Boddy? Maybe he arrested me to stop me from investigating.

Dr. Rogers. He could be Mr. Boddy. What did I really know about him, anyway?

Also, Fiona had mentioned someone else on the lane—a Bill somebody. Rich and powerful. Maybe he's Mr. Boddy. Heck, maybe Marco is Mr. Boddy. Didn't the mafia originate in Italy? Maybe there's some sort of mafia thing going on here.

My head swirled and pounded, and I struggled to follow my own thoughts. My heart raced with anxiety, and time felt like it was standing still. I looked at the clock and was shocked to see that three hours had passed. My head still pounded.

I popped more pills.

Everything got hazier and scarier and made more sense and less sense at the same time.

Mom. What if she's the one doing all this? What if she's jealous that I found out about my real mom, and she wants to ruin this entire experience for me? That would be just like her. She could have come here and killed Don and made everyone think I was crazy, so that I'll have to move back home and let her control every detail of my life. No Eileen for me. No new life.

Mom suddenly walked into my bedroom—*my bedroom? Wasn't I just in the kitchen? How did I get here?* I staggered toward her.

"You," I said, pointing a finger at her. "I figured it out. It was you all along, wasn't it? You killed Don. You spray-painted my house."

"Daphne? What are you talking about? Are you okay?"

"I'm thine," I said. "Thine. Fine." *Why is it so hard to make words?* "But you won't be. You'll be in jail. Just like me. You'll thee. See."

"Oh my God, Daphne, are you on drugs?"

"What? No. Maybe *you're* on drugs." But even as I said it, the tiny part of me, deep inside, that was still slightly lucid, started flashing warning bells like crazy. *Drugs? Is that why I feel like I'm swimming in mud?*

The pills.

And suddenly it made sense, or as much sense as it could possibly make when my thoughts were swirling around my head so quickly that it was difficult to grasp onto one for more than a second. I sat back, intending to hit my bed, but found the floor instead.

"Poisoned," I gasped in disbelief. "Help me. Emerson." And with that, the world went black.

CHAPTER THIRTY-SEVEN

"Something's wrong with her," Janet said frantically. "It's like she's overdosed or something. She said she was poisoned." I could hear the panic in her voice even in my foggy state.

Suddenly, Emerson was looming above me with a frown on his face. "Daphne. What did you take?"

I tried to shake my head no, but the room was spinning, and I felt so disconnected from my body that I couldn't tell if I was successful. I slapped out, but my hands only hit air. My eyes tried to scan the room for a weapon, but I couldn't seem to focus on anything.

"Go away." The slurred sound of my own voice startled me. "I know it was you. I know about the pills."

"What pills?" he demanded.

"The headache pills. You gave me." Everything was spinning faster now, and the blackness threatened to take over again. "Figured out. You poisoned me. Mom, do something!"

Janet gasped. "You poisoned her?"

"Of course not," Emerson growled. "I gave her a bottle of ibuprofen."

"No!" My voice surprised me again. I felt so disconnected from it.

"Poison. I know it. Makes me crazy. Put it in the garbage, Mom. Need more coffee. Need to wake up." My head fell backward again. It felt as if it weighed a thousand pounds.

I opened my eyes and saw Emerson frowning at me as he checked my pulse and shined a flashlight in my eyes. "Stop it," I slurred again. "Too bright. Go away. Poisoner."

"I didn't poison you, Daphne. But maybe someone else did. Let's go." Suddenly, the room was upside down. I realized he had thrown me over his shoulder and was carrying me down the stairs.

"Where are you taking her?" Mom's voice was panicked again as she followed us.

"To the hospital." Emerson's voice was still a growl. "She said she needed more coffee. How much has she been drinking?"

"I don't know," Mom said, her voice helpless. "We weren't speaking. I was in my room. But I know she's been drinking it today. When I went into the kitchen, there were coffee grounds spilled all over. That's not like her at all. She's usually so neat."

"Have you been drinking the same coffee?"

"Actually, no. I'm a morning tea drinker. "

"Get it then. Does she drink it black?"

"Not lately. She's been adding cream and sugar."

"Get both of those, too. Bring all three to the hospital for testing, along with anything else suspicious. Check her cabinets for strange medicine bottles. Look for any homemade snacks or anything that a neighbor may have brought by. Anything you can think of that could have been tainted and that only she has ingested. You should pack her a bag with a toothbrush, pajamas, a fresh change of clothes, and anything else she might need for a few days. Buy her a fresh toothpaste, just in case."

I raised my head slightly and saw Mom nodding, a look of fear on her face. That look, the fear, somehow broke through and touched me somehow.

"I'm okay, Mom," I mumbled. "Just so sleepy. Need coffee. Pack the coffee."

"No more coffee for you," Emerson said, reaching around to buckle me into the truck.

· · ·

SLEEP OVERCAME ME BEFORE WE EVEN MADE IT OUT OF THE driveway. I came to every now and then, responding to Emerson, who kept commanding me to stay awake. But I couldn't. It felt as if I were far away, curled up in a cave to hibernate, and that someone was rolling a heavy stone over the entrance. Everything kept getting darker and cozier, and it was impossible to stay awake, no matter how much he insisted. Dreams beckoned, lovely dreams. Soon, everything faded to black, and even my lovely dreams disappeared.

I AWOKE TO THROBBING PAIN IN MY HEAD AND THE annoyance of bright sunlight. My mouth felt dry, and I struggled to open my eyes or speak.

"Daphne!"

It was Mom's voice. I tried to smile. Tried to force my eyes open a crack, despite the hideous light.

I felt a straw slide between my lips. I drank gratefully, washing away the dryness.

Then I slipped away again.

WHEN I AWOKE THE SECOND TIME, THE PAIN WAS FINALLY gone, and the room was dark. Everything was quiet. My head felt clearer than it had in ages. I pulled myself upright and looked around. I was in a hospital room, hooked up to an IV. Mom was curled up in the recliner beside me, sleeping. I almost hated to wake her. She seemed to have aged somehow since I had last seen her. How long had it been? How long had I been in this room? It felt like an eternity had passed.

"Mom," I said quietly.

Her eyelids flew open, and she jumped out of the chair.

"Daphne! You're awake." She grabbed the cup of water beside my bed and offered it to me.

I drank greedily. Had I ever realized before how perfectly wonderful cool, fresh water was? I would never take it for granted again.

"How long?" I asked.

She glanced at her watch. "About thirty-six hours. Emerson got you here the night before last."

"What time is it? What *day* is it?"

She laughed quietly. "Wednesday, and it's about four forty-five in the morning."

"So, I guess I was wrong when I accused Emerson of poisoning me?" I didn't remember much about that night, but what I could remember was embarrassing.

"You were right and wrong. You were drugged, yes, but it wasn't Emerson—"

"Definitely not me." His familiar voice came from the doorway.

I turned my gaze to him and smiled, but he didn't smile back.

"I'll give you two a minute to talk," Mom said. "I could use a few minutes to stretch my legs and find something to eat."

She stood up and grabbed her purse, squeezing Emerson on the shoulder as she passed by him.

He waited for her to leave, then came to me. "How are you feeling?"

There was a wall between us again, a distance that I despised. Not that I blamed him.

"Better," I said. "Listen, I'm really sorry I accused you of poisoning me."

"Well, I think you were right about being drugged. Just wrong about who did it."

"So who was it?"

He sighed. "I don't know. That's part of why I'm here. This is just a small, rural hospital. They ran a basic drug panel, which was negative. But they don't have the resources to test for much else. Their policy is that when someone comes into the ER strung out on drugs, they do a mandatory seventy-two-hour psych hold and try to wash it out of their system."

I felt panic rising in me. "Are you telling me I'm in a psych hold?"

He grinned. "No. That's their usual procedure. But they make some exceptions for my friends."

I relaxed. "Oh, good. Well, thanks for that."

He sobered again. "You were in pretty bad shape. Whoever did this to you, well, they could have killed you. Your mom gathered up some things from your house that might have been tainted. Greg doesn't have the resources to test them locally, but he sent them to a buddy at the crime lab in Nashville. Hopefully, we'll find out exactly what you were given, and in what. I suspect it was in your coffee, or something you were putting in your coffee. You kept asking for more, and you had been drinking it all day."

I quickly thought back to all the times I had felt so bad lately, the times when I had been hit with horrible headaches or sleepiness.

"I think you're right," I said slowly. "And I drink coffee every day." I breathed out deeply. "Oh my goodness."

He squeezed my hand. "Well, you should start feeling better. Your mom boxed up everything in the house that could have been contaminated with something, even your shampoo. When she decides to take on a project, she's thorough."

"You have no idea."

He grinned at me, and I felt myself relax, until everything he said before sank in and the gravity of the situation hit me. "Oh my word, I could have died."

"Yeah, you could have."

"Has Greg made any progress on Don's case while I've been out?"

"None that I'm aware of, and I think he would let me know of any developments, considering what happened to you. He tested your coffee can for prints, by the way, as well as the can of spray paint—Janet gave it to him," he said, in answer to my questioning look. "No word yet from the crime lab."

"He told me there was a witness who saw me doing the spray-paint thing. Do you think whatever I was drugged with could have made me so out of my mind that I really did that?"

"It's possible," he said honestly. "We won't know for sure until we know what you were given. *If* we can even identify it."

"Hmm." I didn't like his answer. I didn't like thinking that anything could make me so out of control of myself that I might have done something I couldn't even remember. I also didn't like the reality that I might never know what I was being drugged with, or what long-term health effects it might have. Knowing that someone had done that to me was infuriating.

"You'll be okay," he said, as if reading my mind. "Your vitals are all stable, and there's no reason to worry. We'll figure all this out. In the meantime, Janet and I have been talking. She wants to get you out of town and away from all this as quickly as possible, obviously. But you're still technically a person of interest in the case, and Greg hasn't officially given you permission to leave yet. So, we've talked about my staying at your house until you get the all clear to leave. You can both consider me your personal bodyguard and nurse for the time being." He winked, and my heart melted.

"But you have work and animals to take care of," I protested.

"I haven't used a single day of PTO since I moved here," he said, laughing. "I'm overdue. And I'll gladly drag you along to my place when I go take care of the animals. I offered to let you and your mom both stay there, but she politely declined."

I laughed out loud at that. "I can just imagine. She's probably picturing a bachelor pad with empty pizza boxes and dog hair everywhere."

"That's kind of the impression I got from her facial expression," he said with another big grin.

I returned his smile, then reached out my hand and grabbed his. "I really am sorry."

"Shhhh," he said, rubbing his thumb over mine. "Let's just call it even. I accused you of vandalizing your house; you accused me of drugging you. Seems a promising start to an interesting relationship, don't you think?" He grinned again, and I felt the distance between us disappearing. "I will say that I'm looking forward to getting to know the real you. You know, the one who isn't on mind-altering substances."

"I might be a little more boring," I warned.

"I like boring." He leaned down and kissed me gently, closing the distance for good.

"So, how long will I have to stay here? In the hospital, I mean."

"That's up to your doctor, but I imagine he'll let you go late this afternoon as long as you're stable, feeling good, and eating and drinking like normal today. They've already run a basic tox screen and every other test that might explain your symptoms, and nothing came back. Insurance doesn't enjoy paying for someone to stay in the hospital for no reason, so I doubt you'll be stuck here much longer now that you're awake and, well, yourself."

"Good." I breathed a sigh of relief.

Chapter Thirty-Eight

Emerson was correct. As soon as it was clear that I was back to normal, the hospital was eager to discharge me. Mom begged them to let me stay another night, simply for her own peace of mind. I cut her off before she offered to pay cash, because I couldn't stand the idea of another night in the hospital. I was ready to get home. The dark cloud I had felt hadn't dissipated. I knew it wouldn't until I found a way to put this whole thing behind me. The case had to be solved. And while it was tempting to hide out in the hospital waiting for Greg to handle the investigation, I somehow knew it wouldn't work out that way. I sort of liked Greg, despite our run-ins, but I didn't have much faith in his investigative abilities.

We decided Emerson would drive me home in his truck, while Mom went to pick up fresh groceries to replace everything she had thrown away during her precautionary cleanout. I was grateful for that arrangement as well. It had been an excruciatingly long day being confined to a hospital bed, with Mom doing her best to entertain me with gossip about people I barely knew.

The freedom I felt when the fresh air hit my face was even stronger than after my brief "lock up" only two days prior. I vowed never to take fresh air for granted again. I felt positively giddy on the drive home, watching the setting sun light the mountain—*my* mountain—on fire with color.

"What are you grinning about over there?" Emerson asked, amused.

"I'm just happy," I said. "Happy to be alive. Happy to be out of that dang hospital. Happy to be *here,* seeing this gorgeous sunset. Happy to be going home."

"Happy to have a break from your mom?" He laughed, looking over at me.

"That too. And..." I hesitated, wondering if I was brave enough to say the words. "Happy to be with you."

He looked over again and met my eyes, then reached over and squeezed my hand. "I'm happy to be with you, too. You know, I'll miss you when you move back to Arkansas."

And just like that, the mood was spoiled.

"Well, I know Mom is in a hurry to get me back home, but I'm not really ready to go. I like it here. Plus, I still haven't figured out the truth about what happened to my mother. And obviously, I need to figure out who killed Don and poisoned me before they do something else."

"Wait, you're not really considering staying?" he asked, his face grim. "Someone tried to kill you, Daphne. You're in danger here. You need to get away, go somewhere safe, and lie low."

"No." I set my mouth in a stubborn line. "I'm finally thinking clearly again, and I'm going to do what I came here to do. Besides, I don't think whoever poisoned me was trying to kill me at all. Why would they? There's no motive there."

"You're sticking your nose into not one, but two murders. You don't think that's a motive to take you out?"

I shook my head. "Whoever killed Don clearly tried to frame me for it. I think drugging me was meant to help paint me as mentally unstable. Whatever I was on made me feel off. Paranoid. Angry. If I were acting crazy, it would help sell the idea to Greg that I killed Don out of some vendetta. You know," I mused, "What if the witness who saw me vandalizing was lying? What if that, too, was just to throw suspicion my way? We need to talk to Greg to find out who exactly said those things. That might be our killer."

"That's a good point," he admitted. "One worth talking to Greg about. Although this whole thing has just further cemented in his mind that you've been a little, well, unstable lately. There's still no proof that anyone was poisoning you. It's just our personal working theory. We'll either need for something to come back from the crime lab, or for your behavior and personality to drastically, um, settle down to convince him. Or both. He mentioned that you could have even been drugging yourself."

"Well, that's just perfect." I couldn't help rolling my eyes. "Whoever did this successfully convinced half the town that I'm certifiable. Even Katie is giving me the cold shoulder now."

"You and Katie are friends?" he asked, his brown furrowed in an odd frown.

"Yeah. She was actually becoming quite a good friend, until all of this happened and the rumors about me started. The last time I saw her, it was clear that things had changed. It was such a disappointment, because I was really enjoying our friendship. I hadn't had a good girlfriend like that since college. I think we bonded quickly because we both lost our biological mothers at a young age, and—" I could feel the blood drain out of my face.

"What is it?" he asked, quickly switching back into nurse mode.

"No, I'm fine, it's just... Oh, Emerson. I just realized something. I should have put the pieces together a long time ago." I wanted to weep.

"What? Tell me."

"When Katie and I first met and were talking about our pasts, she told me she and her mother grew up in the backwoods of Pennsylvania."

"Your point being?"

"Fiona told me that Don used to be a pastor in Harrisburg. Harrisburg, Pennsylvania. Katie told me that Don got run out of his old church because of an affair. She also told me her father wasn't around much and that he left them completely before her mother died. Emerson, what if Don was Katie's father?"

The ramifications of that washed over him. "But surely Katie wouldn't have... Would she?"

"I don't know. But Emerson, she's been in my house. In fact, right after the murder, she came over to bring me a gift." My heart sank as I realized what she had done. "It was a book. She told me she would make her own coffee while I looked at it. She was alone in my kitchen with plenty of time to drug whatever and open my window so she could stash the spray paint later."

He let out a noisy exhale. "That would also explain something that's bothered me this whole time."

"What?"

"Well, one reason they couldn't officially clear you was that Dr. Rogers never established a reasonable time of death. It's certain, from our perspective, that Don was shot while you were at Marco's. Even a two-hour window during that time would have cleared you. But he was insistent that he couldn't establish one, that he had no way of determining how long Don lived with his wound before he died. He insisted on a ridiculously large window spanning most of the day. It didn't make sense to me."

"He knew," I whispered. "Or he was part of it. Either way. That's why Luke said they were asking neighbors if anyone heard a gunshot, so they could establish the time of death that way."

"And no one did," Emerson added. "But I've been shooting with Dr. Rogers, and I happen to know that he has a silencer for his pistol."

"What about Katie's alibi?" I asked. "She says she was out of town when Don was killed."

"Maybe Dr. Rogers is the one who actually killed Don," Emerson suggested. "Maybe Katie was just part of trying to frame you for it."

"I don't think so," I said, sighing. "My gut says it was Katie. She said she was staying in Asheville that night. Maybe Greg could check up on it, see if there are hotel records or camera footage or something. My gut says that she was in the woods that night. You know, when we were all there for the crime scene, I kept feeling like someone was watching from the woods. It was the eeriest feeling. I think it was her."

"She's in great shape. It would have been easy for her to pretend to leave town, park somewhere hidden on the other side of the mountain, and hike one of the trails up to your place."

"You think?"

"I know. I've been hiking with her. She kicks *my* butt on the trail."

"We have to call Greg."

"I'll call him as soon as we get back to your house, okay?"

I sank back in my seat, reeling from the betrayal of it all. I hated to accuse someone else without proof, but I could feel the truth of it sinking into my bones. Katie, my supposed friend, had killed and tried to frame me for it. She had drugged me.

And I had never seen it coming.

As if nature herself were mirroring my feelings, dark storm clouds appeared out of nowhere over Rosemary Mountain. Heavy rain pelted the truck as the sky turned black.

"You've got to be kidding me." Emerson groaned. "Not now."

We were already halfway up the mountain, but I knew the reason for his distress. These were flash flood rains, certain to cut our road off from the rest of the world until the storm subsided.

"You'd better try to call your mom," he said. "If she's not already on her way, she needs to stay in town. The road is going to flood in no time with it coming down like this."

I nodded and tried to call her. She answered, but the reception was worse than spotty, and we couldn't seem to hear each other at all.

"She can't hear me," I said, worry building within me.

"It's okay. She'll be fine."

I appreciated him trying to reassure me, but the dark feelings were growing by the second. Something felt very wrong.

We pulled up to the house. It was brightly lit. Leave it to Mom to remember to turn on the lights. It should have felt like a sanctuary, a refuge from the storm, but I found myself shrinking from it.

"We'll have to make a run for it," Emerson said. "You sure could use a garage out here."

He started to open his door, but noticed my hesitation. "What's wrong?"

"I don't know. I just don't feel right."

"Dizzy? Headache? What's going on?"

"No, not like that. I can't explain it. I'm just scared."

"You, the amateur detective who just insisted on staying in town to solve the case?" he teased.

"I have a bad feeling."

"Okay. Do you want to go to my place instead?"

I hesitated again. On one hand, yes, I did. On the other hand, if Mom got past the creek before it swelled, we needed to be here. She would be worried sick if she didn't know where we were.

"No," I finally decided. "We need to be here if Mom gets through. I'm probably just nervous because of everything that happened."

"Probably," he agreed. "But just in case, I'll go in first and check everything out."

Lightning struck close enough to vibrate through the truck.

"There's no way I'm staying out here by myself. I'm probably being ridiculous."

"Alright. Then let's run for it."

I nodded, and we both jumped from the truck at the same time. The yard had already turned to mud. My boots sank into it, making the short run to the porch feel agonizingly slow. The rain came in sheets, soaking me to the bones. Emerson grabbed my hand and pulled me forward.

We finally made it to the covered porch in time for another lightning strike that nearly sent me to my knees. I was shivering from the cold. I handed him the key to the front door and stripped off my boots.

As soon as he had the door unlocked, I moved to go inside.

"Hey, wait a sec," he said, grabbing my arm. "I'm going in first to make sure everything is okay, remember? I'm officially on bodyguard duty. Just give me a minute to get my own boots off." He winked and gave me a reassuring smile.

I nodded, still shivering uncontrollably. Any dark feelings I had in the truck seemed unimportant, considering how unbearable the cold was. I didn't want to wait another minute to get warm.

Finally, he nodded at me before opening the door, pistol in hand. The next thing I knew, he was falling, crashing to the floor in front of me. I screamed, then my body lit on fire, and everything went black yet again.

Chapter Thirty-Nine

I woke to find myself zip-tied to a kitchen chair in my living room. I was certain I was dreaming. This was the kind of thing that happened in TV or movies, not in real life. Surely this was just another bad dream, and I would wake up to find myself still safe inside the hospital with Emerson and Mom by my side.

I heard a groan. *Emerson.* I tried to see him, but he was somewhere behind me and I couldn't turn around. I strained my wrists and arms, putting pressure against the ties that bound me, but I couldn't find a weak spot.

"Emerson!" I called out. He groaned again in response.

I heard footsteps and my heart started racing.

"Hey, friend." Katie stepped in front of me. "There's no point in fighting. You won't get out of those."

She stroked my chin with a gloved finger. Even though I had known it was her, had felt it in my core, the sting of betrayal hit harder than I could have predicted.

"Why?" It was all I could ask.

"Why what?" Her tone was faintly amused. "Why Don? Or why you? Can't you figure it out? Aren't you supposed to be psychic?" She moved to a bag that was sitting on the coffee table and started rummaging through it. She pulled out a pill bottle, lighter fluid, and matches. My heart sank. I couldn't move, and I had to assume that Emerson was bound or incapacitated in some way. There was a chance Mom might make it past the creek, although what help she would be, I didn't know. Still, all I could do was try to buy time while I came up with some sort of plan, any kind of Hail Mary.

"I know why Don," I said, forcing myself to be calm. "He was your father."

"So you figured that out." She turned away from the bag and looked at me with an odd expression. It was curiosity mixed with something else—respect? I had gotten her attention, at least.

She turned away from me and went back to her bag. "Well, I suppose it doesn't matter. It's not as if you'll be around much longer to tell anyone anything."

"Wait," I said. "I know why Don, but why me? Why are you doing this?"

She shrugged. "Dave does rounds at the hospital. He told me you were there for suspected poisoning. You kind of messed up my plans with that one," she said, wagging a finger at me and shaking her head. "You weren't supposed to figure that out. But now we'll have to go another route to prove that you went nuts and killed Don, won't we?"

"But why did you have to bring me into this at all?"

"You're the one pretending you have some sort of ESP. You figure it out," she said, shrugging. She never even looked up from her preparations.

"I understand you killed Don to punish him for what he did to your mother—"

"Not to my mother," she snapped, finally looking up. "To *me*. What he did to *me*."

"Oh," I said, caught off guard. "I'm so sorry. I knew Don was a sleaze, but I didn't realize. I didn't know he hurt you like that."

She stared at me blankly for a moment, then began laughing. "Not like *that*. He didn't abuse me. No, he stole my childhood, the life I deserved. He left my mother broken and useless and poor. He could have taken care of us, of *me*. I understand he didn't want her anymore, and I don't blame him. She became such a sopping mess. Vodka for breakfast, lunch, and dinner."

Her voice was pure disgust. "But here he was, living it up in his fine house, wearing his expensive suits, driving his fancy cars. And I, *his daughter,* was wearing whatever worn-out charity clothes were given to me and cleaning up my mother's vomit every night."

"I see," I said.

"But things eventually work out the way they should," she said smugly. "I made sure of it. I decided a long time ago that I was going to take my future into my own hands, and that someday he would pay for leaving us alone and penniless."

"Was Dr. Rogers part of your plan?"

She sat back and eyed me, that smug look still on her face. It was obvious she was enjoying telling me how she triumphed.

"I followed Don from a distance for years. When Dave's wife died, I saw an opportunity to get closer. It wasn't hard to show up at the same convention as him, and it certainly wasn't hard to make him fall in love with me."

She laughed, tossing her beautiful blonde hair behind her. "You know, Don didn't even recognize me? Had no idea who I was when I moved here. Didn't even know his own daughter. But no matter. He's dead now. He paid for what he did, and I got to look him in the eye and watch him die like the pig he is. *I'm* the one living in the nice house and driving the nice car, with the rest of my life ahead of me."

She brought a bottle of pills over to me, along with a notepad and pen.

"Now, I'm sorry about this," she said, though her tone said otherwise. "But I've gone to a great deal of trouble to make sure you take the blame. After all, I plan on living a long, happy life here. So, here's how it's going to go. I'm going to untie your right hand. You're going to write a suicide note. Explain how you killed Don to avenge your dead mother, blah blah blah. Say Emerson figured it out. You're so sorry. Make it look good. You're going to put it in this envelope and address it to Sheriff Morrison. Be sure to lick the envelope when you seal it so it has your DNA on it. Then you're going to take these pills, wash them down with some vodka or wine, your choice, and you'll go to sleep. Don't worry, you won't feel a thing. It's peaceful, really."

"What on earth makes you think I'm going to cooperate with you?"

She gave me a knowing look. "Because you're a softie. And because you don't want your boyfriend over there to suffer. The fire's going to destroy any evidence of anything I do to him while I wait for you to cooperate." She smiled a sickly-sweet smile. "He can have an easy death, like you. Or he can suffer. The choice is yours."

My heart sank because she was right. I couldn't bear to watch her torture Emerson, even if it gave us a little more time. No one was coming. If Mom hadn't made it up the mountain by now, the creek was surely flooded. We hadn't been able to call Greg. No one knew we were in any danger at all. I could try to attack when she let my hand loose, but the fact was that she was stronger, and she would be prepared for it. A tear rolled down my cheek as the truth sank in.

We were going to die tonight. There was nothing I could do to stop it.

"I see we have an understanding," she said, that amused tone still in her voice. How could I ever have liked her? She was smug, narcissistic, and cruel.

"I still want an answer," I said. "I need to know. Why me?"

She could tell that my question was different this time. I wasn't stalling anymore. I had accepted my fate. I just wanted to know. And because of that, this time, she decided to tell me. She looked at me with something like pity in her eyes, like I was an animal trapped in her cage. I had to die, no doubt about it. But she still felt sorry for me, somehow.

"I wish it hadn't had to be you," she said. "You're nice, and it would have been fun to have a girlfriend here. But don't you see? You were like a gift. You came here and told us all about your mother and how you were here to find the truth about what happened to her. You immediately suspected Don, and instead of keeping that information to yourself, you *told* people."

She laughed, lifting her hands into the air. "I had been watching and waiting for so long, trying to find a way to make him pay without endangering myself or my own position here. And here you came along, the perfect suspect. I knew it was meant to be."

She stroked my chin again, and I fought the urge to throw up. "We're like sisters, you and I. We both lost our moms. We both suffered because of Don. And now you'll sacrifice yourself for me. At least one of us will get to go on and live the life we deserve."

Her eyes went starry. "Your death is practically poetic. You're not only sacrificing yourself for me, your soul sister, but you're dying the way your mother did. Sleeping pills and a note. Killing yourself to save another. It's fate." She stroked my hair now, her eyes far off and glassy.

"What do you know about my mother's death?" I asked, desperate.

She looked down at me again, that same pity in her eyes. "More than you do, that's for sure." She paused for a moment, considering. "You were right, you know. It wasn't her idea to kill herself any more than it's yours. You were wrong about Don, though. He knew the truth, alright. But he didn't kill her. Whoops," she said, with a sick grin on her face. "I shouldn't have told you that. It was unkind. Better for you to be at peace, believing your mother's killer got justice."

"Who was it? How do you know?" I cried out. I couldn't believe it. All this time, and she was the one with the answers I had been trying to find. And I was completely at her mercy. She knew it. And she loved it.

"You're new to town, sweetie," she said in a patronizing tone. "I told you I've been watching Don for a long time. I'm a lot smarter than I look. That whole dumb blonde thing opens doors." She winked at me and absentmindedly stroked my chin again. "Everyone thinks Don runs this town, that he's the one with all the power. But they're wrong."

"Like the wizard," I whispered, remembering Emerson's words.

She laughed loudly. "I guess you're right. We don't really have time for this, though." She glanced behind me. "Emerson's stirring, so we need to get this over with."

"Please," I begged. "Please. Just tell me who it was."

"Just tell yourself it was Don," she said, smiling sweetly. "That will make you feel better."

She stood abruptly, indicating that the conversation was over, and headed to her bag of supplies. She brought a knife over and cut the zip tie off just one hand, then balanced the pad of paper on the arm of the chair and stuck a pen between my fingers.

"Write," she commanded. "And make it good. I'll be reading it carefully. If anything looks even a little off, Emerson will pay for it. Then you'll do it again. And again. And again. Until I'm satisfied."

I nodded. I understood. I blinked quickly to clear my eyes from the tears forming and stared at the paper, trying to come up with the right words.

In that instant, I had another vision. This time, I knew it was happening at that very moment. I could see Fiona marching quickly through the shortcut in the woods, bundled in a heavy raincoat, with a shotgun in hand. *Hang on, dear.* I could hear her words in my mind, as clear as day. She was coming. Somehow, she knew I was in trouble, and she was coming. My heart leaped. I just had to delay a few more minutes.

I picked up the pen and pretended my hand was shaking so badly that I dropped it.

"Sorry," I mumbled.

Katie frowned and stuck it roughly back between my fingers. "Don't mess around," she warned. "Get it done."

Not wanting to risk Emerson's safety, I nodded and started writing. I was distracted, listening for Fiona. But she didn't come. The vision was gone, and even though three minutes ticked by as I wrote my note, there was no sign of her. My hope faded again.

"That's good enough," Katie said, looking over the note. "Now the envelope."

I addressed the envelope the way she demanded and licked the seal for her.

Another minute ticked by.

Still no Fiona.

Emerson groaned again in pain.

"I'm afraid it's time," Katie said, tucking the envelope into her purse. "Wine or vodka to wash down the pills?"

"Wine," I said. There weren't any bottles open in the house. Maybe it would take her a minute or two to uncork one. Every delay mattered.

But she was way ahead of me. She pulled out a bottle of red from her purse, already opened. She brought it to me and held it to my lips, tilting it up so that I could take a long drink. Then she started pushing pills into my mouth, one by one. I fought it, shook my head, and refused to swallow. Tears came faster now. I couldn't believe this was how things were going to end.

"I warned you to cooperate," she said, her tone mocking. She went to her bag and pulled that deadly-looking knife back out, making sure I got a good look at it before she walked behind me. I heard Emerson cry out in pain, awake now.

"Stop! Don't!" I cried out.

"Daphne!" Emerson's voice was weak.

"I'm so sorry, Emerson," I cried.

"That's enough of that," Katie said, coming back to me. I could hear Emerson making muffled sounds, as if he had been gagged. I could feel vibrations in the floor as he thrashed, trying to get loose. I dropped my head, tears falling quickly.

Katie leaned over me and shoved another pill into my mouth. This time I swallowed. One, then another. Was this how it had been for my mother?

As if in answer, the back door swung open, and there she was— Fiona, an angel in a bright red raincoat, pointing her shotgun right at Katie.

Katie looked up, shocked. I reacted instantly, using my one free hand to yank the wine bottle out of hers. I swung it across the back of her head with all the force I could muster from my seated position.

It was enough.

Fiona rushed in to cut my ties.

"Emerson," I said, pointing in his direction, as I quickly stuck my fingers down my throat.

Chapter Forty

Like my first Rosemary Mountain storm, this one, too, left as quickly as it had come. By morning, the swelling in the creek had gone back to normal, and the mountain was fresh and beautiful again. The sun shone, drying out my muddy yard and bringing a hint of warmth like we hadn't seen in days.

Mom and I were safely tucked in at Fiona's cottage. Mom hadn't made it past the creek the night before, and I was glad of it. I was grateful she hadn't seen me like that, grateful she hadn't been hurt by Katie. Now that it was all over, I was happy the storm had spared her from experiencing Katie's darkness.

Emerson had also spent the night being monitored by Fiona, and then was sent straight to the hospital when the road was passable the next morning, much to his dismay. He insisted he was fine, of course, but Fiona and I insisted harder that he be checked out. We had wanted to call his buddies that night to fly him out, but he drew the line on that one—said there was no way he would endanger them by making them fly through the storm, just for a minor head wound. He won that one, since Fiona was more than capable of taking care of it.

Katie had used a taser to incapacitate us when we came through the door. Emerson had hit his head on the corner of my coffee table when he fell, making it that much worse for him. He also needed stitches for a minor cut on his arm, the penalty for my not immediately swallowing the pills. He didn't mind. He said a few stitches were well worth the extra time it gave Fiona to get there. Fiona stitched him up herself, and he said she did a better job than some of the plastic surgeons at the hospital. That made her so happy that she immediately went to the kitchen to bake him fresh chocolate chip cookies. Based on his grin and the wink he threw me when her back was turned, I had a feeling it wasn't the first—and wouldn't be the last—time he buttered her up for some fresh-baked goods.

Since Greg couldn't get to the cottage until the creek went down, Joe had temporarily taken custody of Katie. Fiona and I were both uncomfortable with that. But the order had come directly from Greg, and there wasn't much I could do about it.

I asked Fiona how she had known to come that night. She said she had been sleeping and dreamed of my mother. She woke from the dream and knew it was a warning. She didn't hesitate—grabbed her shotgun and headed out in the storm. So, it seemed that my mother had somehow played a part in saving my life that night.

MOM AND I SPENT THE NEXT DAY WITH FIONA. I WANTED TO be at the hospital with Emerson, but on this, he had won again. He said that Mom needed me, needed to see that I was really okay after everything that happened. And he was right. She did need that. So I stayed with her and Fiona, and it was calm, peaceful, and exactly what we all needed. But I would be lying if I said it was what I wanted. It felt like part of my heart was in the hospital with Emerson, and I couldn't truly find peace until he was back on the mountain.

Late in the afternoon, Greg knocked on Fiona's door. He looked uncomfortable.

"Ms. Sullivan, can I have a word with you?"

"There's no need to start being formal now," I said, laughing. "Come on in."

"Are you sure you wouldn't rather talk privately?" he asked, eyeing Mom and Fiona.

"I'm sure. I don't think there is anything you could say that would shock them at this point."

He cleared his throat. "I'm man enough to admit when I'm wrong, and it seems I owe you an apology. I took Katie Rogers into custody this morning. She and Doc Rogers were the first ones who raised concerns about your mental status, and Doc was the one who claimed to have seen you doing the vandalism. I see now that they were just trying to throw suspicion on you. I apologize for giving you a hard time and not believing you when you said you were fine."

"I appreciate the apology, but here's the thing. I *wasn't* fine. I was being drugged, and I didn't even realize it. I wasn't myself at all. At least not all the time. I know that now. You were just doing your job. I can't blame you for that."

He gave me a genuine smile, and I could tell that we were back to being allies of a sort. It was a relief.

"Well, I'd say we have an airtight case against Katie for what she did to you, and I'm pretty sure we'll nail her for Don's murder, too. Deputy Ford processed the scene at your house today while I was questioning Katie. But I'd like to walk you home and take a look at it myself before you clean anything up."

"I'll grab my coat."

Mom moved to come with me, but I stopped her.

"Why don't you stay here with Fiona?" I suggested. I knew there would be some blood, and I didn't want those images to stay with her.

She hesitated. "Well, if you're sure."

"I am."

She appeared relieved, and I knew I had made the right choice. I grabbed my coat and followed Greg out the door.

"So, can I ask you a couple of questions?" I asked as soon as we were alone.

"Go for it," he said.

"What about Dr. Rogers? Was he in on it?"

He let out a long breath. "He says he didn't have any part in planning it, and I believe him. But when it happened, he immediately suspected Katie. He's a smart man. I gather she talks in her sleep some, and he had pieced together that Don was her father some time back, but he never said a word to her about it. When Don was murdered, he couldn't help but wonder, especially when he did the autopsy and saw that the bullet was the same kind he buys for his own gun. He apparently did some checking around to see if she was really out of town like she said she was. When he found out she had left the hotel shortly after checking in and didn't return until the middle of the night, he started covering for her. Obviously, he's been relieved of his duties as the county's medical examiner, and he'll have to answer for being an accessory after the fact. He's cooperating, though. His testimony will go a long way to making sure Katie's brought to justice."

"Hmm." I didn't know what to say. Part of me felt sort of sorry for Dr. Rogers, even though he could have made my own life a lot easier by coming forward.

We walked in silence for a bit, leaves and gravel crunching under our feet.

"Still no new information about Mr. Boddy, I guess?"

He laughed. "Nope, I'm afraid not. But we've got our killer. That may have been nothing, or it may have been an inside joke between him and a friend. His phone is still missing, but I don't think we'll need it to make our case."

We made it to my cottage, and I unlocked the front door for us. I tensed, unexpectedly. The last time I had walked through this door, I had been hit by a taser. Just one more thing Katie had taken from me. I hoped some of those things would be restored eventually.

Even though I'd tried to prepare for it, it gave me chills to see the scene from the night before. The chair was still knocked over, and the floors were stained with wine and blood.

Greg whistled. "I've got to tell you, I've never seen anything like this before. Why don't you go through it and give me your statement about what happened."

So I did. I went through the whole thing, only leaving out my vision of Fiona.

He listened gravely, taking notes. "That pretty much matches what Emerson said as well."

"You talked to Emerson already? Is he doing okay?"

"Yeah, I stopped in on him at the hospital. He's doing fine. Doesn't want to be there. I'm sure you can relate." He had a funny grin on his face. "By the way, I should have told you before. I talked the church into dropping the breaking and entering charges. You don't have to go to court or anything."

"You know, in all this craziness, I had completely forgotten about all of that." I was relieved, though.

"Just don't go breaking into any more offices, okay?"

"Deal."

Chapter Forty-One

With Greg's help, I got the house put back together relatively quickly. He did his best to help me scrub up the blood. There were some mild stains, but I rearranged the rug and the furniture to hide them.

As we finished up, there was a knock on my door. I motioned for Greg to answer it while I fiddled with the placement of my corner chair.

"Oh, hello there, sheriff." Joe's voice was surprised and stiff.

"Joe." Greg's voice was stiff as well.

They both stood awkwardly for a moment.

"I came by to check on Daphne," Joe said, nodding at me. "I'd like to talk to her alone, if that's okay."

"I think I'm about done here, unless you need anything else?" Greg looked back at me.

I hesitated. I wasn't fully comfortable being left alone with Joe, but at the same time, I needed answers. Besides, I had safety in the fact that Greg had just seen him come to my house. If anything happened to me, Greg would know he had been here. And Joe wasn't stupid.

"I'm good," I said, deciding. "Thanks for your help."

"Anytime." He gave me a quick salute, then walked out the door, leaving me with Joe.

Joe faced me. "I think we need to talk."

"I think you're right." I gestured for him to sit, then took the chair I had just straightened and gave him a wary look.

"I just got back from Fiona's," he said. "She confronted me about what you saw the other day. About me and Don."

I nodded.

"Daphne, I swear I had nothing to do with your mother's death." His voice was pleading, and he had pain written all over his face. "The vision you had was true. I was involved with Don. But I would never have stood by and let him hurt your ma. Never."

"Then explain it to me," I said, my voice shaking. "Explain how you were involved with him and what the vision was about."

He hung his head.

"Well, I was the sheriff back then. My wife had left me. Said I was always too distracted by the job and didn't pay enough attention to her. Anyway, she left, and I was paying alimony and child support. We were supposed to sell the house and split the proceeds. But this land is my home. I didn't want to leave, but I didn't have the money to buy her out.

"Anyway, about that time, I suspected Don was embezzling money from the church. I brought him in to confront him about it. He was real repentant. Said he had sinned and it was wrong, but that he had stopped. Said he had already confessed it to the elders of the church, who had forgiven him and put him in an accountability program. But he said that if I charged him, it would ruin his credibility. He offered to let me talk to one of the church elders, who confirmed that he had, in fact, confessed and that they were taking over the finances.

"The elder and Don offered me a cash payment for basically looking the other way. A bribe," he spat out in disgust. "And it was just enough to buy out my house. Not a coincidence, by the way. Don knew exactly what he was doing. He always knew too much about what was going on in town, somehow.

"I shouldn't have taken it. It was the worst mistake of my entire life. But I had already decided to let him off the hook, for some reason. It's hard to explain. Don had a way of convincing people to do exactly what he wanted. The church elder told me the church had no interest in making a case of it and wanted to handle it internally. I was weak, and I wanted to keep my house."

"So you took the bribe," I said.

"Yes." He nodded. "As I said, it was the worst mistake I've ever made. Not just because it was wrong, but because after that, I was under Don's thumb. You see, it gave him power over me. After that, he thought he could do whatever he wanted. Because he could take away my job, my life, with just one phone call. If anyone ever found out I took that bribe, I would lose everything."

"I understand. But how does this relate to my mother?"

"I don't know, I swear," he said, lifting his hands in surrender. "I've already told you I worked with your ma. And I'll admit, one reason I did was to keep her close. I had a big skeleton in my closet, and I wanted to be the first to know if she ever discovered it—not to shut her up or kill her, but just to prepare myself. And maybe I thought if we were friends, she might look the other way," he admitted.

"I see."

"I was reformed, or at least I thought I was. I was serving my community. I was a good sheriff. And I thought if we were close friends, then she might want to protect me. But I was also keeping her close for her sake."

He cleared his throat and stared down at the floor for a minute before continuing. "It became clear pretty quickly that Don wasn't the repentant soul he pretended to be. In fact, I realized that the 'elder' I talked to wasn't a church elder at all. The joke was on me. The man I talked to was just one of Don's underlings, someone else he paid off to continue with his schemes. And his schemes didn't stop. He continued taking from the church, and—" he hesitated.

"And what?"

"I started getting the feeling it was more than that. I didn't have proof. But there was just too much money for a church that small."

"Where was the money coming from?"

He shrugged. "I don't know. I never found out. I wanted to investigate him, while making it look like I was turning a blind eye the whole time. I couldn't ask your ma to help. Didn't want her in danger. I was pretending to be exactly what he wanted me to be—cowardly and under his thumb—but in reality, I was trying to get to the bottom of it. It was during that time period that Eileen died. And after that, things changed."

"Changed how?"

"Don changed. The money stopped flowing the way it had been. He started spending his evenings at home with his family. His mysterious meetings stopped. It's hard to explain, but at the time, I was convinced that he really had changed, that he really was repentant for the first time in his life."

"Why didn't you question him about my mother?"

"I did. Off the record, of course. Like I told you before, there was no proof at all that your mother was murdered. Her death was ruled a suicide, and everyone accepted it as such. But I questioned him anyway. And here's the thing. I don't believe he did it. It was obvious, though, that her death scared him somehow. I never figured out why."

I took a deep breath. I believed him. Despite everything, I sensed that deep down he was one of the good guys. So I decided to trust him with what I knew. I told him about Mr. Boddy and about how Katie seemed to know something about my mother's death.

He sat back, stunned. "I don't know how Katie would know anything about your ma," he said. "But I wish I would have known that when I had her alone in my house all night. One of us needs to talk to her and find out what she knows."

"Can you make that happen?"

"I'll sure try."

"And what about Mr. Boddy? Who do you think he is?"

Joe looked deeply uncomfortable. "I don't know for sure. But I have some ideas. Let me do a little digging, quiet like."

"If we're going to work together, you have to be completely honest with me," I warned. "No more secrets."

He nodded. "I know. And I know there's a chance I might have to pay the price for my sins if all this ends up coming out. But I'm willing to do whatever it takes, for your ma's sake. I want to make things right."

Chapter Forty-Two

There was one more important conversation hanging over my head. I had made a decision the night before when my life hung in the balance, and I needed to break the news to Mom.

When Joe left, I sent a message letting her know that the house was ready for her return. I pulled a fresh bottle of wine from the rack to open for our talk, grateful that she hadn't tossed them in fear of contamination. Her kitchen cleanout had been thorough, but thank goodness, she had left the wine.

I had two glasses waiting when she arrived. I could see the timidness on her face when she opened the door, followed by relief that the house looked normal instead of like a crime scene.

"You rearranged!" she said with false cheer, as if I had a perfectly normal reason for moving my furniture and rug.

"I did. Brightens up the place, don't you think?"

We looked at each other and dissolved into giggles until I had tears streaming down my face. The sheer insanity of the situation was hilarious.

I handed her a glass of wine.

"Drink up," I said. "We both need it."

"We do," she agreed, curling up on the couch and swallowing her glass in moments. I refilled it, then took a seat across from her.

"Mom," I began.

"It's okay, Daphne." She held up her hand. "I know you're not moving back home."

I stared at her. "How did you know that's what I was going to say?"

"I'm your mother." She smiled ruefully. "Besides, you fit here." She shook her head and sighed, as if she couldn't quite believe it. "You fit here like I've never seen you fit anywhere else. You look at Emerson the way I've never seen you look at anyone else, and, well, he looks at you the way I always wanted someone to look at me. And you still have unfinished business here. I can read the writing on the wall."

"So you're not angry?"

"No." She set her glass down on the table and absently picked up a throw pillow, hugging it into herself as if she were seeking comfort. The gesture made me sad. "I'm not angry. I'm happy you've found a place here. I just hope you won't mind if I come to visit sometimes."

"I'd like that," I said.

I meant it with all my heart.

THANK YOU FOR READING DAPHNE'S STORY! I HOPE YOU enjoyed getting to know her as much as I did. Her journey continues in *Murder on the Mountain,* where she and Fiona get caught up in yet another murder...and a search for buried treasure.

Can't get enough of Rosemary Mountain? Sign up for my mailing list and receive Fiona's Hawthorn Tea recipe. You'll also be the first to know about upcoming releases, sneak peeks, and more!

Reviews are invaluable to authors. If you enjoyed Daphne's story, I would so appreciate you taking the time to leave a review at your preferred vendor. It truly means the world.

I would also love for you to come hang out with me on Facebook or Instagram! I love getting to know my readers!

Acknowledgments

This is for my husband, Brandon, who has been my best friend and biggest supporter since the day we met. Thank you for letting me chase my dreams, for being my "alpha reader," for always listening to my ideas, for never batting an eye when I tell you I'm doing yet another crazy thing, and for always being willing to go on new adventures. This book never would have happened without your support and encouragement. I adore you.

I also need to thank my sons, Aiden and Will. You both stepped up, helped around the house, and supported my writing time. You're both my favorite brainstorming partners—I love your crazy ideas, even if I'll probably never actually write a book filled with zombies and werewolves, ha!

Special thanks to the behind the scenes crew that helped work on this book: Candice J., Whitney S., Camille R., Jd H., and Brooke Passmore of BY THE BROOKE DESIGNS.

Candice, your feedback was invaluable. I'm so grateful we met, and absolutely love our writing friendship. Thanks for always being there to chat, and for being such a supportive friend!

Whitney, you went above and beyond the call on this one. Thank you for all the time and heart you put into beta reading. I'm grateful for our life long friendship, and love that we wrote our books at the same time.

Camille, your feedback was incredibly helpful. You helped identify little issues that were bugging me but that I couldn't quite put my finger on. Thank you!

Jd and Brooke, you both brought my ideas to life in a way I couldn't have imagined on my own! Thank you!

Special thanks also goes to Detective Jacob H., for answering all my questions. Any mistakes made by my law enforcement characters are mine, not his—I sometimes chose creative license over best practices.

Finally, a big thank you to my readers, friends, family, and community as a whole. You have all shown me so much encouragement through this, and I cannot thank you enough. I'm so grateful for each and every one of you!

About the Author

Nicole Gardner lives in NE Arkansas with her husband, their two sons, and their two crazy dogs. If she's not at her desk, you'll likely find her either in the garden, or creating teas and tinctures in the kitchen.

Nicole's background is in psychology. This fascination with human behavior and relationship dynamics plays a significant role in her writing and the way she shapes her characters.

www.nicolegardnerbooks.com